BAKER COUNTY PUBLIC LIBRARY

3 7814 00089 6895

D1792375

VS Western NOV 08 1995
Cole, Jackson
Gun-down on the Rio and
Gunsmoke empire

**25¢ fine charged
for cards missing
from book pocket**

Baker County Public Library
2400 Resort St.
Baker City, OR 97814

DEMCO

I've travelled the world twice over,
Met the famous: saints and sinners,
Poets and artists, kings and queens,
Old stars and hopeful beginners,
I've been where no-one's been before,
Learned secrets from writers and cooks
All with one library ticket
To the wonderful world of books.

© JANICE JAMES.

GUN-DOWN ON THE RIO

Two old-time prospectors meet a violent death in a lonely canyon! A group of tenderfoot Easterners are drawn into the sinister scheme of gunslinging outlaws! Gold is the root of flaming evil as gunfire lights up a Texas range. And Jim Hatfield, king of Texas rangers is there for the showdown with mean-eyed Breck Shale.

GUNSMOKE EMPIRE

"Bigjaw" Dave Haley and his crew moved in the richest range in Texas, to bleed the land dry. Their savage butchery had cut black scars across the once fertile land. Decent ranchers gathered their forces to fight. Ranger, Jim Hatfield could sense a powder-keg ready to explode. He knew he had to stop it. And fast.

*Books by Jackson Cole
in the Ulverscroft Large Print Series:*

MESQUITE MARAUDERS and
OUTLAW HELL
PERIL RIDES THE PECOS and
LOST RIVER LOOT
SHOOTOUT TRAIL and
THE LAND PIRATES
TWO GUNS FOR TEXAS and
TIN-STAR TARGET
VAQUERO GUNS and
GUN FIGHT AT DEEP RIVER
RED RUNS THE RIO and
BUGLES ON THE BIG HORN
GUN-DOWN ON THE RIO and
GUNSMOKE EMPIRE

JACKSON COLE

GUN-DOWN ON THE RIO
and
GUNSMOKE EMPIRE

Complete and Unabridged

ULVERSCROFT
Leicester

First Large Print Edition
published June 1985
by arrangement with
Warner Books, Inc.,
New York

British Library CIP Data

Cole, Jackson
 Gun-down on the Rio; and, Gunsmoke empire.
 —Large print ed.—
 Ulverscroft large print series: western
Rn: Oscar Schisgall   II. Title
813'.52[F]   PS3537.C38

ISBN 0-7089-1306-7

Published by
F. A. Thorpe (Publishing) Ltd.
Anstey, Leicestershire
Set by Rowland Phototypesetting Ltd.
Bury St. Edmunds, Suffolk
Printed and bound in Great Britain by
T. J. Press (Padstow) Ltd., Padstow, Cornwall

GUN-DOWN
ON THE RIO

Copyright © Renewed 1970 by
Popular Library, Inc.
All rights reserved

1

Death at Dawn

THE sun rose red that morning, a glaring disc that lifted sullenly into the pale of the dawn sky, bringing its grim promise of the heat of the coming day. The air was still and already hot, laying heavily on the thirst-sickened land. Even the cactus wrens and unblinking sand lizards seemed to feel the ominous oppression of this early hour.

For this morning death had risen with the dawn sun. It was there now on the rock rim of the basin, grimly poised and ready to strike.

Breck Shale sat his grulla at the head of the knot of riders as the red and gold shafts shot across the heat-dried land, waiting. He was a big man, powerful of body and long of limb, and evil glittered in his dark eyes as he stared into the basin below him.

It was a peculiar formation, that basin. Nearly a mile in diameter, it was like a huge bowl, with sheer walls of granite that swooped downward precipitously until they sloped off five hundred feet below on the cactus-studded floor.

It was a place of mystery to all who had seen it, a place feared by the Indians, held in awe by the whites. Tornado Basin, they called it, but it had not been the result of a rending of Nature by a freak wind. It was a crater which had been formed uncounted ages ago by some meteorite which had flamed and roared out of the heavens to plunge into the earth and leave this giant scar.

But there was no wonder in Breck Shale's dark eyes, as he stared into the depths of the crater. His lips were hard and thinned, and there was something of feral savagery in his narrowed gaze.

The swart Mexican who rode at Shale's side pointed a finger, and said grimly:

"Is eet not like I said, senor? Even now, they prepare to leave."

"Looks like yuh guessed right, Gomez."

Breck Shale's dark eyes brooded on the two distance-stunted prospectors breaking camp on the floor of the crater. Behind Shale, Ben Latch, a lean, hard-muscled man with a thin slit of a mouth snorted an oath of impatience.

"Which makes our ride out here worth a lot of nothin'," he growled then. "Breck, I figgered this was a waste of time."

"Yore tryin' to do the figgerin' for this outfit is a good way to get yoreself into a mess of trouble," Breck Shale snapped.

"Slip" Cramer, a runt of a man whose wizened body was a small container for the world of viciousness it held, spoke up in a toneless rasp.

"But if they'd got any gold down there, they shore as shootin' wouldn't be packin' out now. Let's get back to town, Boss. I got a good poker game waitin'."

Breck Shale whipped around in his saddle, his face a stony mask.

"Yuh forgettin' who's givin' the orders for this outfit, Cramer?" he rapped out harshly.

Surprise and quick fear were plain in Slip Cramer's narrow visage.

"'Course not, Boss!" he croaked. "I didn't mean nothin'. I just figgered as long as there ain't nothin' we can do here—"

"There's plenty we can do here!"

The cold ring of Breck Shale's voice

silenced the murmurs that lifted from the gang. They were a hard-bitten crew, gun-hung, cold-eyed—killers by every stamp of the profession.

"Link" Burman, one of them who had not yet raised a protest, leaned forward in his saddle, keen and intent, deadly. Mack Deeven, a bony, cadaverous, pinch-lipped individual, coughed hackingly and waited, a mirthless smile on his twisted lips. "Hack" Wadell's washed-out blue eyes showed a glint of icy interest, but no other expression reached through the hard lines of his sharp face.

"I brought yuh here to do a job, and yuh're doin' it," Breck Shale snapped. "I wasn't wastin' time when I had Pete Gomez spy on them prospectors down there. This is Harvey Britt's spread, and them two jiggers are trespassers."

Slip Cramer chuckled with grim humor. "Then we'll shove 'em off, if that's what yuh want."

Breck Shale jerked his head savagely. "That's the general idea," he said thinly. "Only yuh're makin' shore they won't come back."

Ben Latch's smoky eyes narrowed.

"Yuh don't mean to knock off them two old coots just 'cause they're on the H Lazy B, do yuh? Huh! We can scare 'em so bad they'll never want to see this end of Texas again, without pluggin' 'em!"

Breck Shale's mouth twisted into a chill half smile.

"Yuh goin' soft on me, Latch?" he murmured.

Ben Latch stiffened in his saddle, his slitlike lips thinning out.

"No, cuss it, I ain't goin' soft!" he growled. "I just don't see no sense takin' a chance on killin's that would drag the Rangers in here, that's all."

Shale laughed harshly, humorlessly.

"This won't be no killin' if the bodies of them gold hunters ain't found," he said. "And they won't be found, see? We'll dump 'em in the rocks where even the coyotes couldn't find 'em. I want them two gobblers taken care of so's they'll never come back, savvy?"

Puzzlement was in Link Burman's gray eyes.

"All right, if that's how yuh want it, Breck. But I'm shore wonderin' what we get out of this job."

"Get back!" Shale ordered sharply. "They're startin' up, and we don't want to be skylined." Again his dark eyes glinted, as he swung his mount back from the rim of the crater cliff. He pushed back along the trail that snaked through the granite spires and boulders, then reined in, facing his men, a man on whose own face inflexible ruthlessness was stamped.

"So yuh want to know what this is all about, huh?" he growled. He chuckled, a low, rumbling sound. "All right, I'll tell yuh. Just keep yore lips buttoned, and listen. . . ."

Deep inside the frowning gray walls of the crater, the two prospectors those horsemen had been watching began their slow climb up the tortuous trail. They were a stolid pair, not given to idle conversation, for theirs had been lonely lives spent in the far reaches of an empty country.

Old Bob Gallatin trudged beside his mule with the loose strides of a man long accustomed to such travel. Sweat lay on his sun-ruddied forehead, for here in these depths there was no stir of wind to break the sullen grip of the sun's heat. He worried his cud of tobacco, then spat an accurate stream at a dust-grayed rock. Then, as if he had been considering his words a long while, he said:

"Funny how things work out. You and me, we spent most of our lives huntin' gold. We ought to know our business by now, but here yore son is just out of school, and we're waitin' for him to join us so's he'll tell us what is good rock and what ain't."

They swung around a switch-back, each step moving them nearer to the top of the trail. Old Caleb Tarrant strode along, by the force of long habit drawing on the pipe clamped between his teeth. He was a gaunt man, stooped by toil and the weight of the years he carried, but there was a faint smile lurking around his lips, as though his mind dwelled eagerly on the thought of again meeting his son.

"Times change, Bob," he said. "We know our chore in our way, but a trained man has got it head and heels over us. And Clay's trained. He's spent his time in that minin' school, and he'll tell us a heap we never knowed before."

A shadow came to old Bob Gallatin's faded blue eyes. He frowned against a dark thought that disturbed him. He tried to shake it off, but it persisted as it had persisted ever since he had dropped into Tornado Basin.

"Mebbe," he grunted. "I shore hope so. But I've had a feelin'—"

His words trailed off, for he didn't know to what to lay the ominous presentiment that had hugged his mind so many days. . . .

There was a savagery that was almost animal in the eyes of the men hidden above, as they listened silently while Breck Shale talked. And when Shale had finished, Mack Deeven broke the instant's silence, and his voice came hoarsely.

"Breck, yuh hit it big this time! *Big*, I'll say! This is worth takin' a chance on bringin' the Rangers in!"

But there was a glint of fear in Link Burman's eyes.

"What about Jim Hatfield?" he asked dryly, and his question had the effect of water spilled over a fire, on those men whose minds had become inflamed by greed, listening to what Breck Shale proposed.

"*El Lobo Solitario!*" Pete Gomez breathed in a hushed tone.

"Yeah, the Lone Wolf!" Burman growled. "What about him?"

A snarl rose through Breck Shale's throat and came out with a rasping oath.

"Yuh leave that jasper to me," he grated. "He ain't too tough for a bullet to drop him if he shows up around here. Now pull off the trail and keep still. Them ore-hunters are gettin' close."

Their horses' hoofs muffled in burlap bags made no sound as the outlaws pulled their mounts back into the boulders that flanked the trail. Silence closed in, a still, dead smother that seemed to pulse with the promise of impending bloodshed.

From where Breck Shale sat, the boulders thinned out and sloped down a hundred steep-pitched yards to the level spread of the plateau. Down there the morning breezes shifted, giving a little life to the air, but where Shale's grulla stood there was only heat, waves of it that struck the boulders and swirled around horse and rider.

Minutes passed, tense minutes while the moment drew nearer. The men looked at each other, showing no expression, their hands clamped hard on the butts of holstered guns.

Then from the direction of the crater came the metallic ring of a hoof through the heated air, and Shale stiffened in his saddle, listening intently. A low murmur of voices floated though the heated air, and Shale jerked around to face his men. His voice came low and harsh.

"You, Cramer," he ordered. "Take the other, Latch."

A grin of eagerness split Slip Cramer's thin lips, but no emotion broke through the stony coldness of Ben Latch's narrow face. He was utterly without feeling, a killer of the deadliest breed, a man who had a job to do and was stolidly prepared to do it.

The two men selected as executioners drifted their mounts apart, halting them where a boulder shut off all view of the crater-rim end of the trail. They drew their weapons, thumbs rocking back the gun hammers.

An old man's crotchety growl drifted down the trail to them.

"I can't get over this feelin' that somethin's goin' to happen. I've had it ever since

I went into that dad-blamed hole, and it shore ain't eased up none since we started out."

Another voice spoke up, with a chuckle.

"It's yore rheumatics, and yuh're too stubborn to admit it, Bob. Trouble with you is yuh're gettin' old. Now if yuh had a son like me to keep you young—"

Old Caleb Tarrant's words choked off, as he and Bob Gallatin rounded the side of the boulder and saw the men waiting for them. They read their fate. They knew! They jerked to a halt, leathery faces blanching, seeing death that was inescapable.

Without a word to betray his vicious intent, Slip Cramer's gun roared. Bob Gallatin stiffened under the shock of lead, then stumbled back against the boulder. He held there an instant, then slid inertly into the dust of the trail.

Caleb Tarrant tried to turn, knowing all the while he had no chance. Ben Latch chuckled with icy humor, swung his weapon.

"Yuh're next, mister!" he said in a flat monotone.

And then his gun crashed, to shatter the bounding echoes of the first shot.

Caleb Tarrant lifted to his toes as if he had been jerked by a string. His back arched under the pain of swift-coming death. Whispered words of horror slipped from his lips.

"Why? We didn't . . . We ain't got . . . Why did yuh do this?"

He twisted slowly, relaxing loosely. His eyes bulged; his mouth sagged open as if he fought for words that wouldn't come, and his flame-charred old pipe spilled into the thick dust at his feet. Then as though he were yielding to some powerful urge to sleep, his eyes closed, and he crashed heavily to the earth.

Ben Latch hipped around in his saddle, blowing black whisps of smoke through the muzzle of his weapon. His voice came with a deadly mirth.

"Trouble with you, Cramer, is yuh don't have no etiquette when yuh kill a man. You should always say somethin' to him before yuh cut him down."

Breck Shale swung his horse forward, his face a hard mask.

"We ain't got time to stand around here

and jaw!" he snapped. "Somebody might have heard them shots, and we don't want no company. A couple of yuh take them bodies to the rim and throw 'em over where they'll be buried by a rock slide. Search 'em first. That tall gobbler is packin' a gold poke I want.

"Yuh know what to do next. Get back to the ranch and stay there till it's time to ride. I got another job to do, and I'm leavin' now. I'll meet yuh at Black Rock Gap a week from today at sun-up. The El Paso train will be bringin' that shipment of bullion through that day, so make shore yuh're at the Gap in time to stop it."

2

Philanthropist

THERE were, in a group of squatting men around a huge bonfire, a full hundred work-gnarled individuals whose weathered faces showed a strange mixture of hope and skepticism and sharp interest. They were a hardy lot who had sold their farms and town holdings back East to join the tide of humanity moving to the vast free lands west of the Mississippi.

They were but a few of many, these men, but theirs was a quality strong in all men migrating along the wheel-rutted trails that linked civilization with the wilderness. They knew hope, for this was a land of hope. But they knew fear for the safety and welfare of their families, for this raw new land was one to be feared.

They sat on their haunches, faces painted ruddy under the shifting yellow glow of the bonfire. On all sides of this main gathering place, other fires made red holes in the thick black of the night, and the high-swelled tops of covered wagons showed their gray shapes through the darkness. Back among these wagons, the careworn wives of these men hovered near their sleeping children, and somewhere in the gloom beyond the last wagon the team mules trampled in their restless way.

There was silence this moment, for the deep booming voice of the stranger in the middle of this circle of men had struck deep into the thoughts of the listeners. A murmur of surprise and wonder had run through the men at first but that had died out.

Through the hush came the fretful sobbing of a baby, and the low comforting croon of the mother's voice. But these sounds fell on deaf ears, for the attentions of the squatting men were on this stranger who had come among them tonight with his startling offer.

The man loomed tall before them, and the flickering fire-light accented a bluff and florid heartiness in his strong face. He was broad of shoulder, but his leanness and wiriness spoke plainly of hard-packed power. His jaw was square and walled in by thick burnsides that pointed down almost to his heavy black chin whiskers.

His eyes were dark, always in movement as though made restless by some inner swift currents of energy. A cigar jutted from his full lips, and, standing there, he lit it. After killing the flame of the match, he broke the slender stem under his thick thumb and forefinger. Gray wraiths of smoke curled upward across his face as he waited for a reply to his offer.

Presently a short, square man pushed to his feet and moved past the circle of the pilgrims. He paused there, as though under the grip of powerful emotions. And when he finally spoke his voice was hoarse, carrying both doubt and eagerness.

"Don't misunderstand us for not jumpin' up and down and yellin' our heads off," he said. "Frankly, stranger, you've jolted all the breath out of us with your offer. Just so we'll be sure we didn't hear you wrong, suppose you repeat that proposition."

The stranger grinned broadly, his big hands coming from behind his dark coat to be thrust into his pockets.

"Glad to!" he said heartily. "I came here to offer yuh rich gold claims for a fraction of what they're worth. In my way, I'm givin' these claims to those of yuh who prove yuh're worthy of 'em."

Silence again, and the short Easterner wagged his head in amazement.

"Well, anyhow that proves our ears haven't gone bad," he said hoarsely.

The big man laughed boomingly, then sobered to a grave, businesslike attitude. He fixed his dark eyes on the man before him.

"You the wagon boss here?" he asked.

The short man nodded. "I reckon that's what my friends elected me to be," he admitted. "My name is Sam Winters."

The stranger's lips smiled around his cigar.

"I don't blame you gents for gettin' spooked," he chuckled. "The way I put my proposition to yuh was enough to spook anybody. Suppose we get into this a little slower."

He paused, gathering in the full attention of his hearers, then again his benevolent voice broke through the silence.

"I reckon first I'd better tell yuh something about myself. My name is Harvey Britt. When I came here fifteen years ago

I was just as much a tenderfoot as you men, but a danged sight worse off. I was flat broke, and didn't even have enough money to buy a meal. But this is a good country. It's hard and rough at times, but it's kind to them that need kindness, and I had that showed to me quick.

"I hadn't had a meal for two days when I got to Austin, and I was pretty done in. But a puncher guessed what was the matter and staked me to a meal and some warm clothes. That was the first good turn this State did me.

"A rancher saw me walkin' down the road and gave me a hoss and a job. That was the second good turn, and I made up my mind to be worthy of it. I worked hard and saved my money, and when I had enough for a start I went to the land office and the State gave me a section of ground west of here that I built into the H Lazy B Ranch."

A farmer spoke up enviously from the background.

"Britt, I reckon you was a lucky man to get in here on the bottom floor."

Harvey Britt nodded. "I was lucky, but no more than I want you men to be. I've made my pile. I live in Austin now, and let my men run my ranch for me. But I haven't settled back to take it easy the rest of my life. I know what I owe my start to, and I appreciate it. I've spent the last five years giving help to other pilgrims just as I had help given to me. And that's why I rode here to meet you men."

Sam Winters wagged his grizzled head unbelievingly.

"But these gold claims you mentioned—" Words failed him.

A chuckle rumbled from the philanthropist's throat.

"Like I said, I've got all the money I need comin' in from my ranch. I don't need any more. I got a wire the other day from my foreman saying he'd discovered gold on my land in a place known as Tornado Basin. The basin is rich, and my foreman filed a hundred claims in my name. It's them claims I want to turn over to you men."

Sam Winters' voice came low and croaking.

"Givin' away gold!" he muttered. "I never thought I'd live to see this day come!"

Harvey Britt shook his head at Winters' remark.

"Not givin' it away," he corrected. "Don't misunderstand me in that, men. I've found that money given away is never appreciated. You men all have a little money, or yuh wouldn't have been able to outfit yoreselves for this trip. How much yuh reckon each of yuh can rake up, Winters?"

The oldster frowned slightly. "Not much," he said quietly. "We're all poor men, Britt. We sold all we had back East when we started out here. None of us is worth more than two thousand dollars, that's sure."

Britt grinned. "Which is about what I figgered I'd ask for them claims. My foreman tells me they're worth ten thousand dollars if they're worth a cent, and he's a reliable man. If I gave yuh the claims it would be easy-come, easy-go with most of yuh. I know. I've seen it happen too many times before. So I decided to make yuh sacrifice a little to get much, and by that yuh'll appreciate the gold yuh'll get a heap more."

Sam Winters' lips tightened, and he shook his head grimly.

"Don't get me wrong in what I'm going' to say, Britt," he said levelly. "We're all poor men, and we've had to work hard for what little we've got. We're strangers in a country that's new to us. I won't ask my friends to sink all they've got in gold claims they've never seen."

There was bluff heartiness in Harvey Britt's quick laugh.

"And I'm not askin' yuh to!" he boomed. "The reason I come here was to see how yuh'd take my offer, and yuh've taken it the way deservin' men should."

Amazement was in Sam Winters' tone. "You mean you don't expect us to sink our money in your claims here and now?"

"Without seein' what yuh're gettin'?" Britt chuckled, shaking his head. "I wouldn't ask no man to do that, Winters. You men will do, and the claims are yores when yuh're satisfied they're worth what yuh'll be payin' for 'em. All I want to be shore of is that I wasn't givin' help to men who didn't deserve it, and yuh've proved yuh're worthy of a good turn.

"The route yuh're takin' now will land yuh in Sonita town in three days. My ranch is south of there thirty miles. Drop down there and satisfy yoreselves. If yuh'll do that, all right. If yuh won't I'll hunt up another bunch of men to turn the claims over to. What's yore answer?"

Sam Winters turned. One sweeping glance over the bright faces of his followers was enough. He swung back, his decision made.

"The way you put your offer is fair enough for any man, Mr. Britt, and we're grateful," he said simply.

Britt smiled. "Good! Things like this make me feel like I'm payin' back in a small way the help that was give to me so long ago. My ranch is thirty miles south of Sonita, remember. Yuh'll find Breck Shale there—he's my foreman—and when yuh're satisfied about the claims yuh can close the deal with him. And if any of yuh ain't satisfied after buyin' a claim, let me know, and I'll get out there and see how yuh're doin' in a few days. *Adios*, gentlemen."

He turned then, swinging into the saddle of his giant grulla, and moved away from the fire until the darkness of the night closed around him.

There was silence for a long moment after Harvey Britt had ridden off. The women left the wagons and came forward to join their husbands, their care-worn faces bright and the mist of thankfulness in their eyes.

Sam Winters' daughter, Holly, came to her father's side, a strong and slender girl in a flowing gingham dress. There was a soft smile on her lips as she took her father's hand.

"I'm glad, Dad," she said quietly. "I'm glad for you and all these other people."

"I guess our prayers have been answered, men," someone said in a voice that was hoarse with feeling.

That was all.

3

Blocked Rails

INSIDE the coach of the El Paso Express Ranger Jim Hatfield scraped a match on the sole of his boot and touched the flame to the cigarette he had just nipped between his fine-drawn lips. He expelled smoke from his nostrils, and slumped back in his seat with that strange cat-like laxity of a man who never altogether relaxes his grim vigilance.

He was a big man, well over the six foot mark in height, and with wide, slab-muscled shoulders that tapered down to lean, flat hips. Strong character and tremendous vitality was stamped in every line of his rugged and not unhandsome face.

His skin, smooth and unseamed, showed the touch of the Texas sun and wind. And his were the clear, level gray-green eyes of a man used to looking into the far distances of mountains and plains, or coldly gauging that second-fraction when life and death hung in delicate balance.

Now, his eyes were on those of the man in the seat across from him. He liked what he saw. The young man who had given his name as Clay Tarrant was clean-featured, well-set-up in his neat-fitting store clothes.

"You're a native Texan, I take it," Clay Tarrant said with polite curiosity.

Jim Hatfield smiled with a quirk of his broad lips. He was dressed in the plain but serviceable garb—dark jeans, flannel shirt, neckerchief that could be raised to protect his mouth and nostrils from trail dust, a wide-brimmed felt hat.

"I was born the year Texas decided it would rather be in the Union than stay a Republic," he said in his humorous drawl. His smile broke the gravity of his countenance. "Yuh're new down here, I reckon."

Clay Tarrant grinned and chuckled. "You might think it strange, but I was born here too—near Beaumont. But Dad was a prospector, and Mother was too frail to stand the only life he could give her, so when I was three years old she took me back to Indiana to live." He nodded at the brace of guns that jutted from Hatfield's flat hips. "I've been East so long it's going to be hard to get used to seeing men carry guns around like that."

The Ranger's smile thinned out slightly. "Down here the guns men pack are sometimes the only law they have," he said with grim meaning.

Clay Tarrant frowned faintly. "You mean to tell me this is the only law you have?"

Chill lights filtered into the clear gray-green of Jim Hatfield's eyes.

"We have town marshals and sheriffs and Texas Rangers," he said quietly. "But this is a big country, Tarrant. The few lawmen we have got, have a hard job cut out for them tryin' to keep in line the tough customers that flooded into the state since the Civil War."

He thought of the silver circled star pinned inside the pocket of his shirt, but said nothing about his connection with the most feared and respected law organization in the West—the Texas Rangers. Inborn caution made him keep his identity as a Ranger secret until there was some reason to wear his badge openly, for there were too many bleak-eyed killers only too eager to target a Ranger badge under their gunsights from the cover of the *brasada*.

But caution was Hatfield's least reason for keeping his badge out of sight. He had discovered long ago that he was infinitely more effective as a lawman so long as he was able to pose as an ordinary cowhand.

Conversation lagged as Clay Tarrant pondered Hatfield's grim statement. Hatfield studied the man covertly, liking what he saw. Tarrant had a well-set frame that a few months on the open range would pack with solid muscle. His jaw was clean-lined and strong, and there was a steady, capable quality in the deep blue of his eyes. Tenderfoot or not, he was a Texan, and one to ride the river with, the Ranger decided.

Hatfield turned his eyes out the window, to watch the dun rangeland flow past the coach. The train was moving at a slower speed now, climbing the steep grade that sloped up to the crest of Black Rock Gap. Naked black walls mounted higher on both sides of the coach, dimming the light of early morning, and holding down the gray wraiths of smoke that trailed back from the engine ahead.

The train labored upward through the

pass, then, creaking and groaning, it topped the last rise to pick up speed rapidly as it struck the down grade. Jim Hatfield relaxed into his seat, conscious for the first time of the tension that had closed over him while the train had pulled itself up the grade. He pulled his eyes around at Clay Tarrant's curious voice.

"You acted like you expected trouble."

Hatfield smiled thinly. "Out here a gent lives longer if he is always expectin' trouble," he said quietly. "At least that way he's not caught off balance when it hits him."

Tarrant frowned slightly. "A man being held up by a gang is one thing, but there are a hundred passengers on this train. No gang of outlaws would have the nerve to jump that many at once."

The glint of grim humor did not melt the chill lights in Jim Hatfield's eyes.

"Yeah, there's a hundred passengers on board," he said softly, "but that ain't all. There's a load of bullion in the express car, and gold is somethin' an outlaw will take plumb long chances to get."

Some inner voice of warning sent a whisper to the Ranger's brain. There was nothing tangible to it. It was, instead, some subtle instinct that was an unforgotten sixth sense to him, and it had never failed when unseen danger threatened.

He twisted around in his seat, pressing his face close to the window. The walls of the pass-cut were dropping away to a tangled maze of boulders that flanked the rails. His stare pushed ahead, squinting against the red glare of the eastern sun.

The down-slope of the pass seemed to flow by him like a gray stream, and he could see the train's engine swaying and smoking as the swift-rolling wheels rolled it into a wide sweeping curve. He could see the engineer leaning into the speed wind that whipped past him, his weathered face blackened by smoke and grime.

Even as his eyes caught sight of the engineer, he saw the man stiffen. He half rose, leaning far out of his cabin window, as if staring at some danger down the tracks that threatened the monster of steel and wood under his command. Then the engineer leaned back, straining frantically against a control lever.

The warning of disaster was screamed to

Jim Hatfield's brain. He saw bright splinters of sparks shoot from under the engine's wheels, felt the jolt and jerk of the braked cars jamming into each other. Steel shrieked against steel.

From down the coach, a man shouted in quick alarm.

"Trouble ahead!" Hatfield's sharp yell rang out.

Then, even as the speed of the train began to slacken, he saw a man leap out of the boulders that flanked the tracks. He glimpsed a hard face, saw a rifle leaping up, then it jumped, with a distant roar.

He saw the engineer stiffen under the impact of lead, half turn, then crumple over the sill of his window. His lifeless hand still clung to the brake lever, but there was no longer the strength in it to stop the plummeting mass of the train.

A cry of warning, hoarse and high-pitched, ripped from the Ranger's lips.

"Holdup! Blocked rails! Get braced!"

His hands stabbed down to his holstered guns, but Time swept past too swiftly for him to do anything. The train lurched in full movement, jumped, skewed sickeningly. The whistle screamed even as men screamed inside that hurtling mass of wood and steel.

Jim Hatfield's perceptions were keen and clear to the last. At the first smashing impact of the engine striking the boulders which had been rolled onto the tracks, he saw Clay Tarrant disappear down the aisle of the coach in a limp, skidding roll.

The shock of the crash was like a giant fist that hurled Hatfield to the floor. The window splintered above his head. He heard the jolting roar of cars piling into each other, skidding, twisting, driving. The floor of the coach writhed and buckled under him like a living thing, throwing him around like a leaf tossed before a wind. His head struck some hard object, but he was conscious of no pain.

The smash and thunder of the crash mounted to a chaotic tumult that had no meaning. Time itself seemed to hang suspended that moment, as wooden coaches shattered, as steel screamed on tortured steel, as train wheels left the tracks to plow through dirt and stone.

The roaring ceased as all movement of the train ended, and deathly silence closed in.

As if in a dream, Jim Hatfield became aware that he lay pinned beneath the wreckage of splintered coach seats and piled baggage. He seemed incapable of movement, as if his body had gone dead and only his brain remained alive.

He knew pain then, blinding waves of it that stabbed and slashed across his brain. A red haze swirled before his eyes.

Somewhere in the deep, far distance, he heard the whippy snarl of a gun. From closer at hand, came a woman's whimpering sob of terror.

Hatfield tried to dislodge himself from the wreckage, but his muscles were sluggish and heavy. It was the shifting of his body that brought down the oak stanchion that had swayed above his head. It slid down toward him, splintered end first, and he was powerless to avoid it.

He felt a sharp stab of wood fibres needling into the side of his head. Pain piled onto pain, building up an all-consuming agony that clamped down on his brain like hot irons.

Faintly, but not far away, he heard a man say in a dull, numb tone:

"She's dead, ain't she?"

After that there was nothing but depthless waves of inky darkness around Jim Hatfield.

4

Colt Fodder

JUBILATION flamed bright in Breck Shale's dark eyes, as he watched the train hurtle down out of the pass with ever-increasing speed. He crouched in the boulders, gun in hand, his lips twisted in a cruel, hard grin. He jerked around to face the half-breed, Pete Gomez.

"Yuh think yuh can pick off the engineer, Gomez?" he demanded. "He's shore to see the boulders we rolled out on the tracks when he swings into the curve, and mebbe stop in time—and I want that train to smash up at full speed. We don't want no interference from any of the crew or passengers."

The breed nodded, chuckling. Cold venom was in his eyes.

"Me, I'm best shot een Texas, Boss. I shoot heem when you say, no?"

Shale nodded grimly. He snapped a glance through the boulders. The train was roaring close now, boring through its own smoke, as it swept down the grade. The engineer was leaning out of his small window, square face stiff, eyes narrowed against the whip of the wind. The engine swung into the first bend of the wide curve, and the engineer abrubtly straightened, staring toward the boulders that blocked the rails. Then he threw his hand out to grab the brake lever.

"Now!" Breck Shale barked.

The breed leaped out of the rock like a cat closing in on the kill. His rifle snapped to his shoulder, swung shortly, and roared. He jumped back into the boulders, laughing, as his slug smashed the engineer back into the cab.

The entire train shuddered as the engine struck the heavy boulders. The engine lifted, rolling to one side, thrown from its rails by the impact of the crash. Coach smashed into coach with deafening roars that seemed to split the ear-drums of the outlaws who crouched into the rocks.

Rails twisted and writhed. Smoke billowed. Dust fogged upward in a thick saffron pall as derailed cars plowed through the earth.

Then, almost as swiftly as it had begun, the thunder of the crash faded. In the one moment of sudden silence, the outlaws stood motionless, as if in horror at their own deed. Breck Shale jarred them into movement. He leaped out of the rocks, his yell ripping out harshly.

"Snap out of it, cuss yuh! Yuh know yore jobs. Cramer, Latch, stand guard! Plug the first gobbler that shows his nose. Wadell, bring up the mule. The rest of yuh come with me!"

He broke into a pounding run down the line of cars.

The express car rested at a crazy angle where it had careened off the tracks into the boulders. Its heavy door had been torn open by the impact of the crash.

"Throw out the gold!" Shale's voice rang out. "Hop to it, Deeven! Don't stand there gawkin'. Gomez, you and Burman help him."

The three outlaws leaped forward to climb through the door of the express car. Mack Deeven stumbled into view a moment later, laboring under the weight of a huge bar of gold bullion. He let it drop to the ground beside the car. Link Burman, his narrow face streaked with sweat, staggered to the doorway with another ingot. He dropped it, panting.

"Here's the second, Boss," he called hoarsely. "These things are heavy, but I like this kind of weight. By glory, we've been playin' penny ante a long time! We could knock off one of these trains a month and be rich in a year!"

"Don't get no ideas of yore own, Burman!" Breck Shale rasped savagely. "We're usin' our brains. We try somethin' like this again, and we'd have the whole Ranger force on our necks. We're playin' this safe, savvy? I'm givin' orders for this outfit, and don't forget that!"

He stood there on wide-planted legs, viciousness and evil in his eyes as he watched the third heavy ingot of gold thud to the ground. Hack Wadell and Slip Cramer ran up to pack the gold on the mule. Mack Deeven stepped into the doorway of the express car, his hard face bright with sweat.

"That's all, Boss," Deeven called. "They didn't ship heavy this month."

Shale barked out harshly. "We ain't

wastin' no time squawkin' about that. We're ridin'! Hey, Gomez, come out of there!"

But greed had robbed the half-breed of all reason. He was still unsatisfied with the loot that had been taken. "But there may be money hidden somewhere in here, Boss!" he yelled. "Eef we rob the passengers before they know what happened—"

"We'll risk gettin' our necks in hang-nooses!" Shale rasped. "Come on out of there, cuss yuh!"

The breed jerked his head, his swart face reddening in the anger, his voice strained and hoarse. "Then we spleet here, senor!" he challenged. "You take the gold. For my share, I weel rob the passengers!"

"Like thunder yuh will!" Breck Shale stormed furiously. "Yuh'd get caught and spill yore insides about the rest of us! We're playin' this game safe, I tell yuh, and yuh're ridin' with us right now!"

The breed's head shook. Then he tensed, crouching in the doorway of the car, lips peeling back from gritted teeth. His hand started down—fast—but Shale's Colt was already in his fist.

The weapon came up in a blue blur—roared. Pete Gomez lifted to his toes under the impact of driving lead, his body shivering as if under an icy wind. He swayed, lost his balance, and as if pulled by the weight of his half-drawn gun, crashed face down out of the express car.

"Drag him off in the rocks and cover him up!" Breck Shale whipped out savagely. "We'll use his hoss to help pack the gold. Hustle! Everybody on the train will be comin' out of it any minute."

He swung around, climbed quickly into his saddle. His mount had a bar of gold lashed on it, and the mule carrying the other two weighty ingots was already in movement.

"Get that mule in a run, Cramer!" he ordered. "We'll pull up in a couple miles an' shift the gold to Gomez' hoss. We got to make time till we're out of sight!"

Far above, a lone buzzard wheeled in lazy circles against the high blue of the sky. It closed its wings, starting to drop toward the tangled wreckage of the train, then caught itself, as a few stunned, battered men began climbing out of the coaches. It swung, circling higher and higher into the sky.

In the meantime, back in one of those cars that had hit the boulders with a spluttering crash that had hurled Jim Hatfield into temporary oblivion, the Ranger finally returned to consciousness, with the blinding glare of the morning sun full in his eyes. He lay quietly a long moment, as memory of what had happened to him, gathering his strength, teeth set against the pain that prodded his body. His nostrils were filled with the mingled odors of dust and blood and burned wood, and he could hear low voices all around him.

"We've got tuh get these folks to a doctor," he made out someone saying.

He pried his eyes open again, then blinked them against the hot glare of the late afternoon sun. He sat up, waited grimly until the waves of sickness passed, then pushed slowly to his feet

What met his eyes struck an icy chill through his tall frame. The wreck had occurred in the morning hours, but still so little had been done, except to give what aid possible to the victims, that the damage remained. The rails had been twisted like wires by the force of the crash. The splintered, telescoped remains of the coaches lay along the track bed. The engine had plummeted into the boulders and lay on its side, one wheel still spinning slowly, as if it were the last sign of life in a dying monster. Thin wreaths of smoke feathered upward from the stack.

Cold horror swept through the Ranger as he managed to drag himself to his feet and his gaze moved down the line of wreckage, pausing here and there on knots of stunned passengers who were dragging the dead and injured from the coaches.

A man, his face a mask of blood and dust, moved up to Hatfield's side. The Ranger didn't recognize Clay Tarrant until he heard Tarrant's voice.

"I'm glad to see you alive. I didn't know whether you were dead or not when I pulled you out, and I didn't have time to check. Been busy all day tryin' to save people's lives."

Cold fury at this wanton destruction was like a dark cloud hanging over Hatfield's brain. No more than a dozen feet away, he could see a small, age-stooped oldster kneeling on the ground beside the unmoving body of a woman. The man looked around as if hunting for help he knew could do no good, and his dry, hurt eyes halted on Hatfield's.

"She's dead!" he said numbly. "I caught her when the coach left the tracks, and I felt somethin' snap inside her. She looked at me a long time after I got her out here, but now she don't look at me no more."

Hatfield closed his eyes to shut out the vision of the tired old man who even yet could not believe that the crash had taken his wife from him. And this woman had not been the only one killed in the wreck. Other passengers had died; and many of those injured would die before help could be brought. An oath of helpless fury choked in his throat, to die unuttered behind tight-locked lips.

He caught young Tarrant's arm in a hard grasp, and moved down the line of wrecked cars in grim strides.

"Come on," he growled. "We've got to do something."

He found the train crew in a confused huddle around the derailed engine. They turned as he approached, as if uncertain what moves to make more than had already been done.

"Well, are yuh going to stand there and jaw when all them folks back there still need help?" he lashed at them.

A grimy, thick-shouldered Irishman swung around to glare at him.

"And maybe it'll take the likes of ye to tell us what to do!" he flung back. "'Tis fifteen miles we are from Sonita, and—"

"Eight across country," Hatfield broke in flatly.

Resentment flared in the Irishman's blue eyes.

"So it be eight now! Misther, all we know about this country is the rails we follow. Shure, and we'd be lost in half an hour if we tried to cut through on foot We've knowed that all day."

Hatfield's craggy jaw went hard, and cold lights came into his eyes.

"Well, I won't get lost," he snapped. "I'll go for help. You do what yuh can for the injured, and set a guard to make shore them crooks don't come back."

He started past the Irishman, only to be halted by the quick outthrust of the man's arm.

"Crooks, ye say? Are ye for tellin' us a gang of crooks wrecked the train?"

The Ranger nodded shortly. "That's just what happened," he grated. "I saw them at the side of the tracks just before the crash. They blocked the rails, and shot the engineer when he tried to set the brakes."

A harsh oath ripped from the Irishman's lips, and a short, square-set man shouldered toward Hatfield, his jaw hard and showing a streak of drying blood.

"I reckon yuh're wrong there, pardner," he drawled. "I was on guard in the express car. The crash knocked me out, but when I came to I checked around. The gold bullion wasn't in sight but it's probably buried in the mess somewhere. The mail-bags haven't been touched, that's shore!"

Surprise struck the tall Ranger. His eyes narrowed. "How much gold did yuh have in there?" he asked.

"Three ingots—thirty thousand dollars worth!"

Hatfield knew that gold had been stolen. He had an unshakable conviction of that fact. But why had the mail been left untouched when there was a chance it contained valuables? Why hadn't the outlaws made some effort to rob the passengers? Absently he watched the big Irishman turn and stoop to the engineer's body, then straighten.

"By the Saints, ye're right, Misther!" he burst out harshly. "Mike O'Hara was shot, though 'tis the first time we've known that, and the best engineer ever come out of old Oirland he was, too! If I could lay me hands on the murderin' spawns o' Satan that killed him, I'd bust every bone in their yella hides!"

A look of amazement came into the face of the express guard, and his voice came with an edge of grim puzzlement.

"But why didn't they go through the mail, I'm wantin' to know?" he rasped. "And why didn't they rob the passengers?"

Jim Hatfield's brain was working swiftly now, with the keen insight and perception that had made him the most feared manhunter the length and breadth of the state.

"Mebbe it's because they had what they wanted and didn't want to waste any time clearin' out," he said softly.

He said nothing more to give a hint of the thoughts that were crossing his brain. But they were there, puzzling him. And somehow he knew there was something far more deadly to this than was on the surface, the machinations of some killer more evil and more dangerous than any he had ever met before. To make it worse, the hold-up men by now had had many hours for whatever plans they had made.

But no expressions showed on his craggy face, as he turned away from the train crew.

"You set out that guard," he said "and look after the injured. I'm goin' for help as soon as I've done all I can here."

Young Clay Tarrant moved up to his side as he strode off toward the wasteland that stretched beyond the train rails.

"You may run into them outlaws on the way," Tarrant said, and there was grim determination in his tone. "If you do, I don't suppose there's anything much I could do to help you, but I'll tag along just in case."

5

Gold Rush

WHEN the two men reached Sonita, night was falling. Clay Tarrant walked with the easy strides of a man used to such travel, but to Jim Hatfield crossing eight miles of rough, broken country in tight, high-heeled boots had made his feet feel as if they were bathed in raw flame.

"When I get my hoss out of the livery this time I'll never take my pants out of the saddle again," he said with grim humor.

"You mean you have a horse here in town?"

Hatfield nodded. "My hoss Goldy," he said. "He threw a shoe, and I didn't have time to wait for him to be shod. Had to leave him in the livery here and take the train to 'Paso."

He noticed the puzzled light in Clay Tarrant's eyes, but offered no further explanation. He didn't tell of the killer he had learned was hiding in El Paso, of the fight that had followed when he had tried to make the arrest.

He strode into this different town now with his eyes narrowed. Sonita had changed mightily since he had last seen it two weeks before. It was no longer the drowsing little cow-town that showed life only during the spring and fall round-ups. Now the wide, hoof-riddled street thronged with excited men and women. Horses clogged the hitch-rails, and mule-drawn freight wagons rumbled and growled along the streets.

The town was filled with men he had never seen before—teamsters, cowmen, cold-faced gamblers, and bright-eyed Easterners who were in the hard grip of excitement that pulsed through the air.

Hatfield's keen ears caught the hoarse voice of a prospector striding hurriedly by him.

"Biggest since Sutter's Creek, they say! Washin' out twenty dollars a pan without scratchin' under the grass roots!"

Clay Tarrant snapped a sharp glance at Hatfield.

"Sounds like a gold strike!"

Hatfield nodded, saying nothing. He had

seen it before, although such things were not common in Texas. This was cow country, but the feverish hope for sudden riches had made cattle forgotten here now. Even the staid old townsmen had been caught up by the fire, and fine lines of disgust stamped around Hatfield's lips as he moved deeper into the town.

The strike was new. He could tell that by the high-pitched excitement that reigned. Tonight the town was full to overflowing. Tomorrow it would be a ghost of the past, and somewhere across the hot stretch of the plains another new town would be booming with all the violence that went hand in hand with gold madness.

He caught the arm of a man striding past, turned him around.

"Where's the strike?" he asked.

The man's face was beaded with sweat, and his eyes were hot and feverish.

"Tornado Basin!" he snapped back. He tried to jerk away, but the tall Ranger's grip held him.

"When?"

Anger flared in the man's eyes. "News came to town first thing this mornin'. Gent named Breck Shale made the strike." He bridled, his voice becoming hoarse and savage. "Don't waste any time, hombre! There's a couple hundred fellers ahead of me already—just got to town this mornin' —I aim to get some of that easy money if I've got to hang out 'til daylight to get a chance."

Hatfield released the man and turned to find Clay Tarrant staring at him strangely. Tarrant's voice came low and troubled.

"Tornado Basin! Dad and his pardner left word for me in El Paso that that was where they were heading."

Hatfield's lips became a thin, hard line. He could read the anxiety in Tarrant's eyes.

"Then yuh'd better get to the Basin as fast as yuh can," he said grimly. "If yore dad is in on this strike, he'll need all the help yuh can give him."

Tarrant's smooth face worked under the whip of clashing emotions.

"But the wrecked train!" he protested.

"I'll see that help is sent there," Hatfield said thinly. "There's nothin' yuh can do at the train, and I've got a hunch yuh'll find a big job cut out for yuh at the Basin."

He turned away, leaving Tarrant standing there, to shoulder through the milling crowd. A weathered, sun-beaten sign proclaimed a small building near the general store to be a doctor's office, and he turned in the open door to find a short, paunchy man hastily stuffing clothing into a worn valise.

"You Doc Windell?"

The man nodded without turning. Hatfield's mouth hardened, as he saw the doctor, too, was packing to join the stampede to the new gold field.

"I got a job for yuh, Doc," he said quietly.

The doctor jerked his hand irritably. "Sorry. You'll have to see Doc Standler, down the street."

"Like the devil I will!" Anger did not help Jim Hatfield's frayed nerves. The whip-lash of his voice brought the doctor around, startled. "I ain't got time to hunt through this mob for another doctor. You've got a big job ahead of yuh, and yuh're takin' it."

He lifted the flap of his shirt pocket, baring the silver-circled star. The doctor's eye's snapped to the badge, then lifted quickly.

"A Ranger!" he breathed, surprised.

"Yeah," Hatfield snapped. "And don't get too loose with the information. Get yore instruments, and rustle. The train was wrecked this mornin' at Black Rock Gap, and yuh're needed there bad, for some of them folks have been layin' there since mornin'."

He waited while the doctor grabbed up his black leather bag, and hurried to his horse at the tie-rack outside. Windell mounted, and Hatfield followed him through the crowd in long, stiff strides. He turned in at the livery stable, called, but no one answered.

"Jess, the liveryman, was one of the first to leave town," the doctor put in.

Hatfield bit back an oath, and moved close to the corral gate. He whistled a high, shrill note, and his eyes lighted as he saw the giant golden gelding trot eagerly to him. Goldy was a magnificent sorrel, long and powerful of leg and with speed as well as bottom.

He led the gelding out of the corral, found his saddle in the shed nearby, and strapped it on the mount. He barked a brisk order at the doctor.

"Ride ahead, and don't waste no time! I

got to stop at the telegraph office. I'll catch up with yuh later."

He swung into the saddle, and sent Goldy pounding down the street in a hard run past the motley line of wagons, buckboards and horsemen that was stringing out of the town.

He reined in at the telegraph office, swung out of the saddle in time to catch the clerk, who was throwing a heavy pack on a waiting horse. The clerk looked around as Hatfield caught his arm, a small, bespectacled man with a bony, flushed face.

"If yuh got a wire to send, yuh'll have to get somebody else," he burst out. "I quit my job ten minutes ago, and—" He got no further. His words choked off as he saw the chill glint in the Ranger's eyes. Hatfield laughed harshly.

"Feller," he drawled, "mebbe yuh quit yore job, but yuh're takin' it back long enough to tap out a wire for me," he rasped.

He sent the man stumbling into the telegraph office ahead of him, grabbed up a pencil, and hurriedly wrote on a message blank. He shoved the paper at the clerk.

"If yuh don't want to get tangled up in

a lot of trouble, yuh'll send that wire," he said grimly.

He waited while the clerk read the message back to him.

Captain Bill McDowell,
Headquarters, Texas Rangers,
Austin, Texas.

    Finished job in El Paso. Train wrecked at Black Rock. Part of shipment stolen. Am taking over at once.
Jim.

No more than that, and yet Jim Hatfield knew the rugged old frontiersman at Ranger headquarters in Austin would understand that where one job had been completed, another and even more dangerous task had been undertaken, one which had begun in murder and might end in further great violence.

Hatfield turned out the door, his craggy face a bleak, hard mask. The click of the telegraph key followed him as he swung into saddle, and somehow there was something darkly ominous in the sound.

Impatience weighed heavy on Jim Hatfield's frayed nerves during the ride back to the scene of the wreck. Already the outlaws had many hours' lead, and in spite of the fact their mounts carried the added weight of the bullion, the tall Ranger knew the chances were against him catching up with them before they reached the Border.

They could pick their own route, striking straight through the brush and grasses of the plains, or angling westward into the trackless wastes of hills. And he knew if he were to catch up with them in time, he would have to cling to the faint trail they left on the hard-packed earth in their flight.

No changes had transpired at the wreckage of the train since he had left. Guards patrolled both sides of the tracks with grim vigilance, while the passengers who were able to get about made the more seriously injured as comfortable as possible.

The Irish fireman met Hatfield with a growl of wrath. "The spawns of Satan got all the loot they wanted. Shure and if they'd come back, we'd have let 'em in for all the perdition they deserve."

The doctor paused briefly at the side of the tracks, his eyes traveling the line of the wreckage, moving from one to the next of the injured who had been stretched out in the scant shade.

He turned on the tall Ranger, as he slipped from the saddle, gripping his leather bag.

"Funny how a gold strike will make men forget all that's close to them," he said gruffly. "I'm obliged to you, Hatfield, for makin' me listen to reason. What I can do here is more important than all the gold I might have dug up in Tornado Basin."

6

Murder Trail

LIGHTS glinted in Jim Hatfield's eyes, as he swung Goldy off into the boulders to the south of the rails, the cold, inexorable lights of the manhunter. Here the air was smothered with still, dead heat that bounced from the rocks on all sides of him. He rode slowly, his mind forming grim pictures of what had happened when the tracks had been made in the thick dust below him.

He found an empty shell case where the killer had stood when he had fired his slug into the train's engineer. He swung his mount deeper into the rocks then, his lips thinning out when he saw where the rest of the outlaws had waited.

Each imprint in the dust had a meaning for him. He saw the smaller hoof marks where a mule had been led out of the rocks to be loaded with the bullion. The mule's tracks bent back into the boulders, to be joined by others, and he knew then that he had found the trail of the fleeing outlaws.

The tracks were plain here where the dust was thick and undisturbed by the shifting breezes, and he threaded Goldy through the boulders as rapidly as possible. He reined in sharply, as a dry brown splotch on a rock caught his eye. Blood!

His eyes chilled. He knew none of the train's crew or passengers had fired a shot, so that drop of blood could mean but one thing. There had been a fight between the outlaws, and one of them had been shot.

He nudged Goldy on. The boulders thinned out a quarter of a mile further on, and the trail dipped down into a brush-choked draw. He speeded the golden gelding's pace to a jogging trot, bending low when the tracks faded, straightening when the trail was clear and distinct.

Again and again, his keen eyes picked up the sun-dried brown spots where drops of blood had fallen, and it was nearly a mile from the train rails that Goldy suddenly shied away from a pile of dirt and stone beside the trail.

Hatfield dropped quickly from saddle, his narrowed gaze on the mound of stone.

It was innocent enough in appearance, no different from the other rock heaps that showed along the floor of the deepening draw, but he knew grimly what he would find before he kicked the rocks aside, baring the toe of a man's boot.

He worked swiftly after that, scooping away rock and dirt, until the body of a man lay exposed before him. The face that met his eyes was that of a half-breed, swarthy and evil even in death, thin-lipped, with high cheekbones and a narrow beak of a nose.

It was a face, moreover, that Hatfield himself would never forget, a face that he had first seen on a "Wanted" poster, a half-breed who was wanted for murder, and for whose capture a thousand dollars had been offered.

But it had not been for that money that Hatfield not so long ago had sought the man relentlessly. He had found him, too, hiding in an abandoned line shack. It had been a grimly ironic twist of Fate that at the same time the half-breed had been on a man-hunt of his own—for Ranger Jim Hatfield, the one man in the world that he most feared. Jim Hatfield also had all but finished his career then and there when, in his leap into the cabin after his quarry he had stumbled on rotting boards and been flung headlong before he could fire a shot.

Knocked unconscious, he had come to his senses with the half-breed having the upper hand. Hatfield had been tied, was lying on the floor, unable to move hand or foot while the half-breed had been having a dramatic holiday for himself, taunting the Ranger, threatening him with a shimmering knife, while he held before the eyes of the helpless lawman the poster which proclaimed him killer. To further play up his love for the dramatic the half-breed had dressed himself identically as he was in the picture.

It had looked all up with Hatfield for moments, he was remembering now—and that was when Goldy had come to the rescue. Not gagged, Jim Hatfield had been able to whistle for the sorrel, and with his usual intelligence, Goldy had come barging straight through the open cabin door. The Ranger would never forget the speed with which the killer had sped from the pawing forefeet and bared teeth of the mount.

Goldy had sped him on his way, too, and

finally Hatfield had been able to reach the knife on the floor and release himself. But too late to catch his man. From that moment to this Jim Hatfield had not again laid eyes on the man. Now here he was again—dead. With whom had he been tied up this time? That was one thing Hatfield would have given a great deal to know.

A dark blot high on the dead man's shirt showed where a slug had plowed through flesh and bone. Death had been instantaneous. That fact showed in the lines of horror that were etched rigidly in the man's features.

Hatfield stooped, going through the man's pockets. He found nothing to furnish him with anything more about the dead man than he already knew. He found a few matches, cigarette makings, a jack-knife, a few pieces of change and a greenback with one corner showing an unbroken black stain of ink. He pocketed each thing carefully, for there was a possibility they might lead to the other bandits; then with studied thoroughness, he turned the body over.

Something hard and round rolled under his hand, as he reached for the man's hip pockets. He pulled out his knife quickly, slit the keen blade through the man's shirt, groped inside, and brought out a .45 slug. He stared at it thoughtfully.

"Went through his body, and fell inside his shirt," he muttered. He stared intently at the blood-stained chunk of lead, his lips thin and hard. One side of the slug was etched by a narrow, shallow groove that ran from tip to butt.

"Well, that's somethin' to go on anyhow," he grunted grimly. "Whoever killed this jasper uses a gun with a barrel that cuts a groove out of every slug that passes through it."

He covered the body again, then turned quickly to his giant sorrel. The glint of light on ice was in his gray-green eyes as he mounted and rode on.

The draw deepened rapidly into a granite-walled gulch, as he followed the dim trail. He urged Goldy into a hard run, knowing the outlaws could not have changed their direction here.

For a full mile he hammered between the close-set walls, then abruptly the gulch gave onto a broad, hard-packed flat that was studded with cactus and sage. He was forced to slow his pace as he followed the tracks out on the hardpan. It was dim and indistinct here—a few shallow hoof depressions, disturbed rocks here and there, broken twigs. He lost the trail again and again, and finally it petered out entirely.

But he had its general direction, and determination drove him on. He rode Goldy forward, heading for a notch in the hills a couple miles ahead, and once there, swung out in a wide circle.

He cut the trail again, lost it almost immediately, and sent his mount forward, banking on the wild hunch that the outlaws had not turned off at an angle through the hills.

Sheer luck rode with him when he picked up the trail again, and yet it was not luck alone, for inside his keen brain was a deep knowledge of the character and nature of the breed of men he was following. They did not fear pursuit, or otherwise they would have made some effort to hide their trail.

He repeated the procedure again and again, following the trail until he got its direction, then leaving it to ride his mount ahead a mile or two and slow Goldy there to cut a wide circle until he picked up the tracks again.

The hours wore on, stagnant with the heat that hammered down from the westering sun. The country was growing rougher with each mile he progressed, and he knew that only by taking a wild chance could he catch up with the outlaws before they reached the Border.

He urged Goldy into a hard run, heading for a high barren hill several miles to the south, throwing all his hopes into the chance that from that upflung point he might be able to spot the outlaws.

Sun-fevered wind whipped at his face, and the gray-green of sage and cactus became a blur beneath the hoofs of his racing mount. Goldy ran with the smooth ease of a thoroughbred that was unmatched on the vast stretches of the Texas plains and hills. And he had plenty of bottom. Even under the strain of that long, hard run, he took the swales and coulees, the rock beds and cactus tangles without a break in stride.

Hatfield slowed his mount, as the land lifted toward the high crest of the hill. As he went up the steep pitch, his eyes shifted restlessly across the rangeland that billowed and rolled on both sides of him.

To the east and up toward the north, he could see the long, low-hanging pall of dust that marked the line of men stampeding from Sonita to the new gold findings at Tornado Basin. Townsmen, ranchers, tenderfeet and old prospectors alike were in that line, gripped by the mad fever of the rush. They would settle near the Basin, and a new town would boom with all the violence and bloodshed of the '49 days in California.

Powerful muscles snapped and rolled like cables under Hatfield's legs as Goldy pounded up the steep slope. He reined in on the crest, his narrowed eyes sweeping the south range toward the distant glittering silver of the Rio Grande.

Hope fell from the tall Ranger then. No moving object met his eye to mark the fleeing outlaws. And yet he knew they could not have reached the Border this soon, nor could they have escaped his eye in the draws and gulches that gouged the sun-beaten land. He was too high for that, and even if they had dropped into one of the many gulches he could have seen the gray fog of their trail dust.

His gaze shifted to the west toward the upheaval of barren mountains. But he saw nothing that moved. He pulled his eyes around to the east, halted them abruptly.

He could see them now! Not more than five miles away, they were, a knot of distance-stunted riders who were moving in the direction of the converging point of the gold stampeders. Grim fury drove like a storm through the tall Ranger.

"They must've heard of the strike!" he grated "They're plannin' on mixin' in with the gold hunters. If I don't stop 'em before they get there, may never get 'em!"

Only the gentlest touch of his spurs was needed to send Goldy hammering down the slope of the hill in a wild burst of speed. The flat spread of the range seemed to leap up at him, and at the bottom of the slope Goldy stretched out in his driving, matchless strides.

From the first, Hatfield was sure that the outlaws had seen him even before he had caught sight of them. But they didn't break into open flight as he swept toward them. Instead they separated, spreading out in a long line at right angle to the direction of his approach.

Puzzlement struck the tall Ranger, then dissolved into cold fury as the full force of their deadly plan struck him. They were not going to try to drive him back with their guns. They knew the crash of shots would bring the Ranger help from the line of gold seekers no more than two miles away. Instead, they had turned to Nature, and had found an even more effective block against the attack of the lone lawman—a wall of fire!

A swift-mounting puff of smoke rose from a clump of greasewood where one of the outlaws had halted his horse. Sunlight paled the red flare of flames that spread rapidly under the fanning of the freshening evening breeze.

An oath ripped from Jim Hatfield's lips. There was no more vicious deed on the frontier than burning a range. The fire drove off or killed all food game. It destroyed the forage of saddle stock, became a ravening monster that killed all life that lay in its path.

Hatfield saw the outlaw's rope loop uncoil through the air, drop around the burning bush heap, then the outlaw was spurring his horse savagely across the range. Embers of burning wood sprayed out behind him, catching fire in the sun-dried sage and bunch grass. Other outlaws sped their mounts back and forth, dragging flaming brush behind them.

Along a line of half a mile, scattered fires sprung up, mounted swiftly under the goading of the evening breezes to form a growing pall of smoke. The figures of horses and outlaws became vague and indistinct to the Ranger's eyes as he swept closer to them. He was within a mile of them now, hammering toward them with every atom of speed the giant gelding under him could offer.

But as he sped closer he knew he was powerless to stop the outlaws. He couldn't ask even Goldy to crash through the wall of hungry flame, for by the time he could reach it he knew it would be at least a quarter of a mile deep, and widening with each passing second.

Leaping fires threw a waving ruddy glow into the black clouds of smoke that climbed upwards from burning creosote brush. The outlaws were no longer visible, and Jim

Hatfield knew they had lost themselves somewhere in the tangle of swales and coulees beyond.

He reined up within a hundred yards of the line of the fire, hearing the sullen greedy roar of the flames, feeling the heat even at this distance.

He sat there a long moment, his mind racing. He was in no danger, for the breeze was blowing from behind him, fanning the flames to the east with almost unbelievable speed. And beyond that wall of fire—scarcely a mile and a half away—were the townsmen and prospectors and Easterners who had stampeded toward the new gold field at Tornado Basin. And unless he did something, flaming death would strike down some of those men and women!

7

Range Fire

HATFIELD'S face was a grim, hard mask as he turned Goldy parallel to the line of fire at a hard run. For nearly half a mile he hammered along until he reached a rocky, barren stretch where he knew the wall of flame would be the narrowest.

He pulled his mount in and whipped off his bandanna to blind the sorrel's eyes. He didn't like what he had to do, but he didn't hesitate.

"It's up to you, Goldy!" he said softly. "If we don't bust through here, we'll never make it in time!"

The giant gelding leaped out at a hard run at the gentle touch of the tall Ranger's spurs. Goldy whinnied in terror at the scent of smoke and flame, but didn't falter in his stride.

He hammered on until he reached the

smoldering black stretch the marching fire had left behind.

Heat that came as if from the door of an open furnace rolled around the horse and rider. It scorched Hatfield's face, forcing him to close his eyes in agony. It seemed that moment that his entire body was bathed in raw flame. He couldn't breathe, but still the black, acrid smoke pushed into his nostrils, choking him.

He lost all sense of time. There was nothing but smoke and flame and heat and the dull thud of Goldy's drumming hoofs. It seemed that even the magnificent sorrel beneath him must go down under such torture, but still the animal raced on.

Then abruptly a draft of fresh, clean air struck the Ranger. He opened his aching eyes, saw as if in a daze that he had penetrated the line of flame and smoke.

A chill hand closed over him as he looked ahead. Terror had caught up the gold stampeders. Seasoned old-timers, townsmen, prospectors, ranchers to whom a range fire was nothing new, were alike milling in confusion. Chaos reigned among them.

Some of them had left all their belongings behind to race on foot toward safety.

Others had tried to swing their wagons, only to get their terror-struck teams tangled in their traces. At one side a group of men and women, obviously Easterners, milled around excitedly, helpless in the face of this new danger.

Hatfield swung his horse off at an angle to intercept the fleeing men. His yell rolled out, hoarse and vibrant, as he neared them.

"Backfire, yuh fools! At that crick! Yuh can't outrun this fire!"

The jolt of the tall Ranger's words seemed to shock reason into the men, They halted their mad flight, realizing the futility of trying to outrun the line of fire that was racing toward them before the freshening breeze.

Hatfield swept down the line of them, his yell slicing out over the beat of his horse's hoofs.

"Backfire at the crick! String out and backfire, yuh fools!"

He swept on until he reached the huddled tenderfeet, then slid Goldy to a lock-kneed halt. He hit the ground at a hard run, caught the arm of the first man he met.

"Get spades, rakes—clear off the ground

on the other side of the crick! Scatter and work like sin if yuh want to save yore women and kids!"

The sharp ring of his voice was like a whip-lash that drove the tenderfeet into movement. They leaped to their wagons, whirled to splash through the narrow creek and throw themselves into the Herculean task of clearing off a lane for a backfire.

Hatfield caught a stripling youth by the shoulder, jerked the shovel away from him and threw it to an empty-handed man running by.

"Get help and unhitch the teams!" he ordered. "Yuh'll do more good by gettin' the hosses where they won't stampede when the fire gets close!"

He whirled without waiting to see if the youth had followed his command. He swept the stretch of the range with narrowed eyes. The fire was no more than half a mile away now, a ravening red monster of flame and smoke racing hungrily across the ground.

A single glance told him the men could not hope to clear off space for a backfire in time. The greasewood and sage were too tough to be cleaned away so quickly. And they had to have a broad clean space for the backfire, otherwise the flames would jump the narrow creek.

He spun, caught the closest man to him, and ran to a wagon. He uncoupled a heavy single-tree, grabbed his lariat from his saddle, and uncoiled it with a sweep of his arm.

"Tie both ends to the single-tree!" he yelled to the pilgrim, "and make shore they're tied tight!"

He turned, catching up the middle of the rope, and hitched it around his saddle-horn. He swung into the saddle, and at the hoarse call of the man behind him, sent Goldy forward at a run.

He splashed through the creek, turned up the bank, shouting for the laboring men to get out of his way. The heavy single-tree dragging behind him did the work of a dozen men, ripping loose a wide swath of sage and greasewood and cactus.

A hoarse yell of hope lifted from the men as he swept past them. They leaped out in his wake, clearing out uprooted brush, starting the line of their backfire. Hatfield swept along the creek bank twice before he cut loose the lariat, and dropped from saddle.

He scattered men along the line of fire with firm orders.

"Don't drop back till yuh have to!" he commanded. "Wet blankets, and be ready for any fire that jumps the crick!"

A wall of heat rolled ahead of the marching flames. It was something that took all the strength out of the bodies of the men, and left them fighting on nerve alone. Black clouds of smoke pushed out to thicken the air. The low-hanging sun diffused, became a pale glow through the smoke, then disappeared altogether.

Time hung suspended, lost and forgotten. Men fought with their backs to the creek bank until they dropped in their tracks and had to be dragged to safety. Their wives and children, faces blackened by smoke, their eyes red-rimmed by the heat, revived them, and they went back into the fight with grim stubbornness.

Time and again Hatfield saw the breeze toss burning embers across the creek. He blotted them out with a wet blanket until it seemed that every muscle in his body was made of lead. But still he drove himself on, and not until he felt a hand pulling on his arm, dragging him back, did he realize the heat had abated and that the fires beyond the creek were burning out.

He dropped back, and clean pure air filtered strength into his tired body. He looked around him, and saw a long line of men, smoke-blackened, exhausted, staring grimly toward the wall of dying flames.

A man moved up to him, his grimy face split by a weary grin, and the voice he heard came hoarse and croaking.

"If I look like you, Hatfield, I look like Satan himself!"

Hatfield chuckled. "Yuh shore ain't fit for no party, friend." He stared at the man narrowly. "Cussed if it ain't Clay Tarrant!" he broke out.

Tarrant nodded. Another man, short and square-built, came up, followed by a girl whose leaf-brown hair was disheveled and flecked with ash. Tarrant introduced them.

"Meet Sam Winters, and his daughter, Holly. They're from Ohio. Came down here with the gold rush, but I guess they didn't know they were letting themselves in for this."

As tired as he was, Sam Winters' voice was hearty, as Hatfield shook his hand.

"I'm glad to know you, sir," Winters said. "I guess every man here will want to shake your hand for what you did. If you hadn't showed up when you did, I reckon this would have ended a lot different."

The tall Ranger passed off the man's gratitude with a smile. Winters turned after a moment, to lead his daughter back to his wagon. Teams were being brought up and hitched, and already some of the less heavily packed gold hunters had resumed their march toward the Basin.

Hatfield pulled his gaze around to see young Clay Tarrant following Holly Winters with appreciative eyes. He chuckled.

"Looks like yuh've had yore heart roped already," he drawled.

Tarrant turned quickly, flushing through his smoke and grime. He laughed with low warmth.

"Can you blame me?" he countered.

Hatfield shook his head slowly. "No, I reckon I can't," he said softly. "She ain't enough right now to make any man plumb lose his head, but when she gets that smoke an' dirt from the fire fight cleaned off—"

He didn't finish. A shadow crossed his rugged face, making his wide mouth hard, putting an inexorable chill in his gray-green eyes. Tarrant noticed the change, and waited, saying nothing. When Hatfield spoke, his words were low in tone, grim.

"About the time that fire broke out, did yuh see a bunch of hossmen ride in to join the stampede."

Tarrant frowned slightly and shook his head.

"I was one of the first to spot the fire, and I didn't see anyone until you rode out of the smoke. Why?"

But if Jim Hatfield heard Tarrant's question he gave no answer. He voiced grim thoughts in chill words.

"Then they must have rode south under the cover of the smoke," he muttered. "Probably joined with the crowd at Tornado Basin without bein' noticed."

Tarrant spoke up thinly. "Who are you talkin' about, Jim?"

Hatfield smiled bleakly. "Them polecats that wrecked the train this mornin' and stole thirty thousand dollars in bullion. I picked up their trail at the train and followed it to west of here. They saw me closin' in, and started the fire to get away."

Tarrant's face stiffened, and his voice was sharp.

"They're a gang of killers! You had no business going after them alone. This is a job for the Rangers."

Hatfield smiled, but there was no humor in the uptwist of his thinned lips. He trusted Clay Tarrant, but caution that was even stronger bade him keep his identity a secret.

"When I see a job like that train wreck pulled off I make it my job to go after the killers," he answered calmly. "And while I think of it, don't mention my name to anyone, Clay, and make Sam Winters and his daughter promise the same thing. Don't ask why. Will yuh do that for me?"

Tarrant's voice came without hesitation.

"Sure, Jim, if that's how you want it. And you won't have to worry about the Winters'. But—"

"Don't ask any questions 'cause I can't answer 'em yet," Hatfield broke in grimly. "All I can tell yuh is that them killers came here. Easy money is a magnet for their breed, and the only way to catch them skunks is to keep our mouths shut, and our eyes an' ears open."

They made their camp that night on the flats that footed the uplifted rim of the Basin, and wakened at dawn to find that a town had sprung up around them as if by magic. Everywhere there was the bustle and excitement of men gripped by the raw passion of the gold rush.

Prospectors were already staking out their claims. The wiser heads were looking after the erection of merchandise stores and lunch-rooms. A broad-roofed tent had been thrown up, bearing a sign: "Gold Pit Saloon and Gambling Emporium," and the cold-faced brethren of the broadcloth fraternity were eagerly awaiting victims for their card magic and crooked roulette wheels. Whisky was flowing freely over a pine-slabbed bar to men whose normally tight purses had been loosened by the lure of new riches.

The price of breakfast had gone from two bits to a dollar, and freighters were being swamped with contracts to haul in supplies for the rapidly growing community.

Fine lines of disgust etched themselves into the corners of Jim Hatfield's wide mouth as he moved up the street. The town, only hours old, was giving hint of the corruption which would follow. Painted dancers would filter into the town by sunset. Chill-eyed, tight-lipped gunmen would drift in to join those already present. Communal law and order would be the last to come to break the grip of bloodshed and violence that was as inevitable under such conditions as day.

Shouldering through the thronging crowd, Hatfield saw a score of men capable of wrecking and robbing the El Paso train. But to not one could he direct anything but suspicion.

Nor did any of them show any sign of recognition when they saw him, but he felt no surprise in that. He had been too far from the outlaws to be recognized, unless it was when he had ridden his great gelding through the flames, and that offered but a slim possibility.

8

Boom Town

MID-MORNING had come and passed when Hatfield met young Clay Tarrant on the street. Tarrant's face was grim, and there were troubled lights in his eyes. The Ranger summed the situation up instantly.

"Yuh haven't found yore dad yet," he hazarded quietly.

Tarrant nodded soberly. "It's got me worried," he said. "I've met a dozen men who know him, know he's been out prospectin' but none of them have seen him around here."

"Mebbe he never came here in the first place. Mebbe he got sidetracked, chasin' some ore somewheres else before he got this far. Prospectors are like that."

But this did not stir any hope in Tarrant's eyes. The young fellow said nothing, gripped by his own anxious thoughts.

"What'll yuh do if yore dad don't show up—or until he does?" the Ranger asked.

Tarrant shrugged his lean shoulders. "Sam Winters has asked me to help. He wouldn't know gold if he saw it, and he's buyin' a claim—"

"*Buyin' one!*" The words jumped from Hatfield's hard lips.

Tarrant nodded. "Breck Shale, the man who started the rush, found his gold inside the Basin, not out here. He filed all the claims down there under the name of his boss, Harvey Britt, and Britt gave Shale orders to sell the claims to Easterners only. Shale is down the street now signin' up the buyers."

Chill lights leaped into the Ranger's eyes, and he swung around stiffly.

"That's some deal I want to see about," he growled under his breath, and stalked off down the street.

A crowd of milling men clogged the street in front of the Gold Pit Saloon—prospectors, cowmen, merchants, their angered yells throbbing ominously through the air. Hatfield halted at the edge of the mob, trying by a few words to temper the mounting threat of violence.

Hatred was adding to the flaring fires of fury. They were old-timers, these men, hard-working, hard-fighting individuals who had fought outlaws and Indians and Mexicans to help build Texas. They belonged in this country, felt that it belonged to them, and they had worked themselves up to a belief that they were being robbed of what rightfully should have been their own.

"What has them pilgrims done to deserve them gold claims?" a work-gnarled prospector's voice rang out. "We've took our chances against Injuns and owlhooters for years. Yuh think we're goin' to take it easy when yuh give yore claims to the first batch of tenderfeet that shows up?"

Hatfield fastened his narrowed gaze on the man who stood on the box in front of the saloon. This would be Breck Shale. He studied the man with a deep glance.

Shale was a big man of not more than forty, and in spite of his bulk there was a sleek, hard compactness about him. His face was flat-planed, and in it was a hint of mocking arrogance. His eyes were dark and fathomless. There was subtle, inflexible power in the man, and a full sense of it in the cool glances he shifted over the angered men before him.

"In the first place," he said in a deep, booming voice, apparently continuing an argument that had been going on for some time, "I'm not givin' these claims away."

Out in the crowd, a man laughed with harsh derision.

"Mebbe yuh call two thousand dollars for a payin' gold claim a bargain sale!" he jeered.

Breck Shale nodded, his expression unchanging.

"It's a bargain for these pilgrims I'm sellin' them to," he snapped back bluntly. "You gents around here have been ridin' me too long. I'm speakin' my piece now." He paused, holding the angered men with his dark glance, before he went on: "You men are on private land here, and I can have yuh thrown off if I have to. I work for the H Lazy B. Most of yuh ought to know that. When I found gold in Tornado Basin, I filed all the claims down there under the name of Harvey Britt, my boss."

He went on with level flatness, not offering a chance for interruption.

"Harvet Britt is one of the finest men in Texas. When he come here first he was a tenderfoot without a dollar in his jeans. But the State gave him a section and he built it into the spread you men are on now."

"This Britt boss of yores shore ain't spent much time around here that I know of," a cowman broke in harshly.

"Only because he's got me and my men workin' for him," Shale flung back. "He gave us all a break when we were down and out, and we're lettin' him take it easy in Austin. He gave us a hand when we needed one, and we're glad for the chance to pay him back."

"So practically givin' away his gold is yore way of returnin' favor!" a prospector jeered.

Shale pulled a cigar from his coat pocket, thrust it between his lips.

"We're follerin' Harvey Britt's orders," he snapped "He don't need more money, and he's takin' good care of us. When I discovered this gold, he ordered me to handle it his way. He left Austin and rode 'til he found these men who needed his help just as he needed help when he was a pilgrim new here fifteen years ago. Harvey Britt, I tell yuh again, is one of the finest men in Texas. He's givin' these pilgrims a break just like he did the men in his outfit, and I don't aim to see 'em shoved out of it!"

Someone laughed derisively "Yuh're askin' a big order when yuh try to sell a tenderfoot a gold claim for two thousand dollars, sight unseen."

Shale lighted his cigar, snapped the match between his fingers, then jerked his hand in an impatient gesture.

"Britt laid the proposition to them his ownself. They don't pay anything till they're satisfied with the deal."

Jim Hatfield, making his towering height as inconspicuous as possible while he listened, saw Sam Winters move forward toward Shale.

"Don't think we don't appreciate this chance, Shale," Winters said quietly. "We folks from back East think Harvey Britt is an honest and fine man if we ever saw one, but even if we take those claims, we won't know gold ore when we see it."

Breck Shale laughed heartily. "We ought to be able to get around that, all right," he boomed. "Here's how it stands and it's set up for yore own good. Once yuh take over the claims yuh'll be the only men allowed in the Basin, outside of my men who will be there to protect yuh from outlaws and claim jumpers. But so's yuh all will know what yuh're buyin', I'll let one man go with yuh to check the claims. I hear there's a feller named Clay Tarrant among yuh who is a minin' engineer. Yuh all know him, and he can go along first trip to advise yuh."

A chorus of excited yells lifted from the Easterners. Hatfield touched one pilgrim on the arm, and spoke when the man turned.

"When was it Harvey Britt made this offer to yuh, friend?"

The man frowned slightly, laboring under the grip of his excitement. His voice came hoarse, but distinct, through the tumult of yells.

"Just a week ago today, mister. This feller Shale's right that Britt's the finest man I've ever seen, and if he wants to help us out I don't see—"

But Breck Shale's words came again, silencing the crowd, and drawing the pilgrim's attention away from Hatfield.

"There's only one hundred good claims staked out down in the Basin. Britt is givin' a fair chance to all of yuh. Line up, and I'll take the names of all that's got the two thousand Britt put on the claims. We'll draw out a hundred names and make a list of 'em. That's just to make shore nobody sneaks past the guards I've got on the Basin trail. The guards will let yuh down there when yuh give yore name, and yuh won't pay me any money until Clay Tarrant vouches for the claims yuh're buyin'."

Jim Hatfield turned away as the tenderfeet crowded eagerly forward. Their excitement was something wild and contagious, but Shale's men kept order with grim efficiency. He saw that when an old-timer who had the sun and wind of a hundred prospecting trips on his weathered face tried to slip in among the pilgrims to give his name, one of Shale's men pushed him out.

The names were written on small slips of

paper, and when the last one was taken, the folded papers were dumped into a hat. Silence held them, freighted with the hopes and expectancies of these work-gnarled men from the East.

One by one the names were called out by Breck Shale, and the reading of each brought hoarse echos of exultation. Two men were left out by the drawing, and disappointment showed on their faces as if they had been struck stunning blows.

It was over then, and Jim Hatfield moved down the street, his gray-green eyes cold and brooding. One thing stuck in his mind. The pilgrim he had questioned had said Harvey Britt had made his offer a week ago, but the news of the strike had not reached the men of Sonita town until this morning. But there was an explanation for that. Britt had probably ordered Shale to keep quiet until the pilgrims had appeared on the scene.

And, clearly, Breck Shale was leaving no stones unturned to give the tenderfeet a square deal. Yet disturbed thoughts milled in Hatfield's brain. He could not put from his mind thoughts of the killer gang who had stolen thirty thousand dollars in bullion from the wrecked train, outlaws who were somewhere in this very town right now. He was gripped by an intangible feeling of impending disaster in the making, but there was nothing he could lay his finger on.

9

Crater of Gold

DUSK was coming on when the Easterners strung into the narrow rock defile that led to the lip of the down-trail into Tornado Basin. Clay Tarrant was the last to disappear from the view of those who looked on from the outskirts of the town, and he was followed closely by Breck Shale, mounted on a long-limbed grulla.

Not until the last man had dropped beyond the crest of the curved ridge that ringed the crater did Jim Hatfield move from the doorway of the newly erected general store. He didn't head toward his giant gelding, tied in at Sam Winters' wagon at the edge of town, but swung around the side of the store in long, smooth strides, carrying two heavy coils of rope.

He paused at the rear of the store, his eyes shifting narrowly about. Everywhere parallel to the street, he could see lumber piles, nail kegs—material for buildings yet to be erected. Litter and refuse already marked what before long would be called the town's Tin Can Alley.

But these things hardly caught the tall Ranger's attention. He saw no men, and that brought a grim smile of satisfaction to his lips. He moved away from the store, striding rapidly, until he reached the cover of a deep draw, gouging into the rocky soil. Here he paused, surveying his back trail with the intent caution of a man who knew he might be bringing danger upon himself.

But those left in the town had been too interested in the departure of the tenderfeet to have noticed him. He continued down the draw. When he was a full half mile from town, he turned up the steep, boulder-studded ridge that walled off the rim of the crater.

He moved slowly now, taking advantage of every cover that offered. He made no sound, moving like a shadow as he threaded his way between boulders that still held the heat of the afternoon.

He halted when he reached the crest of the ridge, to lay the coils of rope aside, and throw himself flat on the ground. Below him now was a naked wall of granite which swooped down as if it had been cut by a giant cleaver, a wall no man could go down or climb unaided.

Still deeper into the huge pit—nearly two hundred feet below the rim—the cliff sloped off on a steep incline of rock and rubble. Beyond that was the sage-dotted floor of the crater.

He lay there long minutes while the sun dropped below the western horizon and the haze-blue shadows of dusk gathered more deeply, his keen eyes missing not the slightest detail.

The Easterners had reached the bottom of the trail, and were vaguely discernible in the thickening gloom near a pine-slabbed building that had been set up. There was no sound from below and the silence was strangely ominous.

"Shake is checkin' again to make shore no one got in who wasn't wanted," the Ranger muttered.

Impatience rode him with barbed spurs, but he held back grimly, waiting for the concealing darkness of night to close down. He turned, squatting among the boulders and carefully knotted the lengths of rope together. It was a wild chance he was taking, one based on no tangible suspicion, but there was an urge in him to investigate, one that would not be denied.

Minutes dragged by, and darkness thickened. Above him nail-head stars were beginning to prick through the deep purple void of the sky.

At length he stood up, turned to loop one end of the rope carefully around a huge granite block. He knotted it, tested it, then bent low and moved to the rim of the cliff.

A sweep of his arm sent the rope uncoiling into the black depths of the crater. He had no way of knowing whether it reached the bottom of the cliff or not, nor the time to check. A bonfire was beginning to grow into life where the tenderfeet had gathered, and he knew it would not be long before Clay Tarrant was given his job to do. There were things the Ranger wanted to know before then.

He gripped the rope firmly, then without a sound swung out into space. Directly below the lip of the cliff, the wall curved inward, and for the first fifty feet down the rope, he spun dizzily in empty blackness.

Then his boots touched the wall again, and he steadied himself. He dropped down the rope more swiftly now, lowering himself hand over hand. It seemed the black distance was endless, but at last, panting and nearly exhausted, he felt his feet scrape the base of the cliff.

He took his weight off the rope cautiously, guarding against a careless step that might start a rock slide. The ground seemed fairly firm under his feet.

Rocks trickled from under his boots as he made his way down the talus slope, their sound seeming loud in the night silence. At length the incline leveled off, and he found himself on the dust-layered floor of the crater, ringed on all sides by looming walls of utter black.

As he moved across the level stretch with the inborn caution of an Indian, he made no sound to warn of his approach. He avoided sage and rock that were hardly visible in the thick darkness, working himself closer and closer to the leaping flames of the fire.

The Easterners were milling excitedly around the fire, and the murmur of their voices seemed strange and unnatural against the still of the night. Hatfield dropped flat to inch himself forward to the cover of a clump of greasewood. Here he halted, peering intently through the branches.

Breck Shale came out of the newly erected cabin a moment later, followed by a knot of gun-hung punchers. Hatfield's eyes swept over them narrowly. They were a hard-bitten crew, showing no expression in faces that were ruddy under the flickering light from the fire. In silence the Easterners turned to face Shale.

The big man's fathomless eyes passed over them, pausing intently on each man; then he spoke in a booming rumble.

"I reckon each one of yuh brought yore money?"

A chorus of "Yeahs" gave him his answer. He grinned broadly.

"I just wanted to know," he said heartily. "We ain't got no room for fourflushers down here. Harvey Britt is practically givin' yuh a fortune, and if some of yuh ain't got yore money to carry this deal through there's plenty up above who have, I reckon."

From Hatfield's hidden position, his

shifting glance fell on Sam Winters at the inner fringe of the crowd. His daughter, Holly, stood at his side, and Clay Tarrant was near her, lines of worry still etched in his clean-lined face.

"I'd like to make the test as soon as possible, Shale," Tarrant said quietly. "Night won't make no difference in business like this."

Breck Shale laughed boomingly. "I reckon there's another hundred gents here just as anxious as you, Tarrant."

He sobered then suddenly, and there was something cold and inflexible in his gravity.

"There's just one thing first," he said. "You men are new in this country, but I reckon yuh've heard of the outlaw gangs that hang around the Border. I'm responsible to my boss for all of yuh. Harvey Britt wants yuh to strike it rich. He's helpin' yuh the same as he was helped years ago. But he don't want yuh to lose yore pile to a bunch of crooks.

"So long as yuh're here, yuh've got to agree to this. I had a safe hauled from the home ranch, and it's inside the buildin' back there. I'll stay until yore claims peter out, and while yuh're here yuh'll keep yore gold in my safe. Is that all right?"

Shale's answer came in a babble of yells that rolled through the darkness. The big man waited until silence again came, then turned to one of the men behind him, and took a heavy gold pan.

"We'll make the test then!" he called out.

He moved away from the fire, a powerful stalking man in dark jeans and shirt and hat. Hatfield held to the cover of the greasewood grimly, straining his ears to catch the words that floated back to him.

"We'll take a sample from several places," Shale's voice boomed. "I prospected the whole crater carefully, and it's the same on all the claims, so it don't make no difference where I take the first sample. Here is as good as any."

Hatfield heard the scrape of the pan cutting into dirt, then the clump of boots again. Finally Shale's deep voice floated back to him through the darkness.

"We'll take some more here. A little of this dirt will do. . . . And some over here. That makes four samples from different places. Here's yore pan, Tarrant. Yuh can make yore test now."

Tenseness was in the tall Ranger's body as the men moved back to the fire. He could see their faces against the darkness beyond the flames, bright with excitement and beaded with sweat.

"Bring some water, Hack," Shale called out.

A short, thick-set man came from the knot of punchers, carrying a bucket of water. He set the pail on the ground beside Clay Tarrant, then drifted back to his fellows, no expression on his flat face.

Clay Tarrant's hand trembled slightly as he poured some of the water into the gold pan. He worked the pan slowly in a wavy circular motion. Silence again as Tarrant worked, a silence broken only by the hoarse breathing of the men who looked on.

A minute crawled by while Tarrant worked the pan, then he ceased the motion, and looked into the flame-lighted pan intently. When he looked up, there was a stiffness in his face that bespoke intense excitement within him.

"It's here!" he cried hoarsely. "Gold!

Forty dollars of it if there's a cent—and in only one pan!"

Wild bursts of cheering and shouts ripped from the throats of the Easterners. They leaped around like men gone mad, and not until Breck Shale lifted his arm did silence again close down.

"That ought to be proof enough, gents," he boomed. "Young Tarrant is a minin' engineer from a plumb fine school, and he ought to know gold when he sees it. I'll take yore money now, and yuh'll get yore papers to make the deal legal. And if any of yuh don't get back more money than yuh put in these claims, yuh can have yore money for the askin'."

Jim Hatfield hunched down in a crouch behind the bush, intending to back away from the fire. It was as he took his first step that a harsh voice jarred out from behind him:

"Don't be bashful, hombre. Get out there in the open, cuss yuh, and let us take a good look at yore face for a change!"

The rasp of the man's voice was like a whip-lash that cut through the excited talk of the Easterners. But Jim Hatfield well knew that, as far as he was concerned, life and death were hanging in a delicate balance. All eyes jerked toward the tall Ranger, some showing surprise, some amazement. And in the eyes of the men near Breck Shale was the cold ruthlessness of unfeeling killers.

Jim Hatfield showed only a cool disregard for the gun gouging into the small of his back as he moved into the light of the bonfire. Only in the steeling glint of his hooded eyes did he give hint of thin-drawn nerves and muscles as taut as coiled springs. His smile carried a shadow of ironic humor.

"Howdy, gents," he drawled easily. "Don't let me bust up yore show."

"Thought I seen somethin' move behind that brush over there, Boss," the gunman behind Hatfield broke out. "I circled around, and found this spyin' son gettin' ready to slip away."

Anger darkened Breck Shale's hard face, as he blared challengingly:

"Who in black thunder are yuh, hombre?"

Hatfield's smile changed to one of mockery. From the corner of his eye, he could see puzzlement and indecision on the faces of Clay Tarrant and Sam Winters. Holly Winters was looking at him, her strained face a gray oval against the backdrop of darkness.

"Me bein' sort of touchy about names," Hatfield drawled with deceptive mildness, "I never mention mine 'til I know who I'm talkin' to. Yuh're Breck Shale, I hear, but I ain't met yore gun-slick pards yet."

10

No Return?

SHALE'S flaring temper was like an invisible giant that shook him in it's grasp. A shiver rippled the length of his powerful frame; veins swelled like ropes across his forehead, and his eyes narrowed to pin-points. His hand moved toward his holstered gun, but he halted it with an effort that was apparent to the intently watching Ranger.

Then a subtle change swept over the big foreman, though plainly he was all the more dangerous because of it. He relaxed, and a hard smile twisted the hard line of his lips.

"The man behind yuh is Ben Latch," he sneered. "If an introduction will make yuh feel any better." His words carried a deadly note of derision, He waved a hand without shifting his inky stare. "Over here is Slip Cramer. Next is Hack Wadell, then Link Burman. Mack Deeven is on the far end."

Hatfield plumbed each man with a

penetrating glance. They were killers by every sign of the profession, thin-lipped, chill-eyed, gun-wary.

"And now mebbe yuh'll tell us who you are to come nosin' around on private property," Breck Shale said icily.

Hatfield shifted his eyes. He caught Clay Tarrant and Sam Winters with a glance, held their eyes a brief instant. Everything —perhaps life itself—depended on the meaning he had tried to convey to young Tarrant and the oldster beside him. He poised without moving a muscle, readying himself for whatever might come.

"Yuh can call me Tom Hadley," he drawled easily.

From the corner of his eye, he saw a quick frown on Sam Winters' brow. The Ranger did not like that. He had nothing tangible to go on, but somehow he knew with grim certainty that if his identity as a lawman became known here he would never live to get out of the crater. He moved forward to his toes, as he heard Sam Winters' amazed grunt.

"Why, he told me—"

The quick grip of Clay Tarrant's hand broke off the oldster's words. Breck Shale spun as if jerked by a string, dark eyes glaring. His voice roared out, harsh, strident.

"Yuh know this jasper, Winters?"

Sam Winters' sunburned face blanched in the firelight, but there was no hesitation in his words.

"Only from meeting him on the trail hereabouts. But he said his name was Haskett then."

Hatfield's low chuckle broke the abrupt silence.

"So I gave yuh that name, huh?" he asked Winters. "Looks like I'm gettin' plumb careless with the names I'm throwin' around. Take yore pick, Shale. What yuh call me don't make any difference to me."

Breck Shale turned back, his anger showing in the stiff slowness of his movement. Murder glinted stark in his eyes, but he had a hard grip on himself.

"So yuh're one of them gobblers that picks his own name, huh?" he jarred out. "I had yuh picked for an owlhooter the first time I saw yuh. What did yuh come down here for?"

The tall Ranger smiled thinly, playing his role.

"I figgered I'd get some of this gold yuh're givin' away," he drawled.

"Or mebbe the *dinero* these pilgrims brought with 'em, huh?" Shale rasped.

Hatfield shrugged dispassionately, said nothing. Silence was his best weapon here. He saw the big man flash a significant glance at Hack Wadell, then again he felt the cold impact of Shale's stare.

"How did yuh get down here?" the big foreman demanded.

Hatfield grinned derisively, "Pulled an old Injun trick on yore guards at the top of the trail. They fell for it like tenderfeet."

Breck Shale jerked around angrily.

"Link," he snarled, "take young Tarrant up the trail and see that he gets past the guards. Tarrant, when yuh get back to town, make shore that somebody has a place ready to lock up this outlaw. We'll bring him in after yuh've had time to get things ready for him, seein' there ain't been no time yet to build a juggado."

Clay Tarrant slanted Hatfield a worried glance as he moved off into the darkness behind Link Burman, but if the Ranger saw it he let no expression reach the blank of his face.

From the corner of his eye, he saw Sam Winters start forward haltingly, only to stop at the almost imperceptible shake of Hatfield's head. The oldster was still staring at him undecidedly when the gunmen closed around the Ranger and he was forced out on the trail.

"If he makes a break, shoot him down," Breck Shale ordered his men. "He come here to rob them tenderfeet, and by the eternal he'll pay for it."

Jim Hatfield moved up the trail ahead of the gunmen. They had not removed his weapons, and that was proof enough of their intentions. Murder was taking this dark trail with him. The promise of it was in the very silence of the men behind him.

But why? Was there, after all, something crooked in the deal Breck Shale was even now closing with the pilgrims? But this suspicion went from the Ranger's mind almost as quickly as it came. Clearly there was gold on the claims Shale was selling for his boss. Clay Tarrant was a mining engineer, and he knew gold when he saw it.

Pyrite—Fools' Gold—would have fooled the other Easterners, but not Clay Tarrant.

And what connection could all this have with the outlaws who had robbed the El Paso train of the bullion? None that was in reach of Hatfield's groping brain, but suspicion would not go.

He spoke up easily, trying to startle the gunmen behind him into some illuminating statement.

"You gents are fools," he drawled. "I'm onto the swindle yuh're pullin' on them pilgrims. Cut me in, or I'll spill everything when I get to town."

Mack Deeven laughed with cold derision.

"Hear that, boys? They say a crook always thinks everybody else is a crook. We're not pullin' a swindle on them pilgrims, Hadley, or whatever yore name is. We're follerin' the orders of Harvey Britt to give them back-Easters a start out here. And I wouldn't worry too much about gettin' to town if I was you. We have our own way of handlin' owlhooters on the H lazy B."

Jim Hatfield said nothing more after that. He moved up the trail in stalking strides, every sense keened for that instant when the gunmen behind him would make their play. All doubt concerning Breck Shale's purpose had left him with Deeven's statement. These gunmen behind him were planning his death. They would have no reason to lie to him now, unless from some queer, twisted sense of humor.

Then a new thought came. If by any chance these men were not outlaws, there was nothing to prevent him from giving his real identity. He opened his mouth to speak, but some instinct that had never failed him warned him against it. He moved on up the trail in grim silence.

The trail was a narrow, tortuous thing that snaked toward the break in the wall above in twisting switchbacks. It was when they neared one of those hairpin curves that Slip Cramer's toneless drawl broke the silence.

"I reckon he ought to make his break here, boys!"

At the same instant, Hatfield heard the metallic click of a hammerdog rocking back.

"Take it, feller!" Slip Cramer said.

Every muscle in the Ranger's big body came into play as he threw himself into a twisting side-leap. In mid-air, he heard the roar of the gun. He felt the whippy tug of death against a fold in his shirt, struck the ground, and hurled himself into the knot of gunmen in a low, battering dive.

A hoarse, startled yell sliced through the crash of a second shot.

"Get that devil!"

The full weight of Hatfield's plummeting body smashed into Mack Deeven's chunky frame. Deeven stumbled back under the impact, his gun blaring convulsively into the night sky, as he struck the men behind him.

They went down in a cursing, threshing, tangled heap. Hatfield rolled clear like a huge cat, spun, and broke into a wild run up the trail, hugging the thick darkness of the crater side.

Savage oaths came from behind him, and shouts.

"He's bustin' up the trail!" Yell jarred slumbering echoes from the cliff.

"Gyp! Lee! Plug the jasper headin' up there!"

A gun flared red behind Hatfield as he twisted around the switch-back. He was above the gunmen now, sky-lined for their weapons as he went up the straight incline.

Gun flame blossomed through the darkness below him, and he felt the whip-lash of death against his cheek.

Then he was around the next hairpin turn, and momentarily safe. He slowed his pace, searching the trail for a place of escape. But there was none. The trail was narrow, walled on one side by yawning space, on the other by the side of the crater.

The top of the wall was no more than a hundred feet above him now, and he could see the dark outlines of two gunmen crouching tensely at the lip of the trail. But as visible as the gunmen above were to him, he knew they had not yet seen him in the inky darkness.

He knew with grim irony that, lined against the sky as they were, he could have picked them off with deadly ease. But he made no move towards his guns, for he had no way of knowing yet whether they were fighting for the law or against it. And from Mack Deeven's statement, they might be ordinary punchers filled with hatred for the man they believed to be an outlaw.

A stunted pine, its roots clinging somehow in the shallow soil at the edge of the trail, loomed before the tall Ranger, as he rounded another switch-back. He halted, as one wild hope flamed in his mind. He could hear the boot falls of the gunmen behind him coming more rapidly now that they had less fear of running into a trap.

He bent, grimly testing the slender base of the tree with a hard grip. It felt solid, but if those roots tore out of the soil under his weight—He shut from his mind the thought of what would happen, and swiftly lowered himself over the rim of the trail. The tree shifted slightly, spilling a trickle of dirt and gravel into his face. Would it hold? He held his breath. But the slender pine settled and held.

The gunmen came up the trail a moment later at an alert trot, guns thrust out warily before them. Hatfield could hear their panting breaths as they drew near, and then through the barren branches of the tree, he made out Hack Wadell's narrow features. Mack Deeven came close behind, cursing in a low monotone.

"No moon!" he growled. "And that jasper could be around any of these curves for all we know."

Slip Cramer's high-pitched voice called out.

"Gyp! Lee! Work down towards us—close in on the gobbler. He's in here close somewheres."

"We are!" a voice floated down from above. "We're two levels above yuh. Who are yuh after?"

Ben Latch cursed, then called back: "Some nosey jigger that slipped in on us."

"He didn't get past us."

"He got in somewheres! Shut up, and close in. Plug him for good if yuh see him."

Mack Deeven moved past the pine so close that Hatfield could have reached out and touched the man's boot. Then Cramer and Latch went past with their prowling strides. Darkness shrouded them as they moved guardedly up the trail.

They halted at the switch-back a dozen feet away. From his vantage point the Ranger could see the two guards coming down from above.

A voice snarled a nervous oath.

"Cuss this kind of a job!"

"Who the devil is the hombre anyhow?" complained another.

"Some jasper that figgered on gettin' rich quick."

"He shore didn't get past us."

"Yuh said that before!" Ben Latch's sneering voice. "Tell it to the boss, Gyp. Mebbe he'll see somethin' funny in it."

The two groups rounded a bend to face each other across the level stretch.

"He ain't here!" Mack Deeven broke out harshly. "The tarnation son lost us somewheres down the line."

Slip Cramer snarled another oath.

"He ain't had time to get far," he said then confidently.

They were moving back down the trail now, searching for the least hiding place their quarry might have found. Then Hack Wadell noticed the stunted pine. He moved close to the edge of the trail, looked down, then uttered a short, vicious laugh.

"Well, look who's here! Cussed if it ain't our big nosey man!"

A chill draft fanned up Jim Hatfield's spine, as he stared up at the knot of gunmen. Here was death, inescapable. But he felt no clutch of terror. His mind remained cold and keen, knowing grimly that such a death as was about to be given him could not come from men who respected the law. Only killers of the lowest breed could stoop to this kind of murder, so now, through it all, he wondered what kind of deep game they were playing against the Easterners at the bottom of the crater.

Releasing the grip of his right hand, he dropped it toward his holstered gun. But he never reached the butt of the weapon.

Slip Cramer chuckled.

"Fifty bucks says I can put a gunful of lead in him before he drops out of sight!"

"And waste five slugs!" Ben Latch snorted derisively.

"Yuh'll never get rich that way, Slip!"

And then, viciously, Latch's boot kicked out and down. Jim Hatfield felt the fingers of his left hand go numb, then slip loosely from the trunk of the tree. He jerked his right hand up, but his frantic grab missed. Hungry space claimed him, dragging him down into empty blackness. As if from a great distance, he heard a man's harsh laugh of mockery.

He was vaguely aware of chill night air swishing past his ears. Memories of little forgotten things flickered through his brain with kaleidoscopic swiftness—his first horse, the kicking recoil that had jarred his wrist the first time he had fired a Colt, the way his father had laughed when the heifer had almost dragged him into the branding fire.

Falling . . . falling . . . falling.

11

Killers Take All

BRECK SHALE'S hard face was a gloating mask as he stared at the sheafs of money on the desk before him. The fever of greed was in his eyes, laying a damp sweat on his brow.

"A hundred pilgrims at two thousand a head!" he chuckled. "That's two hundred thousand. Beats handlin' wet cattle all holler!"

The sound of boots clumping outside the building brought him around fast. His hands were near the jutting butts of his guns as the door swung open. Hack Wadell and Ben Latch stalked into the room, followed by Mack Deeven and Slip Cramer.

The eyes of the four men flared bright, as they saw the greenbacks on the desk.

"So yuh got it!" Ben Latch burst out in a low hoarse tone. "I never knowed they printed so much money!"

But if the outlaw leader had heard Latch's remark, he gave no sign of it.

"What about that big jasper? Yuh take care of him? He acted like a slippery customer to me."

Mack Deeven nodded. "He ain't no more, Boss!" he chuckled.

Shale's eyes were like chips of jet. "Yuh shore of that? We can't afford to take no chances now. Yuh plugged him for keeps?"

Slip Cramer laughed thinly. "Well, we made him make his break, all right. But that jasper was a devil, Boss. He took us by surprise—guessed what he had comin', I reckon—and busted up the trail!"

"What!"

"Not so loud, Boss," Cramer spoke up quickly. "Yuh'll bring them pilgrims up here."

"Yuh mean that jigger got away from yuh!" Breck Shale demanded, a hard edge in his voice. "Blast yuh—"

"Gosh no, he didn't get away from us!" Wadell broke in. "That is, not for good. He busted up the trail, and we followed him. Gyp and Lee closed in on him from above, but when we came together he wasn't in between us."

Breck Shale's face was a mask of smoldering fury.

"Don't make me ask what happened!" he rasped.

"When we came together," Wadell went on quickly. "We figgered he'd lost us somewheres on the trail. We cut back, and found him hangin' over the wall from one of them scrubby pines that grow along the trail. Yuh know how big a drop it is from two-thirds up the trail—well, we just kicked him loose and let him fall."

Silence closed in on the room. Breck Shale leaped up from the desk, strode half across the floor, then swung round sharply.

"Did yuh check on him to make shore he was dead?" he ripped out.

Hack Wadell shifted uncomfortably, shook his head.

"We didn't see no sense doin' that. A hundred-foot drop is enough to kill any man, and—"

"By glory, yuh *are* checkin' on him!" Shale grated. "Yuh're goin' back there right now to make shore that jasper didn't come out of that alive. We're takin' no chances in this game"

"What chance would we be takin' if he

was alive?" Ben Latch spoke up thinly. "We got the money, ain't we? All we got to do is slope out of here and—"

"And leave thirty thousand in gold dust behind us?" Shale snarled. "Like fun, we are. We ain't rich enough to leave that much *dinero* here. Yuh're forgettin' Harvey Britt gets fifty per cent of the pile. Now get the blazes out of here, and don't come back till yuh're certain shore what happened to that big gobbler. . . ."

Thin lances of pain stabbing through his body drove the thick black clouds of unconsciousness from Jim Hatfield's brain. He lay quietly, slowly gathering the scattered fragments of his faculties. The realization that he was still alive dawned on him with profound amazement.

The last thing his memory had registered was of the red-hot splinters of agony that had shot through his body the instant his boots struck the ground. He vaguely remembered the plowing skid of his boots, his legs crumpling under him, the numbing impact of his body striking loose dirt and gravel. After that—nothing.

He opened his eyes with an effort,

pushed a dazed glance through the darkness around him. So it was still night! The tall Ranger grinned crookedly. It seemed like an eternity since he had felt his grasp kicked loose from the tree, plummeting him into empty space.

He sat up, testing each arm and leg doubtfully. It seemed that every muscle in his body was a lump of dull, throbbing pain, but there were no broken bones.

He turned, looking toward the cliff behind him, and then he knew why death had missed him. And still it all seemed incredible. He had fallen a sheer hundred feet, but the steep, loose pitch of the talus slope that footed the cliff had saved his life. The sharp angle at which he had struck had helped check the impact of his fall, and the quick loose sliding of dirt and stone had aided further to break the plunge of his body.

A low murmur of voices floated through the air to warn him of approaching men. He pushed to his feet, both hands striking down to his holsters. Somehow his guns had survived the fall and were still in there. That brought a glint of satisfaction to his narrow eyes. This time if Breck Shale's men cornered him, whatever the motive behind their purpose, they would get lead for lead.

He heard the grumble of a voice he recognized as belonging to Hack Wadell.

"My guess is that jasper is some get-rich-quick waddy that figgered he could jump a claim. Just the same I don't like the idea of him nosin' around like he was. And as for Harvey Britt—"

But he didn't finish that. Slip Cramer spoke up, in his tone a note of mirth.

"Well, workin' for the philanthropist, or whatever Shale says Britt is, has its advantages. I never figgered I'd get such a plumb-lot of fun out of helpin' a bunch of tenderfeet."

Mack Deeven chuckled with amusement that struck the tall Ranger as strangely grim and ominous. He could see the men now, outlined faintly against the deeper blackness of the night, moving directly toward him. He pulled both guns, crouching slightly as he waited.

"Reckon that nosey gobbler ought to be above us about here," Hack Wadell growled, his voice low, harsh.

"Yore eyes are bad, Hack!" came Ben

Latch's dry drawl. "It was farther west that we dropped him."

At last the gunmen angled off, and then faded into the darkness. Jim Hatfield moved down the slope guardedly, then as he reached level ground, strode quickly in the direction of the rope down which he had come to enter the crater.

The use of his muscles helped dissipate the stiff soreness in his body. He was hardly aware of the blood that streaked his arms and legs and back from a dozen bruises and rock scratches.

He turned up the talus slope when he came abreast of the spot where he had dropped the rope. He moved up the loose incline with cautious speed, for already he could hear the distant voices of the gunmen working around the cliff, still in search of him.

He reached the the foot of the granite wall, his narrowed eyes stabbing the darkness for the dangling rope. He found it a dozen feet to one side of where he had halted his climb when he had entered the Basin.

He locked his wide lips tight for the supreme effort of the long climb back to the top. His body had been weakened by the shock of his fall, but grim purpose tapped some inner reservoir of strength.

He went up the rope hand over hand, his boots taking advantage of every support the cliff offered. He had reached the overhang of the wall when Ben Latch's harsh voice floated up from almost beneath him.

"Hang it all, that gobbler couldn't have got up the trail without Gyp and Lee seein' him. He's still in here somewheres."

There was no support for the tall Ranger's legs here at the over-hang. He was dangling in space, the full weight of his body on his arms, and he expended every atom of power he could summon as he pulled himself upward.

His breathing thickened and his lungs ached. His arms seemed to be turning to lead. But still he hauled himself up the rope, slower now as his strength was drained by his tremendous exertions. He felt dizzy and weak and sick inside, but there was within him an indomitable will that would never admit defeat.

His vision was blurred and indistinct when at last he reached the lip of the cliff. He paused a moment, gathering the last dregs of his strength, then slowly pulled himself up to the level ground. And the last he heard as he sprawled there, full length, exhausted, was a hoarse voice that floated up to him from the crater:

"Reckon we might as well go back now boys and tell the boss. No findin' that jasper now—he's too well hid. But I *still* say he can't get out of here...."

The pale of dawn was climbing over the eastern wall of the crater when the four outlaws returned to the shack. Breck Shale met them just inside the door, his piercing black eyes reading his answer before he voiced his question.

"So he got away!" he sneered.

Ben Latch nodded jerkily. "Cussed if I know how, but that's what happened," he admitted. "It took us half the night to find where he hit. There was blood all over, but we couldn't find him. We spread out and combed the whole Basin, but we never did see where he went. He's still in here, though. That's shore, for there ain't no way for him to get out except to go past Gyp and Lee. They'll get him if he tries that."

Breck Shale jeered derisively.

"Yeah—mebbe! They didn't get him when he slipped in, did they?"

He fastened hot black eyes on Slip Cramer.

"This is a job for you, Cramer," he rasped. "Get yore hoss and rustle to town. That'll be the first place he'll head for if he gets out of here. And when yuh see him this time, make shore yuh put him out of the way for keeps!"

12

Tangled Threads

ONCE Jim Hatfield realized that he was safe for the time being, on top of the cliff edge, he also realized that there was no time for rest. Grim purpose drove him on, with more now to think about than he had had before. He straightened, quickly pulling the rope up after him.

He left the coil hidden beneath a projecting shoulder of rock, and moved toward the town in long, stumbling strides.

A shadow detached itself from the wall of a building as he neared the end of the street. He jerked to a halt, hands stabbing down toward his guns, but Clay Tarrant's quick call stopped them.

"Jim—it's me!—Clay!"

Young Tarrant moved toward him at a run, anxiety in his face. He halted stiffly before the Ranger, taking in the lawman's battered body with a swift glance.

"What in blazes happened to you?" he said hoarsely. "Where've you been? I've waited here all night for you, ever since I left the Basin."

Hatfield chuckled, but it was with a lack of mirth.

"I've been plumb near in my grave," he grated. "Breck Shale's brother angels was set to plug me. I busted away from 'em, but they found me, dumped me over the cliff."

"They did that!" Tarrant's tone was sharp, intent. "But why?"

"That's what I want to know," Hatfield rasped. "Mebbe they thought I was an outlaw aimin' to rob their pilgrims. They hinted somethin' like that, and I shore didn't tell 'em different. Mebbe they had another reason. That's a hunch I can't get out of my mind."

Clay Tarrant's expression changed, to puzzlement, doubt.

"What do you mean?" he asked slowly.

The Ranger jerked his head "I don't know what I mean," he said flatly. "The whole business is a mess of tangled threads I can't get straightened out. First the El Paso train is wrecked and looted, and the killers that done it hide out hereabouts somewhere. Breck Shale starts sellin' gold claims to pilgrims for his philanthropist boss, and then orders his hired killers to put me out of the way when I get curious. Mebbe they do think I'm an outlaw—I don't know. But there shore is somethin' loco in this somewheres."

"It's not in the gold claims," Tarrant said firmly. "I saw Shale take the samples, and those claims will pay fifty thousand dollars the way that one pan showed color."

"And that's a heap of money," the lawman said pointlessly. "Where-at did he take them samples? I could hear him, but I couldn't see him in the darkness."

Tarrants lips tightened. "They were all twenty or thirty feet apart. I was right behind him all the time."

"Near anything in particular?"

Tarrant frowned. "He didn't seem to care where he scooped up the dirt. Come to think of it, though, he got it all around rocks or brush clumps. But that don't mean anything."

Jim Hatfield's eyes were brooding. "Uh-huh. Mebbe."

Silence built up between them while dark

thoughts worked deep into the Ranger's brain. There seemed no connection between any of the salient facts that troubled him—the robbing of the train, the attempt on his life, the bargain sales of valuable gold claims to the Easterners. And yet he was haunted by a conviction that there was a connection some place, and that when he found it a red holocaust of bloodshed and violence would descend on Tornado Basin.

"I got a job to do, and I shore can't do it standin' here," he growled finally.

He started away, then halted, turning.

"Yuh hear anything about yore dad yet?" he asked.

A shadow passed over Clay Tarrant's face.

"Nothing," he answered wearily. "But he was here. I found this in the dust where the trail crosses the crater ridge." There was bitterness in his tone as he reached into his pocket and brought out an old pipe. He held it to the Ranger. "It belonged to Dad. I gave it to him three years ago when he visited us back East."

Hatfield looked at the pipe intently under the thin light of the high moon. It was a battered, scarred thing, with a tooth-pitted bit that held a dark stain of dried blood. When he looked up, there was sympathy in his gray eyes.

"I wouldn't go lookin' for yore dad any more if I was you," he said quietly. "I don't think yuh'll ever find him—alive."

He didn't look back to see the pain in young Tarrant's eyes. Grimly he plodded on toward the livery barn.

Dawn was pushing its pale flush over the eastern horizon when Jim Hatfield swung his giant gelding down Sonita's main street. He reined in at the telegraph office, dropped stiffly to the ground, his face a haggard mask.

A gaunt, hollow-cheeked man dozed at a desk behind the counter when the Ranger strode into the office. He reached across the counter and shook the man who jumped to his feet, startled, fear in his eyes.

"You the new telegraph operator?" Hatfield demanded.

The man dropped his head in a nod.

"Yeah, but if you're after money—"

"This is no hold-up!" Hatfield broke in. "Get to yore key. I got a wire to send, and tell whoever yuh have to tell to make this rush."

The man dropped into his chair and clattered a telegraph key a moment. He slanted Hatfield a quick glance.

"I'm ready."

"To Captain Bill McDowell, Ranger Headquarters, Austin, Texas," Hatfield dictated crisply. He paused a moment while the telegraph key clattered sharply, "Send information at once on Harvey Britt, now living in Austin, owner of H Lazy B ranch, Brewster County. Jim."

He listened to the staccato rattle of the key until it clicked silent.

"How soon will I get an answer, pardner?" he asked then.

"Inside of an hour if yore party don't delay things," the operator answered.

"He won't," Hatfield clipped. "And don't run around talkin' about this, savvy?"

Sonita town was a ghost of what it had been only a day previously when he strode out into the street. He found most of the buildings boarded shut, but the hotel was still open. He went through the door, and spoke to the clerk idly sweeping the floor.

"I'd like to spruce up a mite" he said.

The clerk grinned at him, and waved a hand.

"Take any room yuh want, brother. Everybody moved out like the place had the plague when they heard of the new gold strike. Mebbe thirty-forty folks left in town, and I reckon they'll be movin' out before long. Yuh can get a bite to eat at Ching Foo's place down the street, if yuh're hungry."

Hatfield nodded and thanked the man. He got fresh clothing from his saddle-bag, washed in one of the hotel's vacant rooms, and after he had eaten breakfast at the Chinese lunch room, he felt immeasurably better.

His first concern had been for his golden gelding. The hotel clerk had been eager to take this job while Hatfield changed clothing and had his meal. Hatfield himself had been unable to attend to Goldy, for the livery barn had been locked when he stopped there.

An hour had passed when the Ranger entered the telegraph office once more. The operator was again dozing at his desk, but he wakened quickly as Hatfield strode in. He grinned wryly.

"Don't get no sleep at all on a job like this," he complained.

"Yuh ought to get plenty if the town stays like it is now," Hatfield said. "Yuh get an answer to my wire yet?"

The man nodded, and handed over a piece of paper.

"Just got in."

A cold glint crept into the Ranger's gray-green eyes as he read the message. It was crisp and terse, and with a thin vein of grim humor that characterized the grizzled old frontiersman who captained the Texas Rangers.

Hatfield read the message slowly, then scanned it again intently, letting the full meaning of the telegram sink into his brain. It read:

> You got a name, but we ain't got the man. Harvey Britt not known here. H Lazy B long suspicioned of handling wet cattle.
>
> BILL.

A thought leaped into Jim Hatfield's brain,

caught a spark, flared into flame. It was only a hunch at best, and yet it could be the key that would unlock this whole murderous tangle—a door that would open on a man of more vicious treachery than any he had ever come up against.

He turned without an expression on his craggy face, and stalked out of the express office.

He didn't see the wizened runt of a man who stepped quickly behind the cover of the saddle shop as he mounted and swung Goldy down the street at a lope. Nor did he see the gun that swept up to level on his broad back.

Slip Cramer's pale eyes were bright with murder, as he squinted down the sights of his gun. His bony thumb rocked back the hammer, then a look of indecision crossed his narrow face.

"Mebbe I ought to find out what that jasper was up to first," he muttered in a low snarl.

He waited until the tall rider had disappeared from the distant end of the street, then sheathed his Colt, and slouched towards the telegraph office.

He strode through the doorway and,

without hesitation, pushed around the end of the counter. The telegraph operator half raised out of his chair, as Cramer moved up to him in his short, choppy steps.

"Hey, you ain't supposed to be back here—" the man began.

"The devil I ain't!" Cramer cut him short. "Hombre, if yuh've got any sense, yuh'll play yore hand close. What was that tall jasper doin' in here? He got a wire, didn't he? I want to see a copy of it?"

Fear flooded into the telegraph operator's eyes.

"But I ain't allowed—"

He choked that off. Unreasoning anger seemed to grip him suddenly. He twisted around, trying to reach the gun inside the open drawer beside him. But he had no chance.

Slip Cramer laughed.

"Yuh blasted fool!"

His gun whipped out of leather, swept up and arced down viciously on the back of the man's head. He didn't wait to see the operator slump limply from his chair. He turned, his pale shallow eyes coldly dispassionate, to riffle through the papers near the telegraph key.

He found what he wanted, read it in a swift glance that brought an oath from his thinned lips.

"So that's who the nosey son is!" he snarled. "Jim Hatfield—Texas Ranger! *The* Jim Hatfield. Well, this is one law job that will land that gobbler's neck deep in the pit!"

13

An Old Man's Pipe

AS Jim Hatfield held his giant sorrel across the broken range south of Sonita, Goldy made time in a distance-consuming lope. He rode loosely in his saddle, his back straight and erect as if he drew some quality of strength from the heat that hammered down on him from the high sun.

He had only a general idea where the H Lazy B ranchhouse lay, garnered in random conversations with the men the day before in the new tent town in Tornado Basin.

He was thinking as he rode—so Harvey Britt's ranch had been under suspicion at Ranger headquarters of handling wet cattle. The thought tightened Hatfield's wide lips, and put a hard set to his rugged face.

Dealers in wet cattle had been one form of outlawry that as yet the Rangers had found impossible to stamp out. The country north of the Rio Grande was too vast, too unsettled to be controlled by so few lawmen. One Ranger could be but one place at a time, and while he was watching one suspicioned rancher, outlaws at a dozen other points could be driving stolen herds across the muddy shallows of the Rio Grande, and returning with herds which had been rustled from Mexican *rancheros.*

Hatfield's thoughts were of such things when he sighted the sprawling buildings of the H Lazy B some distance across the heat-withered range to the west. He swung Goldy off at an angle, reined in to a slower pace as he approached the house cautiously.

The ranchhouse, a huge adobe and frame structure, had been built near a narrow, cottonwood-fringed stream that somehow at this late season had escaped the burning rays of the sun. A post corral fanned out at the rear of the house, and near it were the saddle and tool sheds and other miscellaneous ranch buildings. The bunkhouse, low and solid-looking, squatted well to one side of the main building.

No sign of life greeted the tall Ranger as he reined in at the front of the house. He called a loud, "Hello!" then slipped from saddle when empty silence brought back his echo.

He strode forward, his narrowed eyes shifting restlessly around. He reached the low portico that ranged along the front of the building unchallenged. He paused at the door, every sense keened to catch any warning of danger, but no sound came to break the silence.

Tight-lipped, he tried the door, and was not surprised when it swung open easily. He stepped through the portal, eased the door shut behind him, his swift, all-inclusive stare taking in every detail.

The room was long and broad, with bare walls of adobe and heavy, brown-stained ceiling timbers showing overhead. A set of deer antlers just above the door held a shotgun, and a well-filled rifle rack stood against the far wall.

Hide rugs covered the unfinished boards of the floor, and a heavy oak desk stood in a distant corner of the room. Hatfield strode toward this in smooth, catlike strides.

The desk top was covered with the usual litter of ranch records. A tally book told the Ranger nothing; there were several receipts from an Eastern supply house, and a few mail-order catalogues.

But it was the gold-framed picture on the desk that caught and held Jim Hatfield's attention. It was the likeness of a man who was obviously big and powerful of body—a man dressed in dark town clothes, and bearing the inscription in one corner:

To Breck—from Harvey Britt

Hatfield picked up the picture, staring intently at the image of the man who was said to be living in Austin, and yet who was not known in that town.

Britt's face was strong-featured and square of jaw, showing thick burnsides that pointed down almost to the heavy black chin whiskers he wore. His eyes were dark and showing an inflexible glint even in the picture, and a cigar that had trailed a thin wisp of smoke when the photograph was taken jutted from the man's mouth.

A small, crooked object low in the picture in front of Britt's polished boots caught the Ranger's eye. It proved to be a match that apparently had been broken into a V by the man when he had lighted his cigar before standing for the picture.

"So this is the mysterious Harvey Britt," Hatfield muttered. "The philanthropist who practically gives away rich gold claims and at the same time owns a ranch suspected of handling wet cattle.

"Looks to me like Mr. Breck Shale is doing a little doublecross business on his own hook."

And at that moment, the echo of that thought brought another question to the Ranger's mind. What kind of a doublecross was Breck Shale pulling? Wet cattle? Perhaps. It would be easy with Britt away from the ranch all the time. But where was Britt? *Who* was he?"

Hatfield stood there, tall and gaunt and brooding as he returned the picture to the desk. A faint scowl was on his brow as he glanced through the papers before him. He picked up the last paper, and it was then that he saw the black stain of spilled ink on the top of the desk. A sharp-lined V showed where the ink had failed to reach part of the wood, and the sight of it brought hot lights into the Ranger's eyes.

He reached long fingers into the pocket

of his shirt, brought out the ink-stained greenback he had taken from the body of the dead half-breed at the site of the wrecked train He laid the greenback carefully on the table, shifted it slightly, his lips a flat, hard line across his face. It fitted perfectly.

"So now I know who that breed has been running with, since he got away from me before! He helped pull off the train job—and was one of Breck Shale's men! Shale didn't bother to keep this ink-stained bill when he took all the identification papers out of the half-breed's pockets. Shale sat here and paid off the breed for some job when he knocked over a bottle of ink. The ink stained the desk top everywhere except where this greenback was layin', and I reckon that little mistake will put Shale's neck in a hang-noose!"

He didn't realize that he had been muttering aloud until behind him a harsh voice sneered.

"And yore long nose is goin' to land you in Boot Hill, Ranger!"

Jim Hatfield whirled as if he had been jerked by a string. He caught a flashing glimpse of Slip Cramer crouching in the doorway over leveled guns, and that same instant he threw himself backward in a roll across the desk top.

The room seemed to shudder under the double blast of the killer's guns. In full movement, Hatfield felt the whippy snap of a slug passing through the felt of his hat. Within scant inches of his face as he dropped behind the desk, he saw lead cut a ragged gash through the thick oak top.

Then he was on the floor in a tight crouch, both guns jutting out in his hand. He chanced a quick glance around the end of the desk, swayed back as the hot breath of death roared past his face. He swung his right gun into the clear, shooting entirely by his sense of direction, and raked the doorway with a blast of lead.

Then he jerked erect, his face a hard mask as he threw his left gun up and out. But the killer was nowhere in view. Puzzlement struck the tall Ranger, warning him. He moved away from the desk, placing his back to the thick adobe wall, and waited.

There was no sound to give him the location of the killer. Silence closed around him, pulsing with impending violence, and his nostrils were filled with the acrid tang of burned powder. With his eyes narrow gray-green slits of danger, he edged around the wall to throw a quick glance out the front window. Cramer was nowhere in sight. He scowled darkly, smothered a harsh oath.

"If that polecat tucked his tail and ran, he's got less nerve than I think he has," he growled, under his breath.

He reached the door, leaped across the open space in a single long stride, but he didn't draw the roar of a gun. He kicked the door shut, bolted it, then went cautiously from room to room. They were all empty. Nor did his swift glances through the windows show him the stunted body of the killer.

He returned to the front door, troubled by something he couldn't understand.

"Mebbe he sloped back to warn Shale," he muttered, but that thought seemed hollow and unreal.

He raised the lock-bar with his knee, swung the door open swiftly, gun muzzles high, and himself alert. No moving thing caught his darting glance—too still. The silence grated through him, fraying thin-drawn nerves.

He moved across the portico in slow, prowling strides, his shifting eyes covering the open space on both sides of him. The hot glare of sunlight struck him when he passed beyond the board awning of the house.

He halted there, trying to put himself in the killer's position.

"If I was scared of the hombre I was after, I'd duck back to some hidin' place and plug him from there," he told himself.

There was no concealment ahead of him, except the cottonwood-fringed creek, and his quick-stabbing eyes told himself Slip Cramer had not chosen that place.

Hatfield moved forward slowly, his flicking side-glances touching the bunkhouse and other scattered outbuildings with intent care. He drew near his waiting sorrel, halted, warned by some unfailing instinct that jangled his brain. He moved swiftly, fading to one side, dropping low, spinning.

At that same instant, he heard the *thwack* of lead plowing through the dust where he had stood, the sound followed a second-fraction later by the whippy snarl of a rifle.

His glance shot around, halted on a high knoll a full two hundred yards away. A small figure was outlined there against the pale of the sky—the figure of the killer crouching over a leveled rifle.

"The coyote!" Hatfield rasped. "Figgers he can keep me holed up till help comes!"

Anger drove through the Ranger like a hot flame. He twisted around, lurched forward in a crouching, zigzag run. Twice he heard the vicious whine of lead as he drove across the open space, but his sudden move had caught the killer by surprise. Cramer had expected him to break for the cover of the house.

Hatfield threw himself flat behind the low creek bank, his mind racing. He had known from the first that any attempt to reach his rifle in Goldy's saddle-boot would have brought a slug to the giant sorrel. And armed as he was only with his short-guns, he was helpless unless he got in close quarters with the killer.

He began a slow, stalking movement through the cottonwoods, hugging the creek bank and the deeper shadows of the trees. The rifle was silent now, but he knew that Cramer was waiting confidently for the moment when he would be forced to expose himself.

He followed the creek like a stalking Indian to where it bent sharply toward the foot of the hill. The trees thinned out a hundred yards beyond this point. He lifted his head cautiously above the line of the creek bank, eyes narrowed against the white glare of the sun.

He could see Cramer more clearly now, his wizened body sprawled out on the crest of the hill a scant hundred yards away. A thin splinter of sunlight shunted from the outthrust rifle as it moved swiftly.

Hatfield dropped back behind the bank, shifted his position quickly to one side, grinned crookedly as a rifle slug spurted a miniature volcano of sand where he had been a few seconds before.

He lifted his Colt slowly, raising the long barrel to allow for the distance, and let the hammer drop. He heard a startled yell that ripped from the throat of the killer, saw Cramer roll back frantically out of sight. Hatfield laughed harshly, hurled out of the trees in a hard run.

"Now let's see how yore nerve stacks up!" he snarled.

He saw the killer's head raise over the top of the hill, snapped two quick shots at it. He was close enough now that he could see the gouts of dust his slugs kicked from the ground within a foot of Cramer's head.

Cramer snapped a shot with his rifle, rolled back out of sight, reappeared two yards farther down the slope, his rifle barrel striking out with deadly intent. Fear gave courage to him now, and he crouched there in spite of the slugs that tall Ranger crashed at him. His rifle jumped, roared. Hatfield staggered to one side, feeling for a brief instant as though a hot iron had been laid against his side. But he didn't halt his savage run.

He was quartering the barren slope of the hill now. It was man against man with equal weapons! It was nerve against nerve, with death hanging in the balance!

14

Killers Die Hard

UNDER the sway of terror, Slip Cramer dropped back as the running Ranger shortened the yards between them. Cramer crouched like a cornered wolf, lips peeled back from set teeth, pale eyes slitted.

His rifle crashed again and again, its heavy roar throbbing in the hot afternoon air, but fear and terror sent his slugs wild of their mark. But there was no haste in Jim Hatfield's movements.

He saw Cramer throw his emptied rifle to one side, snatch madly at his holstered guns. The Ranger's harsh yell bellowed out:

"Don't try it, Cramer!"

But the runty killer was beyond reason. His twin Colts jumped as if by magic from their leather sheaths. It was as they flicked level that the Ranger fired.

Cramer's body seemed lifted into the air

under the shock of heavy slugs. He was hurled backward, shivering in mid-air like a leaf under a wind, and his legs gave way under him as they struck the ground, spilling him in a loose heap.

Jim Hatfield's face was like chiseled stone as he knelt beside the killer. Cramer was sinking fast, but there was no melting of the evil that had gripped his soul. His eyes were like those of an animal, red-rimmed, showing pain, horror, unquenchable hatred. His breath was coming hoarse and ragged.

"Well, yuh got me, Ranger. Why don't yuh laugh about it? It's yore chance to crow!"

A faint bitter smile relaxed the stiff line of Hatfield's mouth.

"I tried to stop yuh, Cramer. You made me do it." He bent low to the dying man. "This is yore last chance to square yoreself Cramer. You and the rest of Shale's crowd robbed the El Paso train. I know it—I can prove it. But why?"

But even death could not shake the wizened killer. He chuckled, a low, gurgling sound of mockery.

"Go hang, Ranger," he snarled.

His face was blanching to the gray of ash as death tightened its hold on him. His breathing was shallow and uneven, and a feverish glaze was giving an unnatural brightness to his eyes.

"Yuh want a cigarette, Cramer?" Hatfield asked quietly.

A hungry glint filtered through the shadows that fogged the killer's eyes.

"Yuh mean—yuh'd give *me* a—a smoke, Ranger."

"Shore, Cramer."

But Jim Hatfield didn't reach for the makings. For Slip Cramer was already dead.

Weariness was a growing weight on Jim Hatfield's shoulders when, a little later, he swung Goldy along the trail toward the new boom town. The exertions of the night before, and this day's long ride had been a deep drain on his iron vitality, but the inexorable determination of the manhunter drove him on. It was this same grim courage, this same inflexible resolve to let nothing stand in his way until a job was completed that had made him the most feared of the State's Texas Rangers.

And in spite of his weariness of the movement, there was latent power in his big body. His brain remained keen and crystal clear, and there was no relaxing of the ingrained caution that kept his eyes shifting ceaselessy.

Shadows were lengthening from cactus and sage, as he came within sight of the boom town. There was an unnatural silence about the place, a lack of life on the street that struck an oppressive warning of impending trouble across his brain. It was unnatural in a boom town like this.

Then abruptly, as he drew nearer, he knew! For all of a sudden a sullen, angry roar of voices throbbed over the evening air to his ears A mob! Embittered prospectors and cowmen gathering to move against the man who had disregarded the priority they felt they had to the gold claims Breck Shale had sold to the Easterners. It could mean only that.

The giant golden gelding lurched forward in a hard run at the gentle touch of Hatfield's spurs. The growling rumble of the mob had lifted to a full-throated roar as he reached the first line of unfinished buildings.

He swung Goldy into the empty street,

then reined in sharply, as he saw a lone man running toward him. It was Clay Tarrant, his clothing ripped and torn, a swelling bruise over one eye. Tarrant's voice came hoarsely, as he halted, panting, at the sorrel's head.

"Jim, I'm glad to see you!" he burst out. "I tried to stop 'em, but they threw me aside. I saw you coming up the trail, and got here to meet you as quick as I could."

Hatfield's narrowed eyes flashed over Tarrant, taking in the unmistakable signs of struggle.

"What in blazes is goin' on here?" he demanded. "I heard that mob but... They movin' against Shale?"

Tarrant nodded, his face gray.

"They've heard about the gold in the Basin. The whole town is goin' to try to bust in."

The Ranger's lips pressed into a thin-drawn line.

"They'll get shot to pieces, the fools!" he rasped.

"That's what I tried to tell 'em, but they wouldn't listen!"

Hatfield made his decision quickly,

knowing the death and bloodshed that hung in the balance.

"They'll listen to reason now!" he shouted.

He reached into his pocket, brought out the silver-circled badge, and the fading light of the western sun cast dull red gleams from it where he pinned it on his shirt. Swift surprise came to Clay Tarrant's face.

"So you're a Ranger!" he breathed. And then his hand stabbed out to grab Goldy's reins. "You ain't got a chance, Jim! They'll kill you if you try to stop them. You're only one man!"

"It's only one mob, ain't it?" Hatfield snapped grimly. "They'll be slaughtered if I don't throw them back."

He pulled the reins free of Tarrant's grasp, and sent the giant sorrel down the street at a hammering run. He could see the mob now, moving deep into the shadows that were lengthening from the ridge that ringed the crater. It was a close-packed knot of men, some armed, others carrying only clubs and stones. And above and beyond them his narrowed eyes caught the vague movement of Breck Shale's guards waiting at the crest of the rocky defile where they could hold back an army of men.

It *would* be slaughter once it started!. The guards had every protection in their favor, and the mob was in the open where each man could be picked off with deadly certainty.

Even as the Ranger flashed to the end of the street, he saw the mob roll forward. The guards held their fire a long taunting minute, then the red flare of their shots crashed out.

A scream sliced through the sullen roar of the mob. A man went down as if his legs had been knocked from under him. Another stumbled off blindly to one side, falling, climbing to his feet, falling again until he no longer had the strength to rise.

In the face of that deadly hail of lead that ripped into them from the guns of the guards, the mob surged forward. They were unstoppable by any sense of fear. They were men who had been robbed of all reasoning by the lure of gold that gripped them.

Jim Hatfield's hoarse yell rang out stridently.

"Back! Turn back, yuh fools!"

But as piercing as was his voice, his words were lost in the cacophony of shouts and gunfire. He swung Goldy off, then cut in savagely from an angle. It was a wild chance he was taking, for once he drove in between the mob and the guards, he would be whip-sawed from both sides by flaming lead. But he held his course with unswerving purpose.

He reached the first line of men, swept past them to pull Goldy to a halt in front of the head of the mob. But if they saw him, they gave no indication. They rolled on toward the narrow defile behind him, their close-passing lead flying like invisible hornets.

"Back, blast you! Back, yuh fools!"

He jerked his guns, smashed shots savagely at the feet of the mob leaders. One of the men, a tall, bearded prospector, jerked his gun in a flare of anger toward the lone rider. The gun-barrel blossomed red, its roar lost to Jim Hatfield's ears.

But the tall Ranger felt the shock of the lead. It smashed into the horn of his saddle, ricocheted, screaming past his face. Anger in a fierce tide swept through him. The madness of the mob made them beyond the fear of lead, but they would fear the charge of a horse. That was something they could see.

He leaned low in his saddle, and for the first time in his life, dug spur steel sharply into Goldy's flanks. The startled animal lurched forward like a thunderbolt toward the head of the mob.

The charge of the mob broke under the rush of the giant gelding. Men faltered, suddenly struck by fear. They tried to spin, run, only to trip and stumble, fighting each other. The tide turned as the rear ranks were driven back, and Hatfield followed on their heels, yelling, cursing, firing over their heads until sheer exhaustion halted them at the edge of the town.

One of them turned then, his face showing mingled anger and fear, and an oath of amazement ripped from his lips as he saw the rider coming behind him.

"Gosh-amighty!" he croaked. "This gent that turned us back—he's a Ranger!"

Hatfield faced the men squarely, his rugged face a hard mask of anger.

"What do you think you were pullin' off?" he asked bitingly. "I ought to arrest the lot of yuh. Yuh're on private property, and Shale has every right to keep you out of that Basin if he wants to. Yuh fools! Yuh'd have been cut to pieces tryin' to force yore way down there!"

A rancher spoke up as reason began to take hold in his inflamed mind.

"Mebbe we was fools, tryin' to rush 'em like that," he admitted. "But I reckon we've got a right to be sore. All of us has fought Injuns and outlaws to help make this State, and we ought to have first chance at any new gold fields that's opened up."

"So yuh thought yuh'd stand up for yore rights by committin' suicide, huh?" Hatfield cut in shortly. "Which do yuh think yore women and kids would rather have—you or gold?"

"They shore wouldn't want us if they thought we was too yeller to fight for what belongs to us," a man flung back bitterly.

"So now any gold that's down in the crater belongs to you, does it?" Hatfield taunted. "For law-abidin' citizens, yuh shore forget quick who owns this land yuh're on. Yuh forget that Breck Shale filed on this land legally for his boss, and that Harvey Britt is within his rights if he wants to sell his claims to pilgrims. You ranchers wouldn't stand for anyone tellin' yuh who to sell yore cattle to, would yuh?"

As he drove his arguments home he could see that the mob was wavering with indecision. Men who had faced the Ranger in rigid anger a moment before, shifted uncomfortably, then dropped their eyes under his steely gaze.

"I reckon we've made plumb fools of ourselves, boys," one of them said in a growl.

15

"Who Is the Lawman?"

RAPIDLY the mob broke up, and scattered through the town. A feeling of grim satisfaction ran through Jim Hatfield as he sat his saddle unmovingly. He didn't blame the men for what they had tried to do, but he had known that only by cutting them as deeply as possible could he prevent them from being slaughtered should they make another charge toward the Basin trail.

He looked down to see Clay Tarrant standing close by the side of his horse. Tarrant's face was hard and set, and puzzlement lurked in his steady eyes.

"You was takin' Shale's side in this, Jim," he said quietly. "Those men won't try that again, but they think you're a Judas for turnin' against them."

The Ranger smiled bleakly. "What they think won't hurt me half as much as bullet lead would have hurt them if they'd tried to rush Shale's guards again," he said softly.

He stared at Tarrant intently, seeing things any other man would have missed.

"Yuh're thinkin' Breck Shale killed yore father, ain't yuh, Clay?" he said.

Clay Tarrant's lips thinned, their corners pressing hard.

"Dad wrote me he was coming here to Tornado Basin," he said levelly. "But when I get here he's not around. I find his bloodstained pipe, and the Basin he'd been prospecting filed on by another man. Wouldn't you get the same idea, Jim?"

Hatfield nodded, his face expressionless.

"Yeah, I reckon I would," he growled, "and I don't think I'd be far wrong."

He slipped from saddle and tied Goldy's reins around a hitching post. He turned then, his eyes like chips of ice.

"Let's get goin'," he said grimly.

Clay Tarrant followed him in silence, not voicing the questions he felt. The weight of the day's hours had dragged the western sun below the horizon, and the purple shadows of dusk were thickening.

Without a word, Hatfield led into the

draw that footed the crater's rim-ridge, and at length turned cautiously up the steep slope. He dropped to hands and knees when he neared the lip of the cliff, then lowered himself to his stomach to peer into the gloom-shrouded depths of the crater.

All was silence down there. He could see the faint black of Breck Shale's cabin, its lighted windows like unwinking eyes in the swiftly gathering darkness. A few campfires had sprung into life here and there, crossed now and then by the Eastern gold-hunters.

A vague movement along the Basin trail caught the Ranger's eye, and he saw a horseman—one of the guards—clattering toward Shale's cabin.

"Probably goin' to tell his boss about the mob," the Ranger muttered. He glanced around to find Clay Tarrant's questioning eyes upon him.

"Yuh got a right to know this, Tarrant," he said quietly. "I think Breck Shale and his men are out to swindle them Easterners out of the two thousand dollars each of 'em put in them claims. I don't know how yet, but that's the way my hunch stands."

Tarrant's eyes widened with anger.

"But those fellows are poor men! The

money they put in those claims is all they have."

"Then I reckon they're broke if we don't do something." Hatfield twisted around, picked up the rope, sent it uncoiling like a writhing snake into the darkness of the Basin. He turned on Tarrant then, reaching toward his gun. "Yuh'll need this," he said.

Tarrant shook his head, pulled out the front of his coat to expose the butt of a Colt thrust under his belt. The Ranger's eyes narrowed.

"Can yuh use that thing?" he asked.

"I can make a danged good try," Tarrant answered grimly.

Jim Hatfield chuckled without humor. "That ought to be good enough to plug one of them polecats," he said. "Let's get goin'."

In the meantime the hurrying guard they had seen riding in the Basin had reached Breck Shale's shack down there. He was the outlaw known as "Gyp" Logan. Fear was in Logan's faded blue eyes, and cold sweat beaded his forehead when he reined in his racing mount before the cabin. He struck the ground running, and words broke from him before he kicked the door of the shack shut behind him.

"Boss, there's the devil and all to pay!" he croaked. "A mob of gents from town tried to bust through into the Basin. Me and Lee was cuttin' down plenty of meat when a big gent on a giant of a sorrel showed up and drove the mob back."

Breck Shale slanted a sharp glance at Ben Latch, close at his side. Hack Wadell smothered an oath, but Link Burman and Mack Deeven held silence.

Shale's gaze, dark and fathomless, snapped back to Logan.

"We heard the shootin'," he said dryly. "We guessed what had happened. What about it?"

"*What about it?*" Logan rasped. "That sorrel was just like the one that followed our trail from the train. The big gent ridin' him was the one who gave yuh his name as Tom Hadley. And he was wearin' a law badge!"

The dead silence in the cabin for fear-stricken moments was finally broken by Link Burman's scratchy snarl.

"Some blame sheriff!"

"Sheriff, your grandma!" Gyp Logan

jeered. "I know a Ranger badge when I see one, and that's what this jasper was sportin'. He's Jim Hatfield, shore as fate! I've heard how that gobbler works." He paused, as if to let the hush give strength to his words. "Him and young Tarrant are headin' down here now!"

"*What?*" Breck Shale's single word was filled with meaning.

Logan jerked his hand nervously "He didn't get past us, if that's what yuh're thinkin'." He was a big man, powerful of body, and with a square, jutting chin, but there was fear in his eyes now. "Him and Tarrant worked up the Basin about half a mile from the trail," he went on hastily. "That's about where Hatfield's tracks petered out the night we dumped him over the cliff. He's got a rope to come down there, if I ain't plumb loco!"

Breck Shale's heavy face flooded dark, and fury stormed through his blank eyes.

"And you wasted time comin' here to tell me this, instead of droppin' that lawhound?" he grated.

Gyp Logan's face drained pale. "But listen, boss—I tell yuh he's Jim Hatfield! Yuh've heard of that devil!"

"What if he is?" the outlaw leader snarled "A slug will kill him same as it will any other man. You had orders to keep everybody out of here, cuss yuh!"

"But, Boss—" Logan whimpered, choking.

He got no farther. Breck Shale's hand slashed down in a blur, swept up gripping his heavy Colt. He slid forward with the smooth swiftness of a huge cat, throwing all the weight of his powerful shoulders into the clubbing arc of his gun barrel. Gyp Logan tried to roll away from the blow, but he didn't have a chance. It landed with a sodden thud, hurling him to the floor in a huddled heap.

Shale stepped back, his eyes black pinpoints of anger. At one side, Ben Latch spoke up.

"Boss, yuh didn't have no call to do that."

Shale whirled savagely, red death in his dark eyes. His voice came with the choking rasp of a man with murder in his black heart.

"You crossin' me, Latch?" he flared.

Ben Latch paled, and his body still.

"'Course not, Boss!" he croaked. "Only

with Jim Hatfield on his way here, I thought—"

"I'm still roddin' this outfit," Shale broke in harshly, "and I'll do all the thinkin' for it. Don't forget that, Latch, if yuh know what's good for yuh. Hatfield ain't got nothin' on us. Mebbe he's got an idea, but that don't prove anything in court. If we get spooked and try to bust out of here now, we'd never get half-way to the Border."

"Yuh mean we're stayin' here with *that* Ranger comin'?" Hack Wadell demanded unbelievingly.

Breck Shale nodded shortly. He sheathed his gun, started to turn toward his desk.

"We'll stay till I give the word to leave," he snapped.

"Yuh called that turn wrong, Shale!" That was Mack Deeven's voice, low and deadly.

Shale whirled as if he had been stung, and not a muscle moved in his face as he stared at the gun jutting from Deeven's hand. He raised his burning black eyes with something of utter mockery.

"So yuh're takin' the bit in yore teeth?" he snarled.

"Just that, Shale!" Mack Deeven ground out. "And keep yore hooks away from them cutters or yuh'll take the lead in yore middle."

The killer backed away slowly, every line of his body taut and challenging.

"Keep yore eye on him, boys!" he grated. "Plug him if he makes a funny move. We're cuttin' Shale and Harvey Britt out of this deal right here and now! I got a plumb plenty of his kind of bossin'."

His gun waved menacingly at the outlaw leader.

"You know what to do, Shale," he ordered. "Get that safe of yores open pronto! Don't waste no time doin' it. The two hundred thousand the pilgrims give yuh is already sacked up, and the gold dust they banked with yuh tonight is ready for us to pack off."

One look at the steadiness of that leveled gun, and Breck Shale turned and stooped to the heavy safe. He spun the dial slowly, and the metallic sound of the tumblers falling into place came loud in the tense silence. Shale stepped back as the safe door swung open, keeping his hands clear of his holstered guns.

"Get it, Ben," Deeven ordered.

Ben Latch strode forward quickly, greed bright in his smoky eyes. Greenbacks rustled as he pulled a tightly bound canvas bag out of the safe. Then he was stuffing small, heavy pokes into another bag, his narrow face exultant. He straightened, gripping both bags, and uttered a short, harsh chuckle.

"Gold weighs heavy, but yuh'll never hear me kick about carryin' it," he said with grim mirth.

The outlaws backed away to the door, and Link Burman spoke in a dispassionate grunt.

"What about Gyp Logan?"

"Let him lay," Deeven growled. "We'll pick up Lee on the way, and make the split five ways."

He opened the door guarded, slanted a quick glance into the night. One of the Easterners was passing by, but he seemed beyond the reach of Deeven's low voice.

"Yuh can stay here and say howdy to Jim Hatfield, Shale," Deeven sneered. "Let out a yell to stop us, and yuh'll hang along with us if we get caught." His tone sharpened.

"Let's go, boys! We'll ride for the river and make the divvy at San Jose."

A tight smile thinned Breck Shale's hard lips as the door closed on the outlaws. He stood motionless in his tracks a long moment, listening to the fading hoof-beats of the men who had doublecrossed him. There was no anger in his dark eyes—only a glint of cold satisfaction.

His dark stare shifted to the unconscious body of Gyp Logan huddled on the bare floor, and he chuckled softly.

He turned to pick a keen-bladed paper knife from the desk beside him, gripped it in his strong fingers, then rocked his head to one side, listening intently.

After that, he raised the knife, and moved grimly toward the body of the unconscious man.

16

The Final Link

CROUCHING in the darkness at the foot of the crater wall, Jim Hatfield fought against impatience. Above him he could hear the heavy breathing of Clay Tarrant lowering himself down the rope. He moved down the slope without a word when Tarrant finally dropped clear of the rope. Tarrant strode behind him, matching each move of the tall Ranger, as they went down the treacherous pitch of the talus slope.

"We'll check on the Easterners first," Hatfield said, in a low growl. "They seem to be gatherin' around one fire like somethin's up."

Silently they threaded their way through the sage. To Clay Tarrant, it seemed he had reverted to something long forgotten. He had spent most of his life in Indiana, but he had been born in Texas, and something that was his heritage returned to him as he strode through the night.

He was conscious of the dead weight of the gun thrust under his belt. It was a weapon his father had left with him on a visit East years before, and he had never used it except at an occasional target. But somehow he knew he would not hesitate when the time came for him to draw it on a man.

In this far-flung country, there was no law for dealing with men of Breck Shale's breed save the law of the Colt. The Rangers were carving some semblance of order, but their greatest weapon against outlawry was that of the gun.

Tarrant wondered, with a clutch of anxiety, about Holly Winters. In the few short hours since they had met, an understanding that was deep and powerful had sprung between them. An icy fury stormed through him as he thought of what Breck Shale had tried to do to Sam Winters and the rest of the Easterners, if what Jim Hatfield had said was right.

But instinctively he knew, as the tall Ranger ahead of him knew, that Shale *had* tried to rob the pilgrims of their hard-earned money. But how, he did not know. He had seen rich gold in the dirt samples Shale had taken from the claims. That was a fact he could not deny.

A low murmur of many voices reached the ears of the two plodding men as they neared one of the scattered campfires. They could see the Easterners huddled there, talking among themselves in mumbling tones.

Then men jerked around, startled, as the two approached from the dark. They saw Jim Hatfield, and one of them cursed angrily.

"It's that blasted outlaw!"

They started toward the Ranger grimly, only to halt as Sam Winters spoke up quickly.

"We don't know anything but what Shale and the rest said about him," he reminded. "Let's hear him out before you try anything."

Jim Hatfield halted before the men, reading the anger and bitterness etched in their faces. Holly Winters stood beside her father, her slender body outlined by the flames against the backdrop of darkness beyond her. The girl was the first to see the badge on Hatfield's shirt.

"Why, he—he's wearing a badge!" she exclaimed.

Clay Tarrant moved out, his low voice cutting through the murmurs of amazement that rippled along the rows of men.

"He's a Texas Ranger, friends," Tarrant said. "He's here to help you, if you'll let him."

"So that's why you didn't want me to let out your right name last night?" Sam Winters said gruffly.

The Ranger nodded, his smile thin and cool.

"I wouldn't have lived long if yuh'd spilled my name then," he said. "Shale's men tried hard enough to kill me, as it was. They'd have tried harder if they'd known who I was."

He stared intently from face to face of the men before him, reading doubt and anxiety in every line of their features.

"Yuh act like somethin's wrong," he pressed quietly.

"Something is wrong!" Sam Winters said with a grunt. "It's these claims we bought. Every one of us panned out nearly three hundred dollars' worth of gold today. But late this afternoon it stopped. We couldn't find a trace of color. Our claims just went dry!"

Hatfield's eyes narrowed, but glittered behind the half-closed curtains of his lids.

"Petered out, huh?" he asked.

Winters nodded. "What little gold is left don't amount to the work it takes to get it in," he growled.

The Ranger's voice took on a thin edge. "I'd like to see what yuh panned today, if yuh don't mind."

The oldster's mouth hardened. "We haven't got it. We turned it all over to Breck Shale, like we agreed. I guess he'll show it to you, if you ask him."

"I don't reckon he would," the lawman answered dryly. "Not if what I think has been goin' on is true, he won't."

He didn't put into words the grim suspicions in his mind. He turned, looking around him, then picked up a gold pan.

"These claims couldn't be plumb dry," he said. "I want to see a sample of that gold. Get back out of the way a little."

Silence lay heavily over the men as Jim Hatfield worked over the gold pan. Pan after pan showed a complete lack of color, and it was minutes later when the tall Ranger suddenly stiffened over the dirt he had been washing.

"I reckon this is different from what you found, Clay," he growled.

His eyes were cold and bright as he watched the young mining engineer bend over the pan. Tarrant jerked up sharply, puzzlement in every line of his face.

"This ain't the same as I panned out the other night!" he cried in astonishment. "This gold has already been refined!"

"I figgered it was somethin' like this," Hatfield said icily. "Now I reckon I've got somethin' to say to Breck Shale!"

Shale was standing in the doorway when Jim Hatfield approached the slab pine shack. There was no expression on the big man's face. He just stood there staring at Hatfield with his unreadable black eyes until the lawman halted. He did show surprise, though, when he saw the silver-circled badge on the lawman's shirt.

"So yuh're a Ranger!" he boomed. "I reckon I owe yuh an apology for last night." His voice was hearty, but there was a thin vein of mockery in it.

Hatfield flashed a quick glance around him, searching the shadows for some sign of Shale's men. He saw neither the gunmen nor their horses. His eyes came back to the big man.

"Yuh don't owe me an apology, Shale," he said coldly. "Yuh'd have tried harder to put me out of the way if yuh'd known who I was."

Breck Shale underwent a swift change, showing a flash of anger.

"The devil yuh say!" he blared, "What's eatin' yuh, lawman? What in tarnation yuh got against me?"

The Ranger's answer came like steel grating on steel.

"Wreckin' and robbin' the El Paso Express, for one thing, and murder goes with that," he snapped. "Tryin' to swindle these pilgrims out of their money, for another."

Shale's eyes flew wide, mirroring something Hatfield could not read. The big man showed surprise, but somehow it didn't seem real. The thought puzzled the Ranger.

"Yuh're talkin' yoreself into a lot of

trouble Mister!" Shale said. He said nothing more—waiting.

Hatfield poised his body without apparently moving a muscle.

"My middle name is trouble," he flung back. "Yuh can't bluff yore way out of this, Shale. You stole that bullion from the train to salt these claims yuh sold the pilgrims. I've got a sample of the gold they panned out today. It ain't in it's natural form. It's been refined. Yuh knew these pilgrims wouldn't know real gold dust if they saw it."

"Clay Tarrant shore ought to," Shale taunted.

"He saw real dust when he made his test," the Ranger whipped back. "Yuh took yore samples of dirt from four different places just to make it look good. But yuh'd salted them four places with natural dust, and knew just where to find it."

The big man snorted derisively. "Yuh're makin' a pretty talk, Ranger. Let's hear some more."

"Yuh'll hear plenty!" Hatfield grated. "To keep the pilgrims satisfied while yuh made ready to slope, yuh stole that bullion from the train you wrecked. Yuh filed it down so's it'd look enough like dust to fool the tenderfeet. Yuh took two hundred thousand dollars from these hundred men for the fake claims, then waited till they brought yuh the gold they panned so's yuh could get it, too."

There was only derision in Breck Shale's dark eyes, and the glint of smoldering kill lust. He rolled a smoke with steady fingers, nipped it between his thin lips, reached into his vest pocket for a match.

"And mebbe yuh can prove all that," he sneered.

Jim Hatfield was alert, every nerve keened for that second-fraction when life or death would depend on which man showed the greatest gun speed. He watched the big man scratch the match into flame, lift it to his cigarette.

"I can prove one of yore men was in the gang that robbed the train. An ink-stained greenback yuh left in his pocket will back that up." The Ranger's voice was soft, deadly. "He's dead now—the half-breed yuh buried near the train—Wadell or one of the others will talk—"

The Ranger's voice choked off as Shale

lowered the match to his side, absently snapping it between his fingers. Then the Ranger's voice leaped out, hoarse, vibrant.

"So yuh're—"

He got no farther. Prepared as he was, he was caught off guard by the swiftness of Shale's movement. It came without an expression to betray his intent, the blurred swoop of his hands that flashed his Colts clear of leather. His voice came with a thin rasp.

"Stay put—all of yuh! Make a crooked move and the doors of Hades won't open quick enough to let yuh in!"

He backed away like a cornered animal, set teeth bared in a snarl, narrowed eyes black pools of rage and defiance.

Not a muscle moved along Jim Hatfield's taut frame, as the outlaw backed into the shack. His hands were clear of his gun butts, still, unwavering, fingers sprayed out tensely, as he watched the killer edge deeper into the building.

The quick press of Shale's hard lips warned him. He faded to one side, dropping to one knee with all the speed he could throw into his muscles. He saw the black burst of the killer's shot, the spurt of red, heard the slug whisper past him to spend itself in the emptiness of the night.

His own guns whipped out and up like living things. They bounced, roared, kicking against his palms. He saw splinters shower from the door as it slammed shut under the kick of Shale's boot. He heard the thud of the lock-bar being dropped into place.

At one side, he heard Clay Tarrant's high-pitched yell.

"I can see him through the window!"

Tarrant's gun crashed. The window glass splintered, and from inside the building came the loud smash of a falling object. An instant of utter darkness then was followed by a leaping flare of flame, red and licking.

"I must've hit the lamp!" Tarrant sang out.

"Watch the door!" Hatfield shouted. "He'll be smoked out, and when he shows up he'll be behind his guns!"

But the killer did not come out during the minutes that followed. The flames, fed by oil from the lamp, mounted swiftly, pushing hungrily through cracks in the wall and roof of the hastily thrown-up shack.

Smoke billowed from the shattered window in a thick black pall.

Silence gripped the men who looked on, and Hatfield could hear Holly Winters' low sob of horror. He tried at the door once, smashing against it with all the weight of his body. The lock-bar, eaten half through by flame, snapped, releasing the door, but heat and flame drove the Ranger back.

Dimly through the ugly red glare of the fire, they could see a body sprawled out on the floor. Hatfield's lips pressed tight, and with an effort he pulled his glance away from the body to look into Clay Tarrant's strained face. . . .

At the top of the crater wall, Ben Latch and the men riding with him swung their mounts when they heard a distant crack of shots. They stared into the black depths, and Link Burman spoke up in a low, unfeeling drawl:

"Looks like Breck called another play wrong."

"He's holed up in the shed," Hack Wadell said in a grunt. "But good gravy—look! It's on fire!"

They waited tensely as the minutes dragged by. The flames mounted, piling a red glare against the black of the night. No shots came to show that Breck Shale had been forced into the open by heat and flame.

The fire climbed higher, waving hungry red tendrils through the darkness, then with a distant roar, the roof and walls of the building collapsed.

"Let's get goin', boys" Ben Latch drawled dispassionately. "I reckon that does for Breck Shale."

17

Last Hope

GRIM silence gripped the Easterners as they watched the flames die out among the ashes of the building. Smoke writhed upward in gray wreaths, and the single timber that remained upright looked like a black skeleton finger pointing into the night sky.

Unreadable lights glistened in Jim Hatfield's eyes as he looked at what had become Breck Shale's pyre. He moved forward slowly as the fire receded, kicking through still hot ashes. He stared long at the open safe, smoke-blackened and flame-gutted in the charred wreckage of the house. He heard Sam Winters' bitter growl behind him.

"That finishes us. All the money we had in the world we sunk in them fake claims. We're ruined."

Self-condemnation pulsed in Clay Tarrant's low words.

"It's my fault! You banked on my judgement, and I advised you to buy."

Holly Winters went quickly to Tarrant, standing before him tall and straight and slender, the leaf-brown wealth of her hair framing the pure lines of her face.

"Clay, don't say that!" she cried. "Any other mining engineer would have thought the same. You were simply tricked the same as the rest of us."

"Don't lay the blame on yoreself, Clay," Jim Hatfield advised quietly. "Shale had me fooled till I saw the gold these men panned today. If he'd taken his samples for you to test in one place, mebbe I'd have had a hunch, but it's the first time I ever heard of a crook saltin' a claim in four places. That made it look like he didn't care where he scraped up the dirt."

He was silent a moment, his eyes thoughtful. At length he spoke, in a flat tone.

"This job ain't finished yet. What I'm wonderin' is where the rest of Shale's gang went."

One of the Easterners shoved out of the crowd, a lean, gaunt man with dull, beaten eyes.

"I reckon I can answer that," he said without much interest.

Hatfield turned, a frown on his brow.

"Yuh know?" he asked sharply.

The man nodded dully. "I was passin' Shale's shack, headin' for my camp when they was gettin' ready to leave. Hack Wadell said somethin' about riding to some town, but I didn't think anything of it."

"Where, man!"

The Easterner shook his head slowly.

"I don't remember," he muttered. "I heard him mention the name, but I don't remember it now."

Hatfield reached out long arms, to shake the man.

"Think, man!" he repeated harshly. *"Think!* This may be important!"

"Wait a minute—wait a minute!" The Easterner showed a stir of spirit. "Give me a chance to remember. This quick-and-sudden stuff gets me rattled. What in blazes did Wadell say? I was thinkin' of my own troubles, and didn't pay much attention. The town he mentioned was—it was San something."

"San Jose?" The Ranger's voice was sharp, cutting.

"Yeah, that was it. They was riding to San Jose, and Wadell mentioned a river someway."

"The Rio Grande!" Hatfield cracked out. "They wouldn't be ridin' in that direction unless they wanted to get away from the law. Mebbe—" He stopped short, thinking hard. Then he snapped: "There's a chance that's what happened!"

He spun around, caught a man by the arm, sent him lurching off into the night.

"Bring me a shovel!" he ordered. "And a pick if yuh've got one."

He set to work savagely when the man returned with the tools. He struck bed rock three feet down, cleared off a small space, and grabbed up the pick. The rock was dark in color, strangely soft and rotten, and his second powerful blow broke off a chunk the size of his fist.

He looked up, catching Clay Tarrant with his eye.

"There's a chance Hack Wadell and the rest took the money with 'em," he said. "They hit for the Border for some reason, and it's a cinch they wouldn't have left so soon without the *dinero*. If that's what happened, I think we can get 'em back here. For some reason Breck Shale scared easy when I braced him, but the rest of the gang will know I can't prove anything against 'em. And they'll come back here if they think the risk is worth it."

Clay Tarrant spoke up sharply. "But how?"

The tall Ranger laughed, shoved out the chunk of rock.

"This is silver ore, see—silver ore! They didn't prospect here, and they won't know whether it is or ain't. But when yuh go tearin' through San Jose yellin' how yuh want to buy these pilgrims' claims, them fellers will *think* yuh're tellin' the truth, and that'll be enough to bring 'em back here if I don't miss my guess."

Tarrant's eyes flamed bright. "It might work at that!" he said, with sudden enthusiasm.

"It's a chance," Hatfield grated. "And spread the word when yuh go through the new town up above, just in case they ain't left yet. Don't try to take my hoss. Goldy won't let anyone around him but me. But get yoreself a hoss if yuh have to steal one! Hit straight south from here, ten miles through the notch in the hills. Yuh can't miss the town thataway. San Jose is on this bank of the Rio, and it'll be wide open at this hour."

Clay Tarrant was gone the next minute, disappearing into the darkness toward the Basin trail at a hard run.

Hatfield turned his attention to his heavy guns, reloading them, checking each weapon with practised care. He reseated them lightly in their pouches, and after that, settled back grimly to wait. . . .

Totally unconscious that their robbery scheme might have been guessed by the tall Ranger they were so gladly escaping, the outlaw band that had doublecrossed Breck Shale were jubilant as they neared San Jose.

It was a small town of adobe huts that dozed on the north bank of the river by day, and wakened to iniquities by night. It sprawled its ugly shape on the Border, a haven for the chill-eyed riders of the long trail.

Men rode in and were watched warily, but no questions were asked. For the only law here was that of the gun and the swift-moving telegraph of the outlaw warned the town of any lawman approaching. And when the lawman reached the town, there were men crouching in the deep dark shadows behind leveled guns to wait for him.

"Two hundred and thirty thousand dollars!" Ben Latch chuckled as they saw the town ahead. "That'll make a split that'll put us all on Easy Street. Shore, I think I'll retire."

"Until yuh see another chance to pull off a job," Link Burman snorted dryly. "Where'll we make the split?"

Latch grinned in the darkness. "Me, I want a drink first."

"Then that's just what the rest of us want," Mac Deeven announced pointedly.

"Meanin' anything by that, Mack?" Latch snarled.

"Let it ride," Deeven grunted. "We'll get our drink, then make the split when we get across the river."

There was no more talk after that. They moved quietly into the town, narrowed eyes shifting alertly. A group of men slouched down the street near a saloon, but Latch and the men at his side were given only cursory glances. Link Burman pointed a bony finger toward a small man in the crowd, one wearing a marshal's badge on the front of his shirt.

"There's Dink Freel," he snorted derisively. "Still playin' lawman and makin' his livin' by goin' through the pockets of every drunk he finds on the street."

"Which makes the town look respectable, anyhow," Hack Wadell chuckled. "Let's turn in here and get that drink. My hands are itchin' to get hold of that *dinero*."

They swung in at the hitch-rail, slid to the ground, and moved into the saloon. They got a bottle and pulled up chairs to a table where they could watch their horses outside.

Ben Latch uncorked the bottle and had started pouring a drink into a glass when every muscle of his body froze.

"Get back out of sight!" he snarled. "That pilgrim, Clay Tarrant, has just rode into town."

Hack Wadell's hand streaked toward his gun, but he didn't lift the weapon. He tensed, listening intently to young Tarrant's words float in through the open window. They came hoarsely, throbbing with excitement.

"I got to have money! Where can I borrow money? Tornado Basin is loaded with a fortune in silver, and I can buy every claim in it for fifty thousand dollars. Where the devil is the banker in this town?"

Silence gripped the outlaws, as Clay Tarrant moved on down the street hurriedly, his voice fading out of hearing. Ben Latch's hot stare snapped from face to face of the men around the table, reading the same thought that burned through his own brain.

"We can do it!" he rasped. "Tarrant will spend the rest of the night here and never raise any money. We can beat him back, and take over those claims ourselves."

A stubborn doubt shone in Hack Wadell's eyes.

"How do we know there's silver in the Basin?" he growled.

"Tarrant's a minin' engineer, ain't he?" Lee Nells reminded. "And we never prospected there. I bet them two old coots we killed knowed all the time!"

An oath ripped from Link Burman's bloodless lips.

"I don't like it. Jim Hatfield is there, and that jasper is Satan on greased skids."

"What of it?" Latch raked out. "He ain't got nothin' on us. He's found out we salted them claims, that's shore—he thinks he has! But when we show up he'll figure he was wrong, that they just petered out. He won't think anything about us if we show up ready to turn back the pilgrims' money. And he can't prove anything about the train job, not with Breck Shale and Gyp Logan dead. We're in the clear!"

"What about Harvey Britt?" Mack Deeven grated.

"We'll take care of him when the time comes. Our job is to get them claims back before young Tarrant starts a rush there."

He stared from one to another of the outlaws, his silence his question. Then abruptly, Link Burman lurched to his feet.

"We're wastin' time that's worth a fortune," he snarled.

18

Outlaw's Return

EARLY dawn was chill and clear, and the heavy dew that had fallen filled the air with the pungent tang of sage. Impatience rankled in Jim Hatfield as he looked toward the banners of pink and purple and gold that burned across the eastern horizon. He rose and stretched muscles that had cramped during his brief catnap, and stood there a long moment watching the delicate golden light creep down the crater's western wall as the unseen sun lifted higher.

He turned as old Sam Winters and his daughter approached. Winters' seamed face showed worry as he looked up at the lawman, and the girl's clear blue eyes mirrored deep concern.

"Supposin' them outlaws do show up?" the oldster said bluntly. "What chance have we got? They'll be five against you. The rest of us ain't got any guns."

Hatfield smiled faintly. "I reckon Tarrant will be close behind 'em," he said quietly.

A quick shadow of anxiety settled over the girl's face.

"Clay?" she cried. "You can't be expecting much help from him in a fight like this!"

The Ranger looked at the girl steadily He could read beyond the concern in her eyes. What she felt was more than merely interest in a friend.

"It's a good hunch Shale murdered Clay's father so old man Tarrant wouldn't be around to speak up when Shale claimed he'd found gold here," he said softly. "That's one reason I couldn't keep Clay out of this fight if I tried. Another is what he knows Shale did to you."

A warm flush mounted in the girl's troubled face, and she dropped her eyes under his level gaze. The Ranger smiled.

"Anyhow, I wouldn't worry too much about Clay," he went on reassuringly. "He can take care of hisself in any man's fight."

The minutes wore on slowly, and doubt began to build in Hatfield's brain. Six hours had passed since Clay Tarrant had left the

Basin, and barring some unknown delay, he should have been back in two. The Ranger began pacing the ground restlessly, gripped by an anxiety he didn't let reach his face.

A dozen reasons for Tarrant's absence filtered across his brain, but he shook them off. Tarrant had a level head on his shoulders. He wouldn't rush into trouble unless it was forced on him. Too much hung in the balance because of his lone ride.

Hatfield forced his thoughts into another channel, laying plans for action when—and if—the outlaw gang did return. He didn't have much to go on. He would have to play on the doubts and suspicions of the outlaws, bait them into showing their hand by a bluff.

He had done little more than that to force Breck Shale's hand, and the realization brought a frown to his brow. He had evidence against the outlaws—conclusive evidence in his own mind—but nothing that would stand up in court.

Breck Shale had been quick to fall for the Ranger's bluff, and there was something strange about that. It was almost as if Shale had been eager for Hatfield to force the play. And yet the outlaw leader had died, locked in the building where he had chosen to make his fight. Strangely, the flame-charred ruins of the structure seemed a fitting monument to the vicious man.

A man's low exclamation broke the Ranger's thoughts.

"Here they come!"

He turned slowly to look toward the Basin trail. The outlaws were coming down the snaky path, their haste apparent even at this distance. A thin smile lifted the corners of Hatfield's lips, and without conscious thought his hands moved down to loosen his guns in their holsters.

He counted them grimly as they drew nearer—five chill-eyed killers by every sign of their profession. He couldn't account for Gyp Logan's absence, but his narrowed eyes brightened as he saw Clay Tarrant move into view over the rim of the trail, unseen by the outlaws.

They spurred their mounts forward cruelly, as they reached level ground, and the animals staggered wearily. The dust and lather on them attested to the hard pace they had been driven.

Hatfield spoke a low order out of the corner of his mouth to the Easterners.

"Don't say anything unless yuh have to. Leave the talkin' to me."

Surprise showed on the faces of the outlaws as they reined in their horses and dropped to the ground. Ben Latch grinned crookedly.

"So yuh *are* a lawman after all!" he said smoothly.

Hatfield nodded without expression. "Did yuh have any other ideas about me, Latch?" he asked mildly.

Ben Latch laughed shortly. "Yuh ought to know the answer to that one! Mebbe our ways are rough, but we don't like outlaws on the H Lazy B, and that's what we thought you was. Sorry about that, Ranger."

Link Burman slanted a nervous glance towards the remains of the building.

"What's happened here?" His voice sounded strained against the silence.

Hatfield's face was utterly blank.

"Just a little fire," he drawled.

Ben Latch's eyes narrowed slightly, then widened. He was obviously puzzled, but he tried hard not to show it. His thin lips broadened in a grin that didn't reach his cold eyes.

"We reckoned all along you was an outlaw tryin' to rob these pilgrims," he said easily. "One of our guards saw yuh comin' down the wall on a rope, and warned us. We figgered we'd better play safe and put the pilgrim's money in the San Jose bank vault."

"Did yuh?" Hatfield asked quietly.

From the corner of his eye, he watched Clay Tarrant ride up, and slide from saddle. Tarrant's gun was plain under his belt, as he angled around to halt well to one side of the Ranger. The outlaws seemed suddenly uncomfortable. Latch shook his head jerkily.

"We met a gent in San Jose who said he'd seen Jim Hatfield, the Ranger, in Sonita a couple days before. The way he described yuh, we knew we'd made a mistake about yuh, so we rode back."

Hatfield nodded. "Uh, huh."

Latch's eyelids drew closer together, and knots formed at the corners of his tightening lips. He slanted a shifty glance over the pilgrims.

"How come yuh-all ain't workin' yore

claims?" he asked with a trace of uneasiness.

Jim Hatfield answered for the Easterners.

"Their claims petered out yesterday afternoon," he said, his tone deceptively mild.

The shadow of tenseness dropped from Latch's narrow face, and his voice came quick and hearty.

"So that's why yuh're actin' so funny!" he blurted. "I knew yuh was sore about somethin'. So the claims petered out, huh? Well, Harvey Britt gave us orders to give yuh yore money back if yuh didn't clear a profit. I reckon that'll make yuh loosen up a little."

"That ain't all, Latch," said Hatfield.

"What?"

Hard-gripped anger throbbed in Latch's sharp burst. The tenseness dropped over him again, even more apparent this time. He seemed to read something inexorable and inescapable in the Ranger's eyes. He knew. With a slowness that was almost beyond perception, his body began sinking, his hands over his guns.

At his side, Hack Wadell, Link Burman,

Lee Nells, Mack Deeven drifted clear of each other, eyes slitted and watchful, faces cold, their lips tight and hard.

"What are yuh drivin' at?" Latch said harshly.

Hatfield's voice came in a soft whisper. "They don't like you polecats sellin' 'em salted claims, that's what I'm drivin' at."

"The devil yuh say!" Latch flashed violently.

A shiver rippled the length of his lean frame, was lost in the tensing of muscles. The man was fighting hard to keep a grip on himself. He laughed shakily.

"I reckon yuh're barkin' down the wrong alley, Hatfield," he croaked. "Them claims wasn't salted. If they petered out, we're ready to buy back every claim. So what's the squawk about?"

The Ranger smiled crookedly. "Yuh ought to know, killer," he breathed.

He waited, letting the smothering silence run its course, watching fear and anger and hatred pile up in the eyes of the gunmen. Then without warning, his yell rang out, vibrant, piercing

"Yuh train-wreckin' polecats! Yuh don't

think yuh can get away with a job like that, do yuh?"

The faces of the outlaws blanched to the gray of ash, then flooded dark. The strain of breaking nerves put a quiver in their splayed-out fingers. Their breathing came harsh and uneven.

Again, the Ranger jarred them with his strident yell.

"Why don't yuh ask what happened to Breck Shale, yuh sidewinders? He's dead, that's what happened to him. He thought I didn't have any proof against him—the same as you. You five helped wreck the El Paso Express. Yuh filed down the bullion to salt these fake claims with! You meant to swindle these pilgrims out of every cent they had, but it won't work.

"If yuh want proof, I can give it to yuh. You sent Slip Cramer out to kill me, but his job backfired on him. But he didn't die quick, polecats. He lived to talk!"

19

Red Harvest

FOR mere instants there was taut silence, then as if some inner tension had snapped, the hands of the outlaws flashed toward their guns. Jim Hatfield's slender hands blurred holsterward like twin swooping birds, whipped up, shunting off dull splinters of sunlight. Distantly, he heard Holly Winters' thin-choked scream.

Ben Latch's lanky frame jerked, twisted, went down heavily at the first crash of the Ranger's guns. Hatfield swiveled his weapons, fading to one side of the shots that roared at him from Hack Wadell's guns. He knew he was firing only by the jarring recoil of his Colts against his palms.

Through the fog of powdersmoke that swirled up before him, he saw thin gouts of dust lift from Wadell's shirt under the impact of lead. A look of utter surprise crossed the killer's hard features. His mouth gaped, closed loosely. He took a long, stumbling stride, and crashed facedown in the thick dust.

From the corner of his eye, Hatfield saw Clay Tarrant's slow-drawn weapon swing up. There was no haste in Tarrant's movement, and he was all the more deadly because of it. His face was paper-white, but he showed no more emotion than if he were knocking off tin cans from a fence rail back in Indiana.

His gun bounced with a black burst, the same instant Mack Deeven snapped a quick shot at him. Both men went down, Clay Tarrant with a swift flow of blood staining the side of his face. But only Tarrant climbed back to his feet.

Through all of this, Jim Hatfield had not ceased movement. He saw Link Burman stumble back under the shock of driving lead, catch himself with a violent effort, his guns crashing in his hands.

A red-hot iron seemed to smash through the Ranger's chest, spilling a scarlet mist across his vision. He went down without being conscious that he was falling, and the shock of his body striking the ground partially cleared his senses.

Through the swirling red fog, he saw Burman sinking down as if he were being drawn into the powdersmoke that clouded his lower body. Lee Nells was dodging back wildly toward his horse, his guns jumping like living things in his hands.

Hatfield saw the killer's Colts chopping down on Clay Tarrant, and his yell rang out piercingly.

"This way, polecat!"

Nells spun as if he had been stung. So close together were their shots that they blended into one blatant roar. But Nells was rocking back weakly when his gunhammer had dropped from under his thumb.

A crushing silence closed over the Basin at that moment. Nells caught his balance with a supreme effort, swayed forward, rocking from heel to toe. Pain and horror and surprise mingled on his ashen face. He couldn't seem to understand what had happened.

His eyes rolled from one to another of the outlaws in the dust around him. Amazement crept into his glazing stare. His lips worked slowly.

"Well, I'll be hanged!" he croaked vacantly. "And we came back for this!"

There were plenty of friendly hands to aid the two fighting men who had so valiantly championed the Easterners, and in short order Jim Hatfield and Tarrant were being cared for.

"The bullet struck the badge on your chest, and deflected all the way through your shoulder," Holly Winters said to the Ranger. "The wound is clean, but you'll have a lame shoulder for a while."

There was a twinkle of mirth in Jim Hatfield's eye as he looked at the girl working over him. Her face was still pale and shaken, as pure of line as a finely cut cameo, but there was no tremble in her fingers. Her touch was soft and gentle and swiftly efficient as if death and bloodshed were not in the least uncommon to her.

The Ranger's lips spread in a grin.

"I reckon I'm glad to hear that," he chuckled. "I'm lucky to get a hole in me like this. There's no danger, and still it's serious enough to keep you workin' over me a lot longer than when yuh bandaged Clay's scratch."

Holly flushed warmly, and dropped her eyes under his bantering. He pulled his gaze away from her, and fastened it on Clay Tarrant, sitting quietly two yards away. A white bandage circled Tarrant's head, showing a small red stain where blood had seeped through from the wound above his temple.

His face was drawn and pale, but his grin was firm.

Tarrant scowled slightly. "Suppose yuh stop tryin' not to show how jealous yuh are, Clay," he growled, "and tell how come it took yuh so long to get back."

Tarrant's grin faded as grim thoughts returned to him.

"I went through the boom town outside the Basin tryin' to borrow money like you told me," he said quietly. "That took time because I wanted to be sure the outlaws got the news if they were there. But the big rub came when I got to San Jose. That horse you advised me to steal was too fast, I guess. I beat the gang there."

"They probably took their time, knowin' they were safe," Hatfield said dryly.

Tarrant nodded. "That's the way I figured it. Inside of ten minutes I had a dozen men ready to follow me back here with all the money I wanted to borrow." He chuckled with thin humor. "That put me on a spot. I knew by then the outlaws hadn't reached town yet, so I had to stall out of it the best I could, and get out of sight. I waited a few minutes, and pulled the same thing off again. Those men in San Jose stared at me like I was crazy, and the marshal swore he'd lock me up if I didn't shut up. I got out of town again, and stayed there until the gang showed up. They rode in almost an hour later."

He paused, then went on quietly. "I went into town the third time, and saw the gang take a table near the open window of a saloon. I didn't look toward them, but started propositioning every man on the street. The marshal started after me again, but the outlaws had already heard enough and had slipped out of town."

"Which made yore bluff pay high," the Ranger grunted.

Holly finished tying the bandage in place, and Hatfield stood up, pulling his shirt over his shoulder. He was still gripped by a doubt he couldn't understand, and somehow it hubbed around the death of

Breck Shale. He shrugged it off, and turned his attention to Sam Winters.

"I reckon what we ought to do now is take care of that money," he said. "The gold yuh panned will have to go back to the Express company, yuh understand."

There was a new deep hope in the oldster's faded eyes.

"We're all too glad to get our own money back to worry about that gold," he said gruffly.

Hatfield nodded, and moved to the weary horses the outlaws had ridden. He found the heavy pokes distributed among the saddle-bags on all the animals, lifted them out, and dropped them to the ground.

"That stuff causes more trouble than any other two things," he growled. "Gold is nothin' but gun bait wherever yuh find it."

A rolled slicker behind the saddle of Ben Latch's horse yielded the tightly-bound canvas bag. He tossed it to the ground, listening to the soft rustle of paper money inside.

"There it is," he grunted. "Latch and the rest doublecrossed their boss to get that, but why Shale stayed here until I showed up is more than I can guess. Sam, you can take care of the split-up."

Sam Winters came forward eagerly, and Hatfield stepped back while the oldster stooped over the canvas bag. He slashed a knife through the cords, then gripped the bottom corners to up-end the bag, spilling its contents out on the ground. Hoarse groans came from the onlookers at what they saw. Jim Hatfield's gray-green eyes flamed hot, then turned ice-cold. Through the riot of new thoughts in his brain, he heard Sam Winters' bitter exclamation.

"Paper! Nothing but cut-up newspaper! No wonder Latch and the rest was so anxious to make a deal with us. They planned to give us this bag unopened, then be gone before we caught on."

A man uttered a strangled oath in the still, dead hush. A hundred hopes had been shattered in one short moment, but there was no sympathy in Hatfield's eyes. Another light was there, cold and deadly.

"So that's why Breck Shale was so anxious for me to jump him!" he breathed.

Only Clay Tarrant, standing in stunned silence close by, heard the Ranger's low words. He turned, his face drawn and gray.

"What's that you said?" he asked slowly.

Jim Hatfield's tone sharpened, taking on a sharp ring.

"I said no wonder Breck Shale wanted me to jump him so bad," he repeated. "Shale had planned all along to cross his men by baitin' 'em into crossin' him!"

The Ranger stooped quickly, slashing a knife through the canvas pokes. Dull gray metal trickled from the gash. He straightened, his lips a thin, hard line.

"Lead shavin's," he rasped. "That proves what Shale was up to. Latch and the rest didn't know what they was carryin', or they wouldn't have come back here. If they'd pulled off the deal like you think, Sam, they'd never been able to work a mine here, even if there was any silver ore."

His voice took on a corrosive edge as he looked around.

"Any way yuh look at it, this was Breck Shale's work. He rigged them bags up, then somehow baited his men into double-crossing him. He figgered he'd have the whole pile for hisself that way. Only he didn't get out of the cabin like he'd planned. Mebbe yore slug creased him, Clay, or mebbe—"

Another thought flamed hot in the Ranger's brain. It struck deep, lashing him with its possibilities, bringing a rising oath of anger up his throat to die unmuttered behind hard-pressed lips.

20

Harvey Britt

NO longer conscious of the pain that throbbed from the wound in his shoulder, Jim Hatfield turned abruptly. This was the kind of work that had made him the most feared lawman the length and breadth of the State, and now he found himself on the trail of a man as dangerous as any he had ever met.

The plottings of Breck Shale had been those of a Satanic genius. It seemed incredible that the man now lay dead among the ashes of the burned building.

Hatfield strode through the thick dust to move slowly into the charred remains of the building. He avoided the blanket-covered form among the ashes and, close behind him, Clay Tarrant uttered an oath of distaste.

"I still can't get the picture of that body out of my mind," he said. "Whatever Shale did to the men back there, I guess he paid for it in the way he died."

The tall Ranger said nothing, his eyes hard and bright as he moved slowly through the wreckage. He halted in front of the flame-gutted safe, scraping back the ashes with the toe of his boot. A small metal handle emerged into view. He picked it up.

"What's left of a leather bag," he muttered.

"Probably the one he planned on packing the money in," Tarrant growled bitterly. "But what good would that have done him? He knew we had him cornered when he jumped back into the building and kicked the door shut."

"A wolf always has more than one way out of his den," Hatfield said softly.

He moved on, now following what had once been a wall. The black heap of ashes yielded nothing, but he didn't falter in his intent search. It was where the rear wall had stood that he found two flame twisted scraps of metal. He looked around at Tarrant, close at his side, and grinned his mirthless grin.

"Hinges," he grunted. "Shale planned to slip out through a hidden door he had here in the back wall. Only somehow things didn't work out the way he figgered. Mebbe yore slug creased him. Mebbe he tripped and knocked himself out against the desk. Either way, the lamp was probably knocked to the floor when he fell."

But Clay Tarrant's thoughts were in another channel.

"Then the money he stole from Sam Winters and the rest went up in the fire," he said tightly. "Figuring all this out won't do any good to the men who need that money."

Jim Hatfield said nothing. There was still one question remaining unanswered in his mind, a puzzle whose solution was like a will-o'-the-wisp evading the persistent groping of his brain.

He stood there amid the ashes and lone skeleton upright of the burned building, looming tall and grim and haggard. Deep-etched lines of weariness gave his rugged face a craggy, heroic cast, and his hollow eyes burned with a compelling fire.

To Clay Tarrant, glancing at the Ranger, Jim Hatfield towered on his wide-planted legs, lean and indomitable. Every strong element of this vast frontier seemed a part of the lawman—the unshakable power of the mountains, the inexorable grimness of the deserts, and beneath it all, the strange soft quality of the sun-warmed breezes.

For long-drawn minutes, the Ranger stood there, no muscle moving along the arrow-straight line of his body. Then words came softly, and a slowly expelled breath.

"It could have been that way," he murmured. "It could have been like that."

He turned after a pause, then again all movement of his body froze. He stood there staring toward the trail that snaked down the steep wall of the crater, a thin smile shadowing his lips.

A lone horseman was coming slowly down the trail into the Basin.

The rider came out of the hot glare of the morning sun, it was a man dressed in dark store clothes of an expensive cut. His eyes were wide-set and as black as the ebony gelding he straddled.

He said nothing as he approached. He nodded genially, but no words came from his tight lips. The sharp ridge of his nose and the flat planes of his cheeks were framed in the thick black mat of his pointed burnsides and the heavy beard he wore. His age was as uncertain as the glint in his eyes.

He dropped out of saddle to loom there tall and dark. A strange power seemed to reach out and touch the men who watched him and, standing there, Hatfield was conscious of the bitterness that came like a shadow to the faces of the pilgrims around him.

"Harvey Britt," Sam Winters sighed wearily.

Jim Hatfield stared at the man intently, looking deep into the jet-black eyes and seeing nothing readable. He waited, still smiling faintly, something cold and inflexible about him.

A frown knotted Britt's brow as the silence continued, then abruptly his voice came, sharp and perplexed.

"What's the matter with you men? Don't yuh know how to offer a civil good mornin'?"

A low murmur of anger ran through the Easterners. They stood in scattered knots, truculence in their faces, their eyes clouded with weariness and bitterness. Britt's frown deepened into a scowl, and his voice came with an edge of irritation.

"You've shore changed since I rode into yore camp last week. What's come over yuh anyhow? Yuh act like yuh'd never seen me before."

Sam Winters broke the pilgrims' silence, and his words came with a faint uncomfortable note.

"With all respect to you, Britt, I reckon that's just what we are wishin'," he growled.

"What?" Britt blared. He stiffened, anger and resentment changing his features. He shifted his piercing glance from one to another of the pilgrims, his stare nettled, irascible.

"If this sample is the way they show thanks to a man back East, I reckon yuh'd better all move back the way yuh came," he broke out. "Something's gone wrong here. I can see that. But at least yuh could have showed me a little gratitude before yuh aired yore squawk."

Old Sam Winters cursed fervently.

"What've we got to be grateful about? We sunk our last dollar in these claims of yours, then had them peter out on us the first day."

Britt showed quick surprise. "They did

that!" he said sharply. "But that don't give yuh a call to ride me. I gave Breck Shale orders to refund yore money if the claims didn't pay a profit."

Sam Winters snorted dryly. "What is left of Breck Shale is over there in the ashes of that burned buildin'," he returned caustically. "The rest of your six-gun Samaritans are covered up by that tarpaulin over there."

A single brusk word of amazement leaped from Harvey Britt's lips.

"What?"

"They had a change of heart, you might say," Sam Winters said. "They found it easier to take our money than give it back —if they meant to refund it in the first place."

"The devil yuh say!" Britt jerked out a sudden flare of anger. "Yuh better explain yoreself, mister. Yuh talk about me when yuh talk about my men like that."

"Then I'm talkin' about you!" the oldster flung back violently. "I don't feel like whispering to anybody about the crooks that took two thousand dollars of my money for a salted claim!"

Britt took Sam Winters' blunt statement

as if he had been struck a blow. His face darkened, and veins swelled to stand out like cords across his forehead. He stood there a long moment as if struggling with clashing emotions, then abruptly he spun to face Jim Hatfield.

"I came here to see how the men I'd tried to help were gettin' along," he said harshly. "Instead of gettin' the thanks I'd expected, I stand here and hear my hired help called crooks. Is this man right? Are Breck Shale and the rest dead?"

The tall Ranger nodded, his smile freezing and losing its hint of contemptible humor.

"If they ain't dead, they shore did a good job of actin' like it when young Tarrant here and myself called their hand," he drawled.

Britt's piercing black glance flashed over the lawman's apparently indolent body. His anger seemed a thing of dark, driving passion.

"Why?" he blared. "Yuh're a Ranger, and if yuh was in a fight with my men I want to know why?"

Hatfield's reply came soft and cold.

"Short and sweet—it's for the same

reason Sam Winters mentioned a minute ago. Yore Breck Shale and the rest of his pards were as snaky a bunch of murderers as I've ever run up against. They wrecked the El Paso train, and stole enough gold bullion to file up and salt these claims with. They sold the claims to these pilgrims for two thousand each, then waited till they got back the gold they'd salted into the claims. Shale and his men doublecrossed each other the first chance they got, but considerin' their breed I reckon that ain't nothin' to be surprised at."

Britt took the Ranger's blunt statement, reddening but expressionless. His thick burnsides and beard seemed to bristle around the square, flat line of his jaw.

"So now they're dead," he expelled hoarsely.

Hatfield nodded. "So now they're dead," he echoed.

21

The Town Named Silver Pit

PIN-POINTED and widened, Britt's jet eyes stared at the unreadable shadow of a smile on Hatfield's craggy face. He seemed disturbed about something he couldn't understand. He rolled a smoke with faintly agitated fingers, bit the quirly between his lips. He scratched a match into flame on the sole of his boot, touched the fire to his cigarette, dragged long and deep.

Then he looked around at the Easterners, as if he still found everything hard to believe. He pinched the flame from the match, absently snapped the slender stem between his strong fingers.

"Well, this beats me!" he rumbled. His smile reflected self-condemnation. "It shore does! For several years I've trusted Breck Shale and his men, and I never thought they could do a job like this. But I never checked on them. I stayed in Austin all the time, and gave Shale a free rein out here. He wired me he'd found gold here in the Basin, and had filed all the claims under my name. He must have done that to try to implicate me in his dirty work."

His dark glance slid around to the Ranger's rugged face. Hatfield shrugged wide shoulders and said nothing, that chill half smile haunting his lips.

Harvey Britt pulled his eyes back to the Easterners with an effort, and his voice strengthened as if he felt himself partially responsible for the injustice done them, and was eager to make amends.

"It was through my men that all of yuh lost everything yuh had," he rumbled. "I feel indirectly to blame for what Shale did, and I want to return every dollar Shale stole from yuh. Of course, under the conditions, I'll want the claim deed papers back for my own protection."

Jim Hatfield's flat-toned drawl came before the Easterners could give vent to their wild cheers of gratitude.

"I've been wonderin' how long it would take yuh to get to that," he said softly. His trained body tensed.

Harvey Britt's dark eyes flashed to him,

suddenly hot, startled. His visage burned a deep red, and his voice came in a hoarse stammer.

"W-what!"

"It's taken yuh longer to get to the point than I guessed when I first saw yuh comin' down the trail," the tall Ranger said with a sharp trace of mockery.

Harvey Britt gripped jumping nerves with a hard will.

"Do yuh expect me to believe everything when I hear it?" he brayed. "I knew Breck Shale a long time and had every reason to trust him. I tried to give these pilgrims a hand. I'm tryin' now, but yuh act like—like yuh believe I was in with Shale on this deal."

Hatfield nodded watchfully. "That about spells it out, Britt," he said, with deceptive mildness.

Britt's red features drained to a dirty white, his chest swelling as he dragged in a long deep breath. He shoved his sombrero back with the back of his hand, baring a stiff ashen face that was beaded with sweat.

Hatfield's voice drove on, gathering cold contempt with each word.

"We had a good hunch Ben Latch and

his men would come back, but I got a jolt when you showed up. I reckon yuh heard Clay Tarrant spill his news, and that brought yuh here."

Through the sudden silence, Tarrant's thin words came.

"I met him on the street in the boom town up above. But Jim, you're making a mistake. He's only trying—"

"Britt, yuh fool, there's no silver here!" The Ranger's voice rang out with sudden force. His words struck the big man, shaking him.

"No silver! But—" He caught himself with a supreme effort. "Man, what in thunder are yuh drivin' at?"

Jim Hatfield laughed harshly. "That was just a piece of bed rock I broke off to bluff Ben Latch into comin' back here. I didn't know you'd fall for the same bait, and show up."

His voice hammered on inexorably, giving Harvey Britt no chance to clear his stunned brain.

"I've had a hunch since last night where you came in on this deal, Britt. One of Shale's men said somethin' about yuh gettin' yore cut for their dirty work. But there's more to it than that!"

The rising inflection of his voice had a vast meaning for the big man. His face underwent a violent change, twisting, as if under the realization of what hung in the balance. He made no sound, his body quivering slightly as he poised himself, but even more significant was the strange slow nod of his head—as if he had feared this moment, and now wanted to get it over with.

He knew what was coming. His hands lifted to the front of his black coat, halted, long fingers splaying out tensely.

"All the time, Breck Shale was doublecrossing his men," the Ranger went on. "He was layin' out fifty per cent of every job's take for Harvey Britt, and they never caught on. Shale doublecrossed them on this job, baitin' 'em into robbin' his safe and hittin' for the Border. Then he waited until I showed up. Shale *wanted* me to jump him about the swindle of these pilgrims!"

Harvey Britt slanted a flashing glance around him, marking the position of his horse, of every man who looked on. He rolled to the balls of his feet, swayed back to his heels, stood there, his bent knees dropping him in a slight crouch.

"Shale *wanted* me to jump him, yuh hear?" Jim Hatfield lashed out. "He even set the fire that burned down his shack. He had the whole thing worked down fine, knowin' just what we'd think when we kicked through the ashes. He didn't think I'd wonder what happened to Gyp Logan, the only member of the gang not accounted for.

"Mebbe I wouldn't have thought anything about it, but Breck Shale made a little mistake before he jumped back into the buildin'. He lit his smoke and broke the match between his fingers just like you do, Britt, like yuh'd done when that picture of yores in Shale's office was taken. Britt, you are Breck Shale!"

The big Britt was in movement before Hatfield had finished his accusation. His arm struck up under his coat, his hands clawing out holstered weapons.

The eyes of those who looked on were not swift enough to follow the Ranger's draw. And yet, magically, his heavy guns were there, spouting red flame. Breck

Shale's frame jerked spasmodically under the impact of lead. His guns were up, but he seemed without the strength to rock back the hammers. All the menace left his jet-black eyes, as he crumpled.

His right hand, falling across his face, pulled loose the false beard and burnsides. And the face of the Breck Shale all of them knew was exposed.

The tall Ranger strode forward, stooped, and pulled the gun from the dead man's right hand. He glanced intently at the muzzle, staring at a small dent in the edge of the barrel that raised a slight ridge at the mouth of the bore.

He reached into his pocket, pulled out the slug that had killed the half-breed whose body he had found near the wrecked train, the half-breed who once had so nearly killed Jim Hatfield. He fitted the butt of the slug into the gun's muzzle, smiled faintly as he saw that the groove in the lead matched the ridge in the Colt's boring.

"If I'd got a slug from Shale's gun to match with the one from that breed's body I might have caught on to this jasper before," he said softly.

It was minutes before the onlookers got

their breaths before they could besiege the Ranger with clamoring questions.

"It was the body of Gyp Logan we found in the burned building," Jim Hatfield told them there. "I didn't have Britt and Shale figured to be the same man until Shale made his play. That wire I got from Austin said there was no one there by the name of Britt, and that helped tie in the answer.

"But I didn't really catch on until I saw Shale break the burned match. Then I remembered seeing the picture of a broken match on the floor in front of Shale when he had himself photographed as Britt to help him doublecross his men on their other jobs. But when I finally got the answer, Shale moved too quick for me to stop him."

Clay Tarrant chuckled quietly. "I wouldn't say you moved slow," he said warmly.

The tall Ranger smiled faintly, and went on in his slow mild drawl:

"When I saw the body on the floor of the burned buildin' I thought just what Shale wanted me to think—that it was him who died there. Logan had disappeared, but I didn't figger it was him. That's why Shale —or Britt—started the fire—to destroy Logan so we'd never recognize him. Shale slipped out the secret door with the *dinero*, rustled up the trail and made himself up to be Harvey Britt." He glanced at Tarrant. "He'd have got away clean, too, if you hadn't gone through the town yellin' about the silver ore, Clay."

Hatfield chuckled with satisfaction. "We baited the trap for the gang," he said, "and caught the head polecat I thought was dead. I reckon yuh'll find the money in Shale's saddle-bags. He figgered he could buy back them claims and clear a fortune. Clay, yuh ought to frame that chunk of rock."

Clay Tarrant's smile broadened.

"I am going to," he said, and he looked down at the girl standing close at his side, reading the promise in Holly Winters' eyes that only he was supposed to see. "I didn't get a chance to examine this chunk of rock you pulled your bluff with until a few minutes ago. I'm going to frame it, all right. For two reasons, Jim—for baitin' the outlaws and Shale back here, and because it is the richest piece of silver ore I've ever seen!"

Clay and Mrs. Holly Tarrant often went to that rocky parapet on the rim of the crater wall. From there, Tornado Basin lay broad and deep before them, with its shadowed corners and frowning granite cliffs and floating wreaths of mist when there was a dampness in the air.

In the evening when the clouds hung low in the sky, they could look behind them toward the mining town, with its interlaced steel rails that ran from the ore conveyors, its clutter of rough buildings, the high stacks that trailed their banners of smoke across the heavens.

But mostly, Clay and Holly Tarrant stood close together, looking into the depths of the Basin. Down there lay the glut of iron-roofed buildings and latticed gallows-frames and tool sheds among the waste heaps. It was as if a thunderstorm had washed a wreckage into the Basin. They could hear the boom and rolling echoes of dynamite, the distant ring of hammer and drill, the groan and grinding of the conveyors hauling ore up the wall to the town's stamp mills.

They had named the town Silver Pit.

Most frequently, they visited the rocky promontory at dusk. At that hour the light of day was failing, and the shadows of night were veiling the Basin in their impenetrable shrouds. Ghosts of the past came back then, ghosts of violence and bloodshed, of bitter men, of other men whose love and loyalty was unquestioned, stalking killers who had died as they had lived—by their guns.

And it was then that Clay and Holly always found themselves looking at each other, thinking the same thoughts.

It was always Clay who put their thoughts into words.

"I wonder what danger Jim's in tonight."

For as long as outlaws ruled that vast land north of the Rio Grande, they knew Jim Hatfield would be dedicating his guns to bring peace and law and order to Texas.

GUNSMOKE EMPIRE

Copyright © Renewed 1966 by
Popular Library, Inc.
All rights reserved

1

Hills of Death

THE gentle west wind rose over the wooded summits of the great southwest mountains, impartially caressing both the good and the evil. It sighed through the glossy-leaved stands of live-oak and virgin pine forming the watershed of the Maravilla River, whose system extended hundreds of miles eastward, sustaining a large and prosperous people. It cooled the sweated hides of grazing livestock, growing fat for the market.

To the wind rose a rasping shriek, the groans of small, dark-skinned slaves, toiling with ax and saw, blindly destroying through the feverish, greedy desire of man, the lives of a multitude. Brute overseers, armed with guns and whips, lashed the helpless peons on.

A wide, squat man, whose bulging muscles showed his terrific strength, hurried through the bleeding forest.

"Bigjaw" Dave Haley, boss muleskinner, wore no hat on his shaggy carrot-topped head; red-rimmed eyes burned in his misshapen face, jaw prominent and covered by a thick, rusty stubble. He carried a blacksnake whip with leaden tippets that cut deep gashes in quivering flesh. Corduroy pants, flannel shirt open, showing a hairy barrel chest matted by sweat, and big hobnail shoes completed his get-up. A cut of tobacco bulged out one cheek.

With his grizzly gait he ambled up to a slender, foppishly clad man standing on a fallen giant oak's raw stump. "Hey, Ross! That dude's bin talkin' to the Mexes and I jest seen him writin' in a book!"

Valentine Ross's greenish eyes slitted; he gulped as though his soul distilled a vitriol of hate that seared his throat. He had a face like death, bony sharp, pasty-white despite his outdoor life. Between cruel, ribbon-thin lips he clipped a saliva-stained cigarette. Taller than Haley he weighed half as much, with sharp shoulders and protruding bones. His gray trousers, slim black shoes on dainty feet of which he was inordinately proud, were very neat as was his white shirt with string tie, and plain dark felt hat that was carefully placed on oiled black hair.

"And the Boss is coming tonight," he snarled.

So ferocious was Ross that, though any of the huge, fierce lumberjacks could have broken him in two with their hands, he dominated them and they feared him as they might the devil. For weapons he carried two small-calibre pistols and a narrow keen-edged knife.

Bigjaw's voice was a bear's bass growl; Ross's a penetrating, ill-tempered rasp with a hint of accent. He had mestizo blood, with the worst qualities of both races.

Through the cut forest might be seen slaving Mexicans, faces drawn with anguish, emaciated ribs visible through tatters of clothing. When Valentine Ross moved off his stump, dark eyes rolled fearfully; as Ross passed a group at a rotating saw, he struck out at a peon who was rocking dizzily, plainly sick. The man jumped back with a shriek of terror, the saw snapped up his shirt and in a second it was over, the peon bleeding to death in the mound of sawdust.

Ross did not look back. He moved with a serpent's supple glide, Haley rolling at his heels. They crossed a mountain stream and came to the camp, mostly huts built of logs. A young man in a blue suit, his curly head bare, quickly came out of a shack marked "OFFICE: SOUTHWEST LUMBER CO." But he was not quick enough, for Ross had seen him. He tried to look unconcerned but Ross gulped as he stared into his victim's eyes. He ordered coldly:

"Give me the book."

The young fellow was rattled. "Why, what—" he began.

Ross's signal was imperceptible to the victim; Haley's whip swished, tippets cracking like a gunshot, tearing the young man's eyes. He screamed in agony and Haley rushed at him, threw him, driving a knee into his belly. Bigjaw took a small notebook from the writhing man's pocket and handed it to Ross.

Ross scanned the pages. Then he leaped, snatching up Haley's whip, and began to slash the helpless victim, beat him with a mad strength that made Bigjaw stare in awe.

"This is what spies get!" Ross shrieked. Tiring when he had cut the victim almost to death he threw down the lash, drew a pistol and fired three shots into the dying man.

A horseman, a lean fellow with a cheek badly scarred from an old knife wound, came galloping in. "Hey, boss! Couple Bar W waddies headin' here!"

A short while later two cowboys rode up to an apparently deserted camp. One dismounted, picked a fresh hide from a pile near the racks where fresh beef hung draining.

"Bar W!" he said sharply. Ross emerged from the office. "Looka, yuh danged rustlin' dude," cried the Bar W hombre, "what yuh mean, butcherin' our cows! Yuh've stole too many from us Valley people and yuh got to pay."

"All right—here's your pay," Ross said, with a shrug that was a signal, for guns blasted from the bush into the waddies. The mustangs reared, dashed off through the trees.

Death rode there, wholesale death and horror; and death not only to men but to mighty Texas, threatened by the murderous lust of a man for power.

The west wind descended the eastern slope where the Maravilla swelled from a mountain stream to a wide river watering grassy plains. Through the river's calm beneficence men lived. The wind crossed the main river's valley to Bowietown, lying along the north bank, a typical cowtown with lines of wooden buildings, a big general store, "YAGER'S," and with rutted roads dried by the Texas sun. The wind rustled the trees of the Plaza in the middle of town to cool the excited faces of the crowd assembled there. On the wooden platform sat several of Maravilla's most important citizens, and the honest, toil-hardened Texans listened to their leaders.

Smiling Hank Yager, mayor of Bowie, presided at this indignation meeting. A bluff, square man, teeth easily showing in good humor, thick brown hair awry, brown shirt and pants tucked homily into half-boots, for like many outdoor men Yager liked to be on easy terms with people. His brown eyes were sun-seamed, and he spoke with the bluff heartiness of man to man.

"You heard what happened! Two Bar W men gunned up there this mornin'. Sam Ward's word is gold."

A giant of a man, in rancher's clothes, expensive boots and pants, great Stetson, leaped up, round, honest face red with anger. Sam Ward towered on the dais. He was a great cattle king of Maravilla, loved and respected, head of the Ranchers' Union. The Bar W backed on the western watershed, though the entire range was open and cows from the other outfits grazed the lush hills.

Ward had straight-looking blue eyes, wide-set over a nose once mashed by a horse's lashing hoofs; shoulders broad as a door, arms big as most men's legs. He was an outspoken fellow, a self-made man who had always taken care of himself and his own.

Behind Ward sat his pretty daughter Elsie. Her hair was darker than her father's but she had his wide blue eyes, fresh with youth; a dainty girl in white starched riding clothes. Her features were even, her whole look showed her earnest sweetness. Her face glowed with admiration as she watched her father.

"Boys," boomed Ward, "yuh know me. I come to this country when it was wilderness, nobody here but a few outlaws on the dodge. Done saved my cowboy wages up nawth and bought a quarter section and started with a few runts. Bin here thutty years last October and I have seen Maravilla develop into a wonder spot. We bin lucky here with fresh, plentiful water." He spoke with a simplicity that gripped the hearts of his listeners; they felt his intense love for home.

"I love this land. I jest couldn't live anywheres else. What's goin' on tears me bad as a knife. Them skunks up above are cuttin' off all them trees for miles in sech a hurry they've ruint the hills. They've stolen our cows and used our hosses to dig ditches and drag logs; they've gunned anybody who went up there." He banged a huge fist into his other hand. "We got to act! I'm for it pronto!"

A cheer went up. Alf Betts, town marshal, thumped his wooden leg on the boards. Mayor Yager gave the floor to a tall, gaunt gentleman.

"Senator Ardmore wants to talk, boys."

Senator Rathburn Ardmore stood six-feet-two; thin and angular, bony shoulders stooped in black frock coat. A heavy shock of iron-gray hair waved on his long, triangular head. He spoke with a trained orator's power.

"Gentlemen, perhaps the lumbermen are breaking the law, but is this any reason why we should? I counsel patience and legal means. Austin will help us. A complaint has already been sent the governor. Some of the stock stealing may be laid at the feet of the Mexican bandit, Vasco Torquila. Of course, I'm on your side; the Maravilla is my homeland, and I join with my dear friend Sam Ward, eager to serve you. That's why I caution you to stick by the law."

Mayor Yager stepped up. "Boys, I'm like Ward, in favor of vigilante action and quick. Let's go up and drive 'em out!"

The crowd began to shout and men hurried for their horses, checked their guns. Sam Ward and Mayor Yager rode in the van as a hundred riders headed swiftly for the hills.

Near sundown in the heavily bushed foothills the winding trail came to a great ditch cut into red clay. Earth had been thrown out and the blood-red sun was in the posse's eyes as they bunched up to stare at this deep gully.

The quiet was shattered by a terrific gunfire. Fierce-faced men jumped up from behind the breastworks, and from the bushes at the sides, pouring a withering death into the massed riders. Horses reared as the startled ranchers went for their guns, scattering for cover. Half a dozen fell in the first awful volley. Valentine Ross's high whine, Bigjaw Haley's roar, could be heard shouting orders over the din. The battle opened, and Sam Ward was up front, down in a spewed mass of granite rocks, six-gun spitting hate for the men who were ruining his beloved country.

But the ambush had smashed them; and after a few moments, the fighting cowmen saw Mayor Yager stagger from the rock nest, with Sam Ward limp across his back, head hanging and dripping blood. Yager caught at a horse, dumped the cattle king's body across the saddle, leaped up behind. With a last defiant shot, the mayor rode his friend out of the battle.

Ward's finish disheartened the ranchers; they retreated, the rattled survivors taking to their mounts, harried for a mile by the victorious lumbermen.

Later, back at the Bar W, Elsie Ward stared in wide-eyed anguish at the death-pale face of her father. Yager and others had brought him home, laid him gently in his bed.

"Ride for the doctor, quick," Elsie gasped.

"Afraid he's gone," Yager growled, shaking his head. "Elsie, I'm sorry; I want to do everything I can to help you."

Bancroft Morton, leather creaking, whistled as he headed up into the hills on his pet horse, Black Rascal. He was a bronc buster, expert at taming wild mustangs, meandering from spot to spot in his work. Cool and quiet, Morton had amber eyes and a level gaze. He made a lean, handsome figure in his easy saddle. He wore expensive leather, for his equipment had to be good in such work. He had light, curly hair which he kept close-clipped.

Young, hardly more than a boy, but he was able to take care of himself in a hard world.

He was in the Ord Mountains, and he

had been told in Oklahoma that they were full of wild ponies or strays from the big valley outfits which would pay to have them captured and broken. But as he came in from the north, strange sounds, the shriek of saws, the dim yells of men, the ditch that ran for two miles below, made him swear in disgust.

"Mustangs'll never stick around here," he muttered. Over on the next ridge he saw the figures of toiling men; from a distance they looked exactly like ants.

The soft west wind was in his bronzed face as he sighted a band of horses. "Shore seem tame," he told Black Rascal. His pursuit of the horses took him near the other ridge, and too easily he trapped the horses in a natural corral.

He was disgusted, altogether. "Them lumberjacks are spoilin' this country," he growled.

He dismounted, took his rope, when a sharp command brought him facing about. On a bank nearby stood men, led by a thin, pasty-faced devil whose eyes gleamed green as a cat's. Morton didn't like their looks as they silently stared at him, "Howdy, gents," he sang out, "what's up—?" The thin man whipped out a small pistol and then fired; the bronc buster felt the slug burn his ribs. It spun him about but he grabbed his Colt and let go at them. The horses stampeded and their bodies protected Morton as he quickly mounted and rode away hell-for-leather.

The next morning, his wound roughly bandaged, he sighted across rolling prairie where steers grazed thick, the low-lying buildings of the big Bar W. He pulled into the yard, before him the wide-sprawled ranch, a rambling, one-storied house, barns, bunkhouse, corrals, with the Maravilla River close at hand.

Ban Morton stopped at a rear corral; a tall hombre with a leathery, saturnine face looked slowly up at him.

"Howdy," Ban said. "My name's Morton. Say, who's boss here?"

"I am, Nevada Lewis," the saturnine hombre growled. "What of it?"

Morton dismounted, stretched his legs.

He moved with the queer, stiff gait of the bronc buster, as though he were unused to walking.

A young woman appeared from a kitchen door and Ban Morton stared. In that first look at Elsie Ward, the world suddenly changed for Morton; his lips opened and he tensed. She went to a line, took down some fresh, clean bandage cloths, went back inside. There was such a dejected droop to her girlish figure Morton was deeply affected.

"Nevada" Lewis didn't miss his reaction.

"Old Man's bad hurt," he said to Ban.

"Nevada," Ban Morton drawled, "I'd like to talk to whoever's runnin' the shebang here. It's important."

Lewis shrugged. "There's some gents inside if yuh want," he said coldly.

Morton stalked to the front porch and went up. The door was open and he came face to face with Elsie, as she was crossing toward a large side room. Through the doorway, Morton glimpsed a great figure flat in a bed, and several men sitting round him.

As Elsie stared into his eyes, Morton heard a deep voice growl, "While we were up after them skunks, Torquila raided the Dot O and Runnin' T thirty mile south. We got to do somethin' 'bout that Mex bandit. Nuthin's safe any more."

Ban took off his hat. "My name's Ban Morton, ma'am. I rode here special to warn yuh of what's goin' on up above, in the hills. Lumbermen up there are cuttin' yore timber off and it's goin' to ruin yore entire range."

"Thank you," said the young woman. She seemed to like Ban Morton's appearance and his honest voice. "Come inside— some of our friends are talking about what to do."

She led him to the side room and said: "This is Ban Morton. Mayor Yager, Marshal Betts, my father, Sam Ward, Senator Ardmore—" She introduced the various ranchers of Maravilla, who watched the young stranger with a cold suspicion, until he started to speak to them.

"Gents," he began, "I saw what them lumbermen're up to. It's worse'n yuh know. Once they cut off all that timber it means yore whole range for hundreds of miles is ruined. Rains'll pour off the hills, gully yore land, carry off topsoil, yuh'll have floods when it rains, droughts when it don't, no river to speak of. I've seen it happen up nawth and it's terrible."

"What would you advise?" Yager boomed.

"Send a complaint direct to the guv'nor; the State won't allow sech destruction. Yuh'll need to act fast, too, or it'll be too late. S'pose, Miss Ward, yuh write it out and I'll take it to the telegraph office myself."

The ranchers were in dire straits, a whole people seeing the end of hope and life, with death bearing down on them.

2

A Ranger Hits the Trail

CAP'N BILL McDOWELL of the Texas Rangers, rugged old frontiersman that he was, whose hide was said to be tough enough to snap back at a bowie knife, restlessly paced the confine of Austin Headquarters. He was in a disturbed mood.

"A terrible mess," he muttered, "and a big one."

He slammed a gnarled fist into a calloused palm. "Yessir, Hatfield's the on'y one kin handle it, if it can be done—"

A familiar tread caused him to swing, and he swore as his game leg twinged; too old to ride the Danger Trail now, Captain McDowell had a hard time holding himself in at news of atrocities against Texas.

"Hatfield!" he boomed, facing the cool, tall man who silently appeared before him.

Though six feet, Cap'n Bill had to look up to meet the gray-green, steady gaze of his star Ranger. Jim Hatfield was bronzed by wind and sun and rain, his rugged features quiescent but giving a hint of his terrific power. He had very wide shoulders, a lean-muscled body tapering to a fighting man's slim hips where hung two Colt .45s, blue-steel, that could flash into action with lightning speed.

"Yes, suh," he drawled.

At sight of Ranger Hatfield, at sound of that soft but compelling voice, McDowell felt reassured. He knew that the strength of a fighting panther was in that long body, that the heart beat with a flaming courage that never quailed.

Under the wide fawn Stetson showed jet-black, gleaming hair, the Ranger's whole mighty being radiating perfect health, steady nerves ever fully controlled. No man could match Jim Hatfield's speed in action and McDowell knew he had a diplomat's brain to coordinate with his marvelous physical power.

"Steel and hick'ry and coiled chain-lightnin'," McDowell thought as he eased down in the big fellow's company.

Hatfield's face was in repose softened by a wide, good-humored mouth but

McDowell knew the deadliness with which the Ranger struck the enemies of Texas. In terse sentences the captain outlined the trouble gripping Maravilla.

"It's a big country, Jim, large as some eastern states. Puzzles me, too, how it's got so bad 'thout us hearin' much. Some complaints come in on this Vasco Torquila, the giant Mex bandit raidin' down there and I meant to send a man down. But this here land ruination Miss Elsie Ward speaks of in her personal telegram to the governor is new. Talks like we knowed all about it. Seems a passel of lumbermen 're cuttin' the timber off the Maravilla watershed and that concerns Texas. It's a big job in itself; but if private parties is allowed to cut timber thataway, there's no sayin' how far it'll reach. May mean ruination and anarchy in the state, so get goin'."

The cool Ranger's voice had a mildness to it that had fooled more than one blustering and now defunct gunman:

"Callate them hills 're where that forester disappeared, Cap'n!"

McDowell jumped, slammed the desk so the inkwell leaped. "By golly, Jim, yuh're right. Figgered mebbe he'd got hisself lost or gone over a cliff. But Sheriff George Godey of Brewster County wired he can't locate him. Yuh can trust Godey down there, he'll give yuh aid."

Hatfield didn't reply and McDowell laughed inside. It was not the Ranger's way to ask aid; information was another thing, but when Jim Hatfield was ready he found a way to strike, strike with the unerring, deadly aim of a bullet.

"Been sev'ral murders there, of cowboys," added McDowell, "Elsie Ward's pa, Sam, was most kilt, the citizens went up to attack the lumbermen, had a battle, and got beat off, 'cordin' to Godey. It's bad when people take the law into their hands; yuh'll hafta straighten that out. And don't forget Vasco Torquila. Hustle now, hell's roarin' in Maravilla!"

Hatfield saluted; he asked no questions but strode out, door closing quietly behind him.

"Well," thought McDowell, "I'm glad it ain't me he's sicked on!"

In the brilliant sunshine Goldy, Hatfield's pet sorrel, nuzzled his master's hand, feigning to nip his sleeve, ears back. Hatfield's voice soothed the magnificent gelding, and he mounted, sitting the saddle with a master rider's ease. He carried his blue-steel Colts in oiled, supple holsters that would not drag; a Winchester snugged in a boot. The gray-green eyes shone for he was happiest when he was in his way, at work.

Jim Hatfield headed southwest for Maravilla and the legions of death.

While Jim Hatfield rode, a conference took place outside the office of the Southwest Lumber Company. The yellow moon peeped through the pines, and a ray struck the evil face of one who dominated the brutal crew.

"That bronc buster got word through," he growled, "and the Rangers know. They'll come."

"Let 'em," snarled a narrow-shouldered dude, tapping his knife. A bear-like hombre snapped a bullwhip.

"Watch," the chief insisted. "We need time, time to make our hook-up, get this timber out. Then we'll have control and to hell with everything. The Rangers 're the only thing we have to worry about. Fat Phil is taking care of Bowietown."

"Okay, anything you say, Chief, but you won't object if I call you up here to look at a dead body or two?"

"So long as it's not yours," and the chief grimly added, "the Rangers are a diff'rent proposition. I've done all I could to hold 'em off. Remember, I know more than you do, that's why you're workin' for me. I'll see to the Rangers myself."

"These ranchers are a nuisance," the dude growled. "I got fifty thousand foot of oak and pine ready to go out; but they're ambushin' our teams to the railroad. We got to be able to haul farther to the east now."

The chief cursed. "I'll break them, once and for all," he declared furiously. "I must have Maravilla, to hook up the whole shebang. I'll wipe that Union off the map!" . . .

Ranger Hatfield, on Goldy, both showing the strains of their incredibly fast trip from Austin, stared through the bush fringing the bluff. Heading for the Bar W and Bowietown, Hatfield had stopped at sight of the chase across the plain. One man was fleeing before a dozen, until the lanky fugi-

260

tive's lathered horse had hit a gopher hole and crashed, sending the rider headlong in the grass.

The angry voices of ranchers who had seized the fugitive had drowned out the faint sounds of Hatfield's stealthy approach; in the purple shadows cast by high mesquite with star-white blooms and thorny granjeno the Ranger saw them swarming about the quaking prisoner.

"String him up!" a harsh voice insisted, and the cry was chorused, echoing in the verdant rangeland.

The sky was a ruby-red dome, the sun a great ball on the western hills; steers grazed beyond and insects hummed in the death of the day. The aromatic odor of sage and creosote tinged the exhilarating, sweet air.

"There's a good oak tree over there," a cowboy growled. "We'll teach yuh lumberjacks a lesson yuh won't forget!"

Hatfield was intrigued. He ran a long-fingered, slim hand down the line of his fighting jaw.

"So," he mused, "he's from up there! And I callate these'll be Bar W hombres takin' revenge." An idea had come to his clever brain, and he swung a booted foot to the earth, touching Goldy's muzzle to warn the sorrel to stand quiet.

Silently Jim Hatfield moved up to where he looked directly down on the necktie party. The victim, held by a dozen men in cowboy garb of Stetson, chaps and boots, wore a corduroy suit and he had lost his helmetlike corduroy hat when he fell; the Ranger noted his mutilated cheek. His sunken eyes rolled in terror and he shook at the imminence of lynch death.

"Don't, gents, please. I'm innocent."

"Innocent, hell!" a rancher snarled, slapping him. "I seen yuh myself up in the hills when Sam Ward was ambushed. We're goin' to string up every one of yuh we snaffle. Yuh was spyin' around the Bar W jest now. Why, that hoss yuh was on has a Bar W brand on. That's 'nuff to hang yuh."

They weren't wasting any motions. A 40-foot lariat had been strung and tossed over the limb of a high oak tree close to the bluff where Hatfield crouched.

"He may not deserve savin'," thought Hatfield, "but I need a quick introduction and this looks like it." He had made his decision and action came instantly with it. He was not the man to miss such a chance to obtain information; the only hitch was the fact that he did not wish the ranchers to identify him as yet.

Hatfield did not descend among them but stayed back among the bushes, on the commanding eminence of the bluff, where rotted shale formed a slide. He drew his two six-guns, and the clicks as they cocked under his thumbs were lost in the shuffle. But the incisive command he uttered froze every man in the circle.

"Reach, gents!"

These were men who knew what a gun meant. Hands reached high even before their eyes rolled around. In the gathering gloom they saw the glow of the Lone Wolf's eyes, the glint of the hypnotizing Colts.

Hatfield kept his voice gruff; the intervening bush effectually hid him.

"Sorry to spoil yore party," he drawled. "You, Scarface, grab that chestnut and pull him up here." His all-seeing eye caught the slight move of a cowman who thought he was hidden behind a comrade's body. A six-gun barked and the bullet spat through Hatfield's Stetson crown. The echo was the

Ranger's gun, roaring blue-yellow, and the homber uttered a sharp yelp:

"Shot my gun outa my hand!"

The precision shot jolted all idea of resistance out of them, and they just waited, as the lean hombre willingly shoved from the death ring, grabbed the rein of the powerful horse Hatfield had indicated, and came scrabbling up the slide.

"What now?" Scarface gasped, as though the rope already cut off his breath.

"Mount and ride. I'll follow."

The instant Hatfield swung, the cowmen went for their guns and fired into the bushes where he had crouched. The slugs snapped the leaves, but the angle prevented them from striking the Ranger as he mounted Goldy, swung and galloped after the man he had saved.

"Quickest way for a look-see up there," he mused, as Goldy loped in the swift trail west taken by Scarface.

The pursuit was begun. The Bar W men yanked their mustangs up the slide and came hell-for-leather on the trail, whooping it up and firing wildly. Hatfield had made a good choice, the chestnut could run like the wind and Goldy had to spread himself to stay at the flying hoofs. They ran several hundred yards before the infuriated lynching bee really started, and the pair in front began to gain for they could zigzag through the rising bushy hills.

The last rays of day died and they rode for miles under a rising yellow moon. The ranchers finally quit in disgust, unable to trail wraiths in the night.

Panting, the scar-faced hombre swung in his saddle, eyes rolling in his narrow head.

"Thanks, mister. Yuh saved my life."

"Okay," drawled the Ranger. "I been too close to it myself to let a man stretch hemp."

Scarface seized this hint that the big man on the golden horse might be outside the law. He began to draw out Hatfield in what he thought a subtle manner, about his past. The Ranger by his terse replies let Scarface gain the impression he was on the dodge.

It was subtly done and Scarface, too, felt grateful, with the noose so close behind.

"Say, mebbe we kin use you. What's yore name?"

"They call me Frisco Jim."

"Okay, Jim. Tag along with us and you'll be in clover. We're goin' to take Texas to hell 'fore we're through, and there's plenty in it." Scarface, wiping the sweat of death from his lean cheeks, was boastful.

"How use me?" asked the Ranger—he would draw out Scarface if possible but could not damage his standing by showing too much curiosity.

A look that was near to fear came over Scarface's countenance. He seemed to draw back and he muttered, "*He'll* tell you, Jim. Take my word for it, there's money and good money."

Plainly Scarface was a subordinate and afraid to talk too much. Hatfield shrugged, aware that he must step carefully or Scarface might grow suspicious.

A million stars powdered the sky. A million night creatures sang a song of mystery. The brush and trees rustled in the softness of the wind and beyond, the river placidly flowed through the gorgeous valley it created. Far up above, ahead, Hatfield saw tiny yellow specks in the forest that were lights.

It was midnight when they reached the camp of the Southwest Lumber Company. Alert guards patrolled the trail; three times were they challenged as they rode the fragrant, winding ways. From the dense thickets a hard voice demanded:

"Yes? Who's that?" The intonation was staccato, each word carefully articulated.

And each time Scarface replied the same way, by rote: "S.—W.—L.!" The two riders went through.

They forded the stream, up onto the space where stood the shacks. Hatfield looked over the camp. Fully awake men, with rifles, stood about, and through the trees he saw more dark figures, silver sheen of moonlight on gun barrels, by what seemed to be a large stockade. A few yards before the central hut, marked, "OFFICE. SOUTHWEST LUMBER CO." burned a red fire; lanterns hung on wooden pegs in the logs.

As the two dismounted, turned their horses into a rope corral, a bony figure slid from the office.

Danger was here, permeating the scented air of the pine woods. Hatfield could smell it. Hundreds of guns were ready to turn on him. The eerie shadows, grim faces under corduroy helmets, powerful figures in pants of the same material and gray flannel shirts, and a confused moaning that came from the stockade, would have shaken most men. Hatfield, cool, unperturbed, but alert, took in what he could.

The pasty-faced devil staring at Hatfield snapped, "Scarface! Who's that with you?"

Hatfield didn't like the voice any more than the man's appearance. It was an unpleasant, penetrating snarl, but plainly the dudish-clad hombre was a power in the camp.

"Ross," cried Scarface, "this big jigger saved me. I connected with our man at the ranch. It's fixed to cook Ban Morton, he's as good as dead. But when I was leavin' a Bar W waddy reckernized me and they had the rope hung when this feller stuck guns on 'em. I won't go down that way no more, boss; they know me now. As for ridin' to Bowie and seein' Fat Phil, that's out too. Jim here's new; mebbe he can take over the job."

"Shut up," snarled Ross. "You'll do what you're told, Scarface." He stepped up to Hatfield, fixed his cattish eyes on the placid countenance of the officer, whose easy carriage was almost contemptuous, that of a reckless gunman who thinks he can take care of his hide. Indeed, Hatfield was figuring how much he could find out before Ross found him out. The ruby light glowed on the fish-belly skin of Ross's narrow face. Hatfield read him as a master foe, and he wondered how well Ross read him.

Beyond a brief glance at the shacks, at the dim outline of the stockade off among the trees, Hatfield did not go; he was too clever to show curiosity.

For a moment the two men confronted one another and while not a move the Ranger made was wrong, Valentine Ross went as much by instinct as by appearance. But if the boss suspected anything he did not show it, beyond a gulp. He seemed to accept the tall jigger at Scarface's valuation.

Plenty of armed men around, watching the scene; at a word from Ross they would have run in to pour death into the Ranger. Scarface talked excitedly:

"Say, Ross, this feller kin move like light. He's on the dodge, name's Frisco Jim. Picked me away from them ranchers neat as you wish to see. I told him mebbe we could use him."

"Maybe we can," replied Ross smoothly. "You boys look worn out. Turn in, take your friend to that hut over there so you won't be disturbed." And to Hatfield he added, "Make yourself at home, pal. Welcome."

Was there, mused the Ranger, a sarcastic tinge to Ross's voice? He gravely thanked him. Crouched close at hand, in the shadows, he glimpsed a hogshead figure with rusty hair and beard; by his clothes, the blacksnake whip tucked under one arm, Hatfield guessed he was a muleskinner, and he heard Ross call him "Bigjaw."

Still Hatfield sensed the danger; he also sensed an expectancy. Save for the sough of wind in the trees, the peaceful murmur of Nature, faint crackle of the fire, there was quiet; then, as Hatfield swung to follow Scarface, a shrill, anguished shriek, the cry of a tormented soul, rang from the stockade in the woods; and a moment later two shots cracked, the voice ceased.

Hatfield looked there; then was aware Valentine Ross watched him. He shrugged, pretending to find nothing strange in this. The odor of fresh sawdust mingled with the smell of burnt wood; below, the Maravilla gurgled in its stony bed.

"C'mon," Scarface ordered nervously,

touching his new pal's sleeve. "Let's turn in. I'm plumb wore out." He led the way along a path, north from the collection of huts to a log shack. Sleeping men were inside and Scarface found the Ranger a vacant bunk at the left of the doorway.

The Ranger lay down. Scarface closed the door. As the Ranger's eyes grew used to the gloom, the heavy breathing of sleepers in his ears, he noted the single small window a few feet away. He composed himself to wait, marshaling in his clever mind the events which he had observed. It was not his way to leap before making a thorough investigation and the set-up here looked huge, far-reaching.

It was not long before Scarface, wearied from fright, joined the snorers. The Ranger dozed, one ear open. About an hour later he heard sounds outside that brought him up on his elbow.

"Snap! Snap! Snap!" Not human sounds, those. "Whips," he decided. He heard cries of pain, and they were human. The stamp of many hoofs, the vibrations of the earth under the tread of many men and beasts, came through the bunk supports to his body.

"This is what Ross was expectin'," he thought, and silently rose, feet on the earth floor, and started for the window.

Scarface seemed asleep. Hatfield peered from the small, unglassed window opening and could see the fire near the office, and off to one side, Valentine Ross. The space before the office was crammed with men and animals, and Ross was talking to a man mounted on a great bay stallion, a giant form in flowing black serape, countenance shadowed by steeple-peaked sombrero gleaming with rows of pearl buttons.

All Hatfield could make of the Mexican's features were the darker blobs of mustache and beard; the spirited horse pivoted and the Ranger looked on the broad expanse of the rider's back as he spoke with Valentine Ross.

His eyes swept the armed, mounted gang of bandidos, an army of them on shaggy little Mexican mustangs; they slouched in the saddle as they pulled up at the Southwest Lumber Company's camp. Small men, colorful in dress, with fancy boots adorned with great roweled spurs, those who wore boots, for some had spurs tied to their ankles, feet bare. Leather pants to protect the legs in the thorny chaparral; above the belt they looked like guerilla soldiers, two X-crossed belts heavily laden with cartridges, side-arms of pistols and knife, rifle slung under a leg.

The majority favored the high pointed Mexican sombrero, though some wore old army felts. Fierce of face, with the cruelty of their Indian strains, raiders and killers by heritage, who followed the giant on the stallion.

They acted now as vaqueros though not herding cows but men, a massed column mounted on mules, hemmed in by the armed force. The victims cringed from the lashes wielded by the shrill-voiced bandidos. At a harsh command the peons swung toward the big stockade among the trees.

A cold fury hit Jim Hatfield. A glimmer of what the Southwest Company might be up to flashed across his brain. "Got to stop it," he muttered. And suddenly, engrossed in the strange proceedings outside, Hatfield realized he was not alone. Warned by a sixth sense, a vivid instinct that more than once had saved him from death, that was developed from his wild existence and the extreme danger he was in so much of the time, he whirled as clawing fingers dug into his left arm.

3
Slaves

"DON'T shoot, Jim!"

The fierce movement of the Ranger, the great strength of his rippling muscles, startled the hombre who had caught him. It was the man with the scar on his cheek and he gasped as he fell back under the sharp jab of the Ranger's Colt muzzle, rammed into his belly.

A sleeper roused and growled, "What the hell's that?"

Scarface's reply determined his fate. He said, "Aw, go back to sleep. It's jest Torquila bringin' up another gang."

Torquila! Captain McDowell had mentioned the Mex bandit who was taking advantage of the existing upset, to strike the Maravilla ranches and settlements raiding as he pleased. And here Torquila was connecting with the Lumber Company!

Still wary, still ready to blast his way

out of there, Hatfield pretended to relax. "Who's out there?" he demanded.

"Sh, quiet," whispered Scarface. "Put up yore gun, Jim old boy. I know yuh're only curious, but fer Gawd's sake don't let nobody else ketch you snoopin'. Ross'd soon kill you as not; he's okay but if he even smells spy he'll finish you. Git back to bed."

"Awright," drawled Hatfield. "But I got to watch my hide, pard. I ain't lettin' a posse slip up on me, savvy?"

Scarface sighed with relief, and Hatfield wondered if his new pal were as unsuspecting as he seemed. Hatfield lay down and Scarface did, too.

"I better work while I got the chance," the Ranger mused, as he lay with head in clasped hands. He was eager to make use of every instant in the enemy camp, aware Valentine Ross was not the sort to be fooled long. The cold-faced boss of the lumbermen must have an extraordinarily keen mind; Hatfield knew how tough and unruly lumberjacks were and that the dudish, skinny Ross could maintain himself over them only by a tiger ferocity, and extra-sharp mental equipment.

He stared at the small rectangle of the window, faintly red from the fire by the office. Then, against the frame, he caught a dark, roundish object slowly rising, that stayed only an instant and then ducked down. It was the top of a man's capped head. Someone was standing guard out there.

"Ross *is* suspicious," Hatfield decided. "Checkin' me, shore as hell's hot!"

The sentry must have heard some of the low-voiced talk between Hatfield and Scarface; it did not matter how much. He would have seen the Ranger's outline in the window. It changed the aspect of the situation; every instinct warned Hatfield. Ross had a couple of hundred armed men around to say nothing of Torquila's army.

The heavy breathing of the 'jacks in his ears, the odor of their sweated bodies in his flared nostrils, he watched the window for the guard. After while he came up on his elbow and eased his booted feet to the dirt.

"Hey, Scarface!" he whispered.

No answer. The tall man rose, a wraith in the darkness, tiptoed to the lean hombre's bunk. Scarface was asleep.

The window was too small to let him

through. He pulled a .45 cartridge from a loop in his belt and tossed it out of the little opening so it clinked on the sill and rolled on the ground outside. With a panther's movements he reached the door; it creaked on its leather hinges as he pulled it open.

Now the space around the office seemed deserted. The bandits and Ross's men had herded their captives off through the trees. Hatfield looked back at the window and, as he had counted, the noise the cartridge had made had drawn the sentry to the window, giving the Ranger a few moments to get out the door.

Timing his exit perfectly, he closed the door and slid around the far end of the shack, and down the west side. Pausing at the southwest corner he peered along the south end. The guard was back at the southeast corner, watching the door, after he had investigated the sound Hatfield caused at the window.

"Like to have a look-see at that office," he mused, calculating his play. So far the only hitch was the sentry, the others having gone over the compound.

The Ranger started, one foot after the other, feeling the dirt. He was within a yard of the crouched man, a hulking 'jack in corduroy and round cap, whose rifle leaned against the hut wall, before the guard heard him. The man swung with a gasped curse.

"What the—!"

The Ranger launched his powerful body through the intervening space. He glimpsed the 'jack's bearded, open-mouthed face as his steel hand closed like a vise on the hairy throat. The fellow was strong, a fighter, hard as nails, but the Ranger's terrific attack knocked him back against the chinked logs; his cry was choked off by the long, inexorable fingers.

The man lashed out with a fist, hit the Ranger in the face, but the impetus of the officer's lunge was not checked. Hatfield drove a knee into the lumberman's belly and a dull crack sounded as the Ranger laid a heavy Colt barrel on the guard's head. It took all the fight out of the 'jack; buffaloed, he went limp, and Hatfield dragged him into the bush and flitted toward the office.

A lantern burned inside. The clearing fire was low; beyond stood a bunch of ponies, and there were saddled mustangs near, mounts kept ready by Ross and his crew. Coming up in the end shadow,

Hatfield made sure he could duck into the hut unobserved; and then he was in. The lantern flickered on a table made of rough-cut sticks and an oak slab. His swift eyes took in the hanging clothes, the single bunk, and a brown suitcase pushed under it.

"Figger that forester snooped round here," he decided, "and didn't get far with Ross."

His slitted glance quickly discarded most of the furnishings. He came to the bunk, pulled out the suitcase. On one knee, a Colt laid beside him, he went through the contents. Some shirts and toilet articles. Then he found a small black notebook with a dried brown stain on its cover.

"Blood," he muttered. And inside the leaves was a silver badge marked, "STATE OF TEXAS. FOREST SERVICE."

"That's it," he said aloud, and opened the report book. Hasty scrawls showed on the first pages: "Ran into SW. L. Co.'s camp. Ross, the boss, gave me a job when I said I was after work. Showed me State lease to cut timber." Next: "These men are killers! Some real 'jacks but they're in cahoots. Cutting fortune in live-oak and pine, no heed for future growth. Must get evidence."

There wasn't any more. "Ross caught him huntin' that evidence," thought Hatfield, shoving the badge and book into a capacious hip picket. "Wonder why Ross saved these?"

There were papers that intrigued him at the bottom of the bag. A lease from the State to cut timber, signed by the governor, and he found a large sheet that puzzled him, for he stared at it for some moments, vertical creases in his bronzed brow. It was, he concluded, a rough, hand-drawn map of central and south Texas, two wide lines running north and south that cut a great swathe in the outline of the state, reaching across the Rio Grande into Mexico. Yes, there was the Maravilla River, an uneven line from west to east. And small letters dotted about with no apparent system: "T", "C" right under it at the spot where stood the mountains he was in. Farther north, an "O" and to the west another "C" and two "I's".

"Now what the—" he muttered, and staring at it, suddenly he threw the papers back into the bag, grabbed up his gun and jumped over to the door.

He was cut off. Right on the office were Ross, Bigjaw Haley, Torquila and the mob of armed 'jacks and bandits.

Caught, Hatfield crouched to the side, back so he could not be seen unless someone actually stepped into the shack. He had a flash of Ross as the boss hustled, not into the office, but on past it. On Ross's flank strode the giant Torquila, and Hatfield glimpsed the cruel bearded face, dark as an Indian's, the cape flowing out in the speed of his movements. They headed, the whole bunch to the hut where Hatfield supposedly slept, and gunmen ringed it. Ross, a lantern raised, kicked in the door.

"Rouse up, you big jigger!" he bawled.

The Ranger slipped outside, swung to the south end of the office, toward the bush. "He's gone!" Ross yelled. "Spy, spy!"

Starting away, Hatfield bumped into two lumberjacks hurrying from the stockade. They wore corduroy, roundish caps pulled low and heavy hobnail boots.

"Hey," demanded one, "where you goin'?"

"Tim!" cried the other, "it's the guy they figger's a spy!" And he bawled, "Ross, Ross, here he is!"

Both went for their guns. Hatfield's Colt flashed with the speed of legerdemain, hammer back under thumb. Tim, weapon coming to shooting level, crashed with a slug in the thigh, his bullet driving into the dirt between the Ranger's spread feet. The second let go and Hatfield, swinging his gun, felt lead burn his ribs. Then his firing-pin hit again and the 'jack whirled, clutching his punctured throat as he lost all volition, to fall across the writhing body of his pal.

Loud shouts rose as the whole camp roused and started for the Ranger.

Hatfield headed for the saddled horses on the other side of the fire. As he passed through the ruby light circle they saw him and a howl of hate rose. Blasting guns crashed in the scented night air and he heard slugs spitting in the leaves and needles, thuds as they hit tree-trunks or spurted up dirt. One bit a chunk from his boot, then he was among the mustangs, the animals dancing with alarm at the gunfire.

The Lone Wolf grabbed a fast looking

black, vaulted into the saddle, slammed a fist down between the laid-back ears as the unruly beast reared and, knocking the horse into running position, lined out south through the forest. He preferred not to call Goldy into that death hail; the seconds delay in bringing up the golden flash would have meant destruction for both Goldy and the Ranger.

The bank of heavy guns, furious howls of the enemy followed him as he zigzagged south through the woods. He urged the black on by a low crooning. The creature recognized the masterful but friendly sound so that he calmed enough to give his best. The cries of hatred made a horrid din as the pack mounted to tear after the spy.

Hatfield cut down a slope carpeted by pine needles, cut up by rock formations. The going was shadowed, almost blind. Here and there moon rays like silver streams penetrated the trees; an owl hooted eerily near at hand, as he swung in his saddle to empty a Colt back at the mob.

"Jest as well I left that sleepin' hut," he mused, his nerves unshaken by the narrow squeak. Yes, Valentine Ross had suspected him, must have mentioned his distrust of the tall stranger to Torquila and they had come to investigate. They would have killed him had he not consented to a thorough search and questioning; they would have found his Ranger star, snugged in its secret pocket.

The mob was in full hue-and-cry on his trail; he headed the big black on south, crossed the swift Maravilla, and came onto a trail leading toward Old Mexico, sixty miles away. He rode with a masterful recklessness unmatched by other horsemen, the wind whistling past his ears. The mustang, once realizing the power of the rider drove on at a breakneck speed.

Hatfield heard the leaders pounding behind, some hundreds of yards in his rear. He looked back. "Wonder how long they'll keep a-comin'?" he mused. "It'd be handy if I was back at the camp, with most of 'em gone."

Icy daring, allowed the Lone Wolf to weigh such an angle, at such a moment. He would try, and he slowed her rounding the next turn. Choosing a spot where a stony formation hid rocks he swung the black up the steep bank into the trees.

Back in the deep shadows he dismounted, stood by the mustang's head with a hand over the beast's quivering nostrils. The leaders of the hunters swung into sight, he saw their heads and shoulders as they rode in the trail gully.

Torquila was among the first, great figure with cape sweeping back in the wind of speed. His bandits bunched on his heels, all wild, crazy riders; the lumberjacks, not so good in the saddle, straggled along. After a few minutes he apparently had passed.

The ground close around Hatfield was too cut-up to ride on; he led the pack to the trail, mounted and galloped back toward the Southwest's camp.

In the firelight he saw that only a few men had stayed behind. There was a way open among the trees; in the far distance north, was the office and shacks. After crossing the Maravilla, Hatfield swung toward the stockade, the black walking through a forest lane.

Fluffy bits of white clouds swiftly swept across the face of the moon, dotting the earth with passing shadows; the sky was milky with stars, and the sweet west wind softly brushed the stern, rugged face of the tall Ranger, intent on his duty. The Maravilla gurgled innocently over its stony bed as though determined to deliver its sustenance to the people who depended upon it.

He came near the enclosure, dismounted and left the black with reins dragging, crept in foot by foot toward the stockade. From what he had observed he concluded the law of Texas was being flouted, beyond the killings and violence laid at the feet of the Lumber Company. It was big, bigger than it had sounded, and Jim Hatfield was not the sort to miss such a clue. Alone against a multitude, the Ranger meant to ferret out every crooked angle of the situation.

Crouched in the dense bush shadows, Hatfield watched the armed men slowly patrolling the square walls of the palisades. Downwind, he caught the stench from the corral, the fetid odor of uncared-for humanity, like the hold of a slave-ship. His eyes turned dark with rage; he could guess the treatment suffered by the unfortunate workers at the hands of the Southwest Lumber Company.

Behind Ross were other criminals, he had concluded from his swift survey. "Want to know who wangled that State concession to cut this timber. And how come we was so late gettin' word of all this. Now what's that funny map with all those letters mean?"

Someone had delayed reports on the feverish activities of the Southwest, so they had had a free hand for some time before Austin was aware of what went on.

Every instant lessened the Ranger's chances of escaping with his life. Enemies seethed about him, eager to kill. His run had branded him a spy, there was no explaining now; it was cinched. But through his trick of rescuing Scarface he had gained valuable information, though Vasco Torquila had been quick enough to demand a full investigation of the big man posing as an outlaw.

"Smart Mex," mused Hatfield, "Hafta see him again."

Flat on his belly in the fringe of bush outside the stockade clearing, he heard moans of sick men; some were praying, others cursing. The high, rough poles of the palisade stuck fifteen feet into the air, barbed wire strung along the top. Barred gates faced him at the south where lounged half a dozen 'jacks, pistols in open-flapped holsters, rifles across their knees. He could hear them talking.

"Oh, they'll ketch him all right," one was saying. "Scarface got fooled, but not Ross, no sir. Betcha that bronc buster Morton sent him up to spy on us. By this time tomorrow we'll be fryin' that bronc buster's liver and we'll add that big jigger's."

"Yeah, that Morton's caused us plenty trouble," another 'jack growled. "I mean to take a crack at him myself. Why, when them cowboys ambushed us on the road the other day I nearly got shot! That was Morton's idee and he was the one that telegraphed Austin. He done it hisself, so there was no chance to stop it."

Hatfield listened, ticketing every bit of information. But he could not linger; he had but a few minutes in which to act, and he crept around to the north, where he saw the black shapes of rocks sticking up close to the middle of the poles. A sentry, moonlight gleaming on metal Winchester barrel, came slowly along past the rocks, and paused for a word with his mate at the corner before swinging to stride back.

The Ranger saw the wholesale crime. He

must check up on it and meant to do so while he could. He came erect as the sentry again passed along his side, swung with his back to the Ranger for a few moments. Seizing the opportunity, Hatfield scuttled across the narrow strip of moonlit open space, and ducked down between the rocks and poles before the guard turned to come along once more. The sentry passed Hatfield's hiding-place; he was almost entirely hidden in the black space. As soon as the 'jack was a few yards off, Hatfield put his lips to a space where two of the strong pine poles were wired together, and in a sibilant whisper, spoke in Spanish.

"Juan, Juan. Juan, Juan!" He expected, by use of this common Mexican name, to get a reply.

"Si, I'm here," a weak voice answered.

"You're Juan from—?"

The Mexican peon groaned, "Juan Gonzales from Avalo. Help us, we're sick, dying!"

The peons close inside were rousing, growing excited; voices quivering with hope chattered eager questions.

"Sh! Quiet" warned the Ranger, but the guard swinging back, heard the sounds, and uttered a warning shout that echoed through the woods. He ran toward the spot where Hatfield crouched in the rocks.

"Hey, what's goin' on inside there?" he bawled,

The bunch up front had heard the alarm and were running in answer to the sentry's call. The guards along the other sides, too, were bearing down on Hatfield from either flank. The Ranger came up on his knees, opened fire as the nearest 'jack threw up his Winchester. The long rifle slug smacked the rock, the flaming flare stabbing the Ranger's eyes; spattered fragments of stone cut his skin. But the steady Colt muzzle did not move as the Ranger raised thumb off hammer.

The 'jack threw up both hands, rifle flying off to thud on the dirt. Hatfield swung right, the acrid smell of burnt powder in flared nostrils, the glint of the fighting man shining in his slitted eyes.

He laid three .45 slugs into the oncoming enemy, dropped the hombre from the right before he could shoot. A third, close on him, let out a shriek as he saw his mates fall, and he went down on one knee, pumping bullets wildly at the rocks. Lead cracked the stone, one ripped the crown of Hatfield's Stetson as he rose up to run for the trees.

The main bunch was rounding the corner of the stockade. Hatfield emptied his Colt at the rifleman, sent him jumping back to his friends. He dropped his empty pistol into its holster and drew his second weapon. Hitting the trees he looked back, gun up. They sighted the dark, moving figure and whooped as they swung their muzzles on him.

Bullets hit the trunks of the pines, ripped the underbrush; Hatfield was cut off from the black mustang and he heard yells from the camp, knew Ross and Torquila were back.

Warm sweat of exertion rolled down his skin; he wiped it from his eyes for clear vision, and took a deep breath of the aromatic, cool air. He gave three shrill whistles, repeating them as he hustled west though the woods.

"There he goes! That way!" a lumberman shrieked.

The madness of murder burned them; a fury that drove them after the Ranger as a pack of hounds hunts down its quarry, hoping to tear him to pieces. And suddenly, before him, Hatfield saw the end of the covering woods.

Far as the eye could reach, bathed in moonlight, stretched a scene of desolation. The silvered sky shone on miles cleared by the Southwest Lumber Company's greedy vandalism; bleeding, ragged tree stumps, blackened spaces where bush had been burned, the wreck of Nature's loveliness, hills and dales ripped open by the greed of man, mad for money. Piles of trimmed logs stood here and there, ready to be hauled away for sale.

He cut north, repeating his whistle; they were after him, and Ross, Torquila, most of the mob were mounted. One glimpsed him against the lighter space and bullets whirled about him. He swung to fire back, hold them.

Jim Hatfield, in his perilous work as a Texas Ranger, had been in many tight spots in his fight against the evil of those who sought power and wealth through unlawful means. He had ridden the Rio with Death as his mate; had seen the river run red with the blood of victims of Mexican raiders; had faced the Ghost Rider, and had run against the terrible power of city thieves who sought to pirate the rich oil lands of Alamita. He had fought against aroused Indians whose fury devastated the Border. But the Lone Wolf had never come closer to bloody death than when, with icy nerve and mad daring, he had ridden straight into the face of hundreds of hostile guns, commanded by the Southwest Lumber Company.

A hint of grayness was in the eastern sky; dawn, dawn that would make escape altogether impossible. Texas needed him, and Maravilla, bleeding from the awful thrusts of its powerful enemy, cried for his aid. He could not fail!

A shrill whinny sounded, and a golden ghost horse, saddle on, galloped up to him. Goldy had jumped the rope barrier holding him below the camp, had come in answer to his master's call.

"Good boy," muttered the Lone Wolf as he hit the saddle in a flying leap, and urged the sorrel north along the jagged line of the bleeding woods.

Under him, long legs locked in the familiar seat, the great sorrel paced off the yards in a businesslike gait. Nothing but a death bullet could stop Goldy now.

Hatfield lined the sorrel out, let Goldy have his head, as he ran before the howling army of killers who sought to take him and tear him to shreds for daring to interfere with their deadly plans.

4

Captured

BANCROFT MORTON had never been so happy as he was at the Bar W. Sanguine by nature, he was seldom downcast. Save for his intense love of horses little else had possessed him; an expert bronc buster is always in demand and he could find work when he wanted it, but his wanderings had been aimless. Now his life had a purpose.

Sam Ward lay, unable to move, in his old tester-bed, lovingly tended by Elsie. The chief of the Maravilla cowmen had not died; sore wounded, he was too tough to quit. Suffering, a bullet lodged close to his spine at one side, and too dangerous to be removed as yet, Ward could still smile at the soft-handed young woman who nursed him with such deep devotion. He could still command the ranchers who looked to him as leader.

Lately had ridden up young Ban Morton

and Morton had proved his devotion to the cause. He had pointed out clearly the danger to the Maravilla range once the watershed was denuded, a strong point against the lumbermen. Aided by old Sam's shrewdness, Morton had figured out telling blows against the Southwest Lumber Company, such as sending waddies, armed with rifles, to harry at long range the mule and horse teams commanded by Bigjaw Haley.

Cut logs were being hauled to the railroad, and the wagons brought back liquor and food supplies on the return trip. The big outfits of the Maravilla had each contributed half a dozen riders who were ordered by Ward not to close with the enemy but to make it too hot for them to get through, blocking delivery of the timber. Hitting and running, they had forced Valentine Ross to hold back his output and even now the rancher's band was lying to the north, watching for the lumbermen.

That morning, as Jim Hatfield was pursued by the infuriated army of Torquila and Ross, Morton left his bunk early as was his habit. He went out and washed at the pump, then strolled to the kitchen. Guards had been placed around the ranch, on Ban's advice, to prevent any surprise attack by the 'jacks on Sam Ward.

Through the night a ring of them rode in the moonlight. The Bar W had fifty punchers, all tough fighters. The night guards were now coming in, to get some food and sleep; the day punchers were rising. Elsie was up. Her face was drawn and Ban Morton was saddened to see the terrible strain she was undergoing but she smiled on him and gave him a pert little nod that touched him with its sheer courage.

At her invitation he helped himself to coffee, fried potatoes, bacon and biscuits left by the cook on the lean-to stove, and she sat down with him while he ate. She brushed back a wisp of dark hair that had strayed over her long-lashed blue eyes; dainty of body as she was she had exhibited a marvelous strength in the ordeal that had come upon them.

"We jest can't let them 'jacks cut any more of that timber, Elsie," said Ban. "They've ruint miles of the watershed awready. Yuh saw in the cloudburst the other day how roiled the river got; even 'fore the tree roots rot out a heavy downpour'll wash off the topsoil."

She sighed. "It's awful, Ban. But what can we do, till we get help? They've so many men up there and they seem to know every move we make."

Morton took a gulp of the warm, brown coffee. The familiar kitchen odor, the joy he felt in Elsie's company and her trust, thrilled him with a deep content. He was eager to help the ranchers.

The injury to their chief, Ward, was a serious blow from which they were just recovering. Demoralized by the disastrous defeat that day, they had taken little action since. The bold raids of Vasco Torquila kept the Vigilantes skipping from spot to spot, and the ranch owner dared not leave his home with too small a guard for the fear the giant bandit would strike.

"I figger we ought to drive every steer we kin round up away from the west sections, Elsie," Ban Morton told her. "That'll make it harder for them dawgs to rustle 'em, anyway."

"Let's ask father," she suggested.

When he was through eating Elsie led Ban Morton through the cool, rambling house to the side bedroom where Sam Ward lay in the old-fashioned mahogany bed carted out from Missouri when he had first come to the Maravilla. Ward, a wadding of bandage on his wound, lay on his side, stiff and uncomfortable He listened to Ban's idea and nodded.

"Tell Nevada to start this mornin'. Morton, we got to save Maravilla. Now I've thought it over I see I was foolish to go off half-cocked the way I did; I jest led my friends into a death trap. I should've organized more keerful. Sheriff Godey's comin' down this afternoon, and I reckon the Rangers'll be here pronto. Then we'll act."

"It wasn't yore fault," Ban told him, seeing Ward's inward distress, that he blamed himself for the fiasco. "Anybody would've done the same. I'll help with the drive today."

He nodded and went out into the hall, and Elsie following him, touched his arm. "Be mighty wary, Ban. If they catch you they'll kill you. That bullet that went through your hat the other night makes it plain."

"Yeah, it's a cinch somebody don't like

me hornin' in here. But I'm safe enough on Black Rascal."

She was standing close to him, and the words they spoke were calm and emotionless; yet, behind the matter-of-fact speech their hearts spoke. Elsie looked up into his youthful, pleasant face. And Ban Morton was overcome by an emotion he could not resist; he seized her and kissed her, and she put her arms around his neck.

"Elsie—I love yuh," he whispered.

"I love you, Ban dear. You've been wonderful."

Someone cleared his throat behind them, engrossed as they were in one another. Ban Morton swung, saw a lean, saturnine hombre, Nevada Lewis, standing on the long veranda; Lewis had seen them kissing through the open door.

"'Mornin'," Nevada drawled. "Jest comin' for orders."

Ban Morton frowned. He was rattled, caught that way kissing his girl, and he didn't like Lewis much. Nevada spoke very little and seemed to resent Morton's presence at the Bar W, for Ban had usurped the foreman's natural rôle as Ward's favorite.

"Orders're to run in all the cows from the west range," growled Morton.

Nevada Lewis nodded. Elsie went back into her father's room and Ban, with his stiff-legged gait, strolled out. He went to the round corral where ranch horses were kept for use at night, and roped a hard-mouthed buckskin, a fast horse but a bad actor, that he was gradually gentling. Black Rascal he had turned out in a grass pasture down by the Maravilla and like most cowboys Morton never walked any distance if he could ride.

Reaching the pasture, a large enclosure on the river, it was some minutes before he looked over the two hundred mustangs inside and realized his pet was missing.

At first he was not alarmed; maybe some hurried nighthawk had roped Black Rascal. He rode back to the corrals and looked in the barns, but the handsome horse wasn't there, either. Nevada Lewis was standing outside the bunkhouse, and Morton limped up to him, as the foreman doused his whole head in a bucket of cold water.

"Seen my hoss?" Ban demanded.

Nevada slowly dried his dripping face and hair with the community towel before he spoke. "Why, no," he drawled. "He missin'?"

"Yeah. And the man who took him will never steal another," Ban slowly declared.

The foreman shrugged. A calf bawled in the distance; mustangs stamped in the pens. Punchers were up, to a new day of toil on the range. The familiar sounds of the ranch were in Morton's ears as he swung, heart grieving at Black Rascal's disappearance. He kept hoping his pet would gallop up, as he went around asking various men if they had seen him. No one had.

The pasture was not far from the house and guards had been out all night, but the nighthawks lay in close to the buildings and a clever thief could have slipped through.

As Morton went to mount the buckskin, riders appeared from the east, dust rising under the clipping hoofs of their animals. He waited.

John Ogalvie of the Circle 5, east of Bowietown, George Keith of the Running R, to the north, and Mayor Yager galloped up. Ban knew them all, leaders of Maravilla, able lieutenants of Ward.

"Howdy, Ban," sang out the hearty

mayor, grinning at the slim bronc buster. "How's Sam today?"

"'Bout the same and still chipper," replied Ban. He liked the big mayor who always had a kind word for everybody.

They dismounted in front of the house, and Yager slapped Ban on the back. "We're goin' to hit them lumbermen snakes and pronto, no fooling," growled Yager. "Come to talk it over with Sam."

Ban trailed them into Ward's room. After greetings were over Yager said, "Sam, we're collectin' every fighting man in Maravilla. We could muster four hundred, arm 'em, and attack those devils and drive 'em out pronto."

To their obvious surprise, Ward shook his head. "They're too strong set up there, Smiley. We sorta got 'em cinched for a while and I'd rather wait'll the Rangers get here and make shore there's no mistake like before."

Ogalvie looked at Yager, and the mayor scratched his head. They were, Ban Morton decided, rather dashed at Ward's lack of enthusiasm for their plan. And some doubt, too; Morton thought they might be wondering if his injury had broken the big rancher chief.

"I'd like to get my hands on them," growled Yager.

"Well, Sam," John Ogalvie said slowly, "I still think we could wipe 'em off the map but—" He shrugged. Keith nodded; these men were the sort who would be loyal to the death.

Ban Morton was restless; he couldn't forget Black Rascal. "Gotta find him," he muttered.

"Godey's comin' today," Ward said, "and I'm hopin' the Rangers'll soon be down. Then we'll hit."

Morton slipped away from the conference and mounted the buckskin, straightened the unruly beast out, and rode over to the pasture. To his surprise Nevada Lewis rode up to join him as he was casting around.

"That's a fine hoss of yores," Lewis growled. "Don't blame yuh for worryin'." He began to help Ban hunt for traces.

The dirt was cut up by countless hoofs but Nevada, riding a widening circle, ran on some fresh prints a few hundred yards west, close to the river bank.

"How 'bout these?" he sang out.

Ban trotted the buckskin over and got down. Black Rascal had a groove in his left front shoe and sure enough there was a mark like that in the soft spot.

"Led by two men," remarked Morton. "One on a white with a throwout to his left hind laig." There was a white horsehair, and the hoofprint told him the animal's idiosyncrasy.

"Want me to ride with yuh?" asked Lewis.

Morton shook his head. The foreman had work to do and Ban wanted to follow that trail alone. Nevada nodded and swung back.

Ban Morton shoved the buckskin west, eyes on the rising hills with their stands of live-oak and pine. His keen vision made out the line of that great ditch, here and there where the foliage did not obscure the view. As he drew nearer he glimpsed toiling ants he knew were hundreds of peon laborers, working on the ditch.

"In a hurry to get it through," he muttered, "but they can never use it with us hamperin' 'em. They must know that."

Cows ranged the grassy, well-watered

sections. The land was lovely, with greens and browns, and the star-white blossoms of the high mesquite, here and there a sandy cactus flat where flourished giant ocotillos, and prickly pear with green-and-purple fruit. Lines of stones had caught the wind-wafted seeds of granjeno and the bushes grew in dense hedges, like walls.

Feathery huisache trees turned their leaves to the gentle wind; a road-runner scampered from the man's path; the whir of a giant rattlesnake sounded and the buckskin nervously jumped aside. The odors were sweet, and mixed with the rich damp earth and grass smell and the aromatic odors of creosote and sage. Crows cawed on his flanks; a bunch of cows threw up their tails and thundered off at sight of him. The sky was a deep blue dome where burned the brilliant golden ball of the sun.

The Maravilla was a gorgeous land, a happy home. But over it hung the gigantic, clutching greed of man. Terror was smashing that happiness, destroying the people of Maravilla; like a swift-growing cancer, threatening to spread throughout mighty Texas.

Morton swung northwest, meaning to

come up from that side; he was on guard, ready for trouble with the lumberjacks. Suddenly a rider darted out from a wall of thorny granjeno, off to Ban Morton's left. He let go with a pistol and Morton heard the whistle of the bullet past his head. The man ahead was on a big white and Morton noted the outflung left hind leg, even as he saw the shiny black horse led by a rope behind.

"Black Rascal!" he cried. Morton forgot caution at sight of his pet; he dug in his spurs and lined the buckskin out in mad pursuit.

For a mile they flew on. Morton was gaining. The going was uphill, rocky in places, and the bush thicker and wilder. Morton fired several times, but dared not aim too close for fear of hitting Black Rascal. The horse-thief now and then would swing and send back a bullet but the jolting speed of the chase prevented careful aim.

Morton galloped right into the trap. The buckskin, traveling full speed, hell-for-leather, was violently swirled around, neck giving a sharp crack as lariats settled over him, thrown from the bushed sides of the draw. Hidden men had tossed those deadly nooses, with unerring skill; while two roped the buckskin, bringing him around, falling, others circled the bronc buster, who was exerting every ounce of skill to maintain his seat at the buckskin's mad jerk.

The buckskin went down and Morton hit the ground running. The lariats tightened, pulled him down, too, with a thud, and, wind knocked out of him, he found his arms completely helpless because of the binding ropes.

Men in peaked hats, leather chaps, some barefoot with spurs tied to their ankles, who wore crossed ammunition belts over khaki military jackets; swarthy of face, dark of eye, ran upon him, yelling in triumph. Vaqueros turned bandit, they could throw a reata with deadly skill. A bunch of them fell on Morton before he could wriggle out of the loops. He was kicked, goaded with needle spurs; they cursed him in Mexican, laughing at his anger, at his attempts to fight back.

He knew he had, through his deep love for Black Rascal, run into this death trap. They tied his wrists and legs, threw him across Black Rascal's back like a sack of flour, and headed north for the lumber camp. And well up toward the hills a man with a bear's wide, powerful body, reddish of hair and beard, clad in dirty corduroy, bullwhip under his arm, met them.

"Got him, huh?" growled Bigjaw Haley. "Nice work, boys. The boss'll be glad to see this polecat." He lurched to the helpless Morton, fierce, red-rimmed eyes glaring into the bronc buster's face.

Ban Morton set his teeth, determined not to let them see he was suffering. His look evidently angered Haley for Bigjaw snatched his whip and slashed Morton's body with the lead-tipped lash. A wave of red agony swept Ban. Black Rascal reared and snorted wildly.

"C'mon, bring him along," ordered Bigjaw.

Morton glimpsed the workers at the deep ditch; they were driven by brute overseers, mule-skinners assigned to this job, for Morton's plan prevented them from delivering their timber now. The workmen were Mexicans, ragged, the misery of death in liquid Latin eyes. Thin and peaked, goaded without mercy, they dug into the red clay. Hundreds of horses and mules drew rough scoops or wagons of dirt, banking the sides.

But Ban Morton had little chance to observe the activity. They crossed on a rough bridge of logs roped together by rawhide and started on up the wooded slopes. Bigjaw Haley led; a dozen Mexican bandidos surrounded the prisoner.

"You ain't got long to live," railed Haley, spitting a brown tobacco stream from his rusty-bearded lips. "Once the chief gits his hands on you you'll wish you never was born. You'll be glad to die."

Morton hid his fear, held himself with a tight rein. Hope was gone; they would kill him, evidently after some torture, promised by Bigjaw Haley.

"What's the idee?" he demanded.

"Why, whippersnapper," said Haley meaningly, "we'll larn you not to fool with real men. You've horned in on our game and you got too many cute idees. Besides, the chief don't like you personally."

Only one very thin chance remained; when they turned him loose he would run or maybe snatch a gun and shoot a way out. It was awful to die, now he had found life's purpose; he kept thinking of Elsie, and sternly told himself not to be a fool; he'd go soft if he dwelt on that . . .

The lurching of Black Rascal as he plodded up the rocky slopes toward the Southwest Lumber Company's main camp, hurt Morton's ribs and belly. But he was sure the hastily wrapped ropes on his legs were also loosening under the strain and he kept expanding and contracting his calf muscles, cords biting the flesh, "If I could get that loose," he thought agonizedly. . .

He kept working at the leg bindings, pulling one leg up a little, then down, movements hidden by the motion of Black Rascal; after a while the tighter loops slipped and he figured he could pull his feet out of his boots and so be able to run.

"Hey, mister," he groaned, feigning deep distress, "lemme down. I gotta rest. I'm dizzy as hell."

Bigjaw Haley just laughed, spat tobacco juice.

"You'll be a sight dizzier tonight," he promised.

Ban Morton closed his eyes, let his head go limp, as though fainting. Through lowered lashes he saw a rock pile to the north, fringed by heavy granjeno bushes.

Maybe, once on his feet, he could dive through behind the stones, for cover to run.

When Black Rascal gave a lurch that way Morton slid off the horse's back, as though senseless. He hit the ground, and as the following bandits swerved their shaggy mounts to avoid colliding with Black Rascal who had naturally stopped when his rider fell, Morton kicked off the loops and leaped up.

He dived head first for the thorny bushes, that scratched his skin; his hands were still tied behind. His quick act caught them off guard, but as Morton came up on his knees in an effort to get around behind the rocks, where he would stand a chance of running, Bigjaw Haley swung his long lash, spurring his horse, at Morton.

The leaded tippets viciously wrapped around Ban's throat and head, biting into his cheeks he was violently jerked backward, and fell on his side. The whip came free and Haley struck again, across the back of Morton's head. With a howl of rage Haley leaped down and began to lash Ban across the back.

A red miasma of pain, pain too great to bear, engulfed Ban Morton. Merciful darkness hit him and he lay quiet as the burly muleskinner tore into him, ripping his clothes off with terrible blows of the lash.

"The chief kin have what's left," yelled Bigjaw.

5

The Other Side

"WELL," mused Ranger Jim Hatfield, "it worked once—why not now?"

He raised his Colt, and took aim.

After shaking off his pursuers early that morning he had spent some time hidden in the dense bush north of the Lumber Company's camp. He had slept a few hours to make up for the lost night.

Having observed the devastation of the Ord Mountains and hills to the west through which the Southwest Company had cut, noted from a height the rough, winding trail they had formerly used to cart the timber north to the Southern Pacific at Lenox, he had started east for the Bar W and Bowie, to organize efficient resistance and ferret out several mysteries which he had come upon. There was that map with the fine lettering; the stoppage of the messages to Austin; the peon workers, brought in from Mexico by Vasco Torquila, a very important angle.

Hatfield knew he was bucking an extremely powerful combine, that could command a multitude of guns. He did not miss the activity on the east slopes, where the great ditch was being pushed through, and observed that it ran from close to the Maravilla toward a natural arroyo that led north for many miles.

"Not a bad idee," he decided. "Got to give 'em credit. Save a lot of time and tough haulin'. Draggin' them heavy trees across cut-up hills ain't easy. Only the rancher'll stop 'em."

Far-off shots attracted him and from a commanding bluff he had looked down on the capture of Ban Morton. He recognized Bigjaw Haley and the semi-military figures of the bandits, and he guessed their victim was a member of the opposition. Then the gray-green, shaded eyes narrowed, as he recalled the words he had overheard concerning a young bronc buster named Morton.

"Callate they've got him," he muttered. He had meant to stop at the Bar W and warn this Morton.

"If I pick him away from them, it oughta give me a quick introduction to the ranchers. 'Sides, from the way Haley acts, he'll be killed shore."

It had taken him some time to work down where he could cut their trail as they climbed into the hills. He left Goldy back a way in the bush and hustled up behind the rock pile, where Morton made his attempt to escape.

The Ranger had gained a lot by snatching Scarface from the cowboys; he expected to gain again by saving this decent looking fellow from Haley, who was lashing him to death. The Maravilla people would be suspicious of a stranger till he proved himself, and Hatfield, not wishing as yet to announce himself a Ranger, knew he must act swiftly, for Texas. Thinking over that queer map he had seen in Ross's suitcase had given Hatfield a hunch. Perhaps the men behind the Southwest Lumber Company might have more than local plans.

Bigjaw Haley had his thick right arm raised, the bullwhip snapping overhead, as Hatfield drew a steady bead and put a bullet through the center of the wide wrist. Haley screamed as the smashed tendons let go and the whip flew from his unnerved fingers.

The shot, with its echoing report, electrified the bandit gang. With shrill yells they unshipped their guns to fight. Hatfield, Stetson down to his gray-green eyes, the crown just showing over the top of a flat boulder, blasted the bunch of them with his bullets, and two men fell off their mustangs.

The rest began shooting at him, but he had good cover and they were in the open. He picked off a third as they tried to stand; the survivors, appalled at the sudden slaughter and the screams of wounded, swung their hairy ponies, dug deep with spurs, and rode off into the south bush.

Bigjaw Haley, dazed, sat down hard, holding his bleeding, stubby wrist. His bearded jaw sagged, brown saliva dripping from gaping lips. Hatfield, Colt up, vaulted the boulder and slid down the slope to the prostrate figure of Ban Morton.

Haley stared wide-eyed at the tall figure of the Ranger, whose gun emitted a faint, uneven trickle of smoke. Fear flashed into the reddish eyes as they fixed on the great fighting man. Haley had never before realized he had nerves in his wide, stocky body, but he began to shake as though with ague, and a stifled screech welled in his hairy throat.

He groveled in the dirt, crying for mercy: "Don't kill me, mister. Don't!" He had never acted that way before, had considered himself too tough to crack. But he had seen this big jigger fight off the whole gang the night before, and get away with it. In addition, the torn tendons of his punctured wrist took all the strength out of him.

Hatfield paused an instant, staring at the strange sight of the broken muleskinner. "Next time, Haley, I'll kill yuh." It was a plain statement of fact and Haley believed it.

A bullet from a bandit, in ambush a hundred yards south, spanged on a stone a foot from Hatfield's big boot. He fired at the smoke spurt. He had to get Ban Morton out of there and, lifting Morton, he tossed him across the big black horse who stood quietly, nosing his master. He grabbed Black Rascal's bridle and led him around the rocks into the thick bush.

Haley began crawling for cover. The bandits, seeing Hatfield retreat, regained heart and came riding back, shooting into the mesquite, madly yelling.

Down behind a granite boulder, safe from the big jigger, Bigjaw Haley regained his aplomb. "Get him, get that feller," he howled, but he did not show any part of himself.

Hatfield quickly yanked Black Rascal to the spot where Goldy, the magnificent sorrel, waited. The Mexicans were coming through after him, but they had to dismount and lead their ponies for some yards before remounting, the ground too rough to ride.

A lariat still dangled from Black Rascal's saddle horn, the one used in tying Ban. Hatfield took a few turns to secure the unconscious man. This delay, and reloading his Colts, allowed the bandidos to come up. He heard them in the bushes and leaped at them, both guns blaring. A man shrieked a Spanish oath; slugs ripped around Hatfield as he crouched, throwing lead at the enemy. His bold stand routed them again, and they fell back.

Hatfield jumped to Goldy, mounted the golden sorrel, who was impatiently stamping, and started east out of the hills.

The growth was thick, and the ground uneven, and at his heels like a pack of raging dogs came the remnants of the bandits, harrying him at a distance for they feared his deadly guns.

The lovely face of Nature, the green of the trees, the blossoms, yellow, red and white of the bush, and the pastel shades of the rock formations made an ironical setting of the fierce guerrilla fight that raged down the slopes. Gorgeous-hued butterflies flitted up from the flowers, the bees and ants pursued their busy tasks without taking note of the man-made hell close upon them. On all this, the sun smiled benignly, as though the fury of man did not exist.

The staccato bark of the guns echoed along the hillsides. A bullet bit a piece out of Hatfield's left arm; he bound a strip of his shirt around the wound without slowing, for he was aware he must get down across that ditch and on his way toward the ranches eastward before the lumberjacks organized pursuit. There were many of them off to the south, and they must have heard the shooting and Haley's powerful shouts.

A look at Black Rascal told him he was a super horse, capable of high speed; but Ban Morton was still out, unable to grip his saddle, and that meant the run would be slowed. Goldy kept sniffing, wishing to open up as they came to the arroyo, a deep dry ditch, in former times the Maravilla's bed, but now filled only during heavy rains. Some natural change had sent the river into its present course.

Dimly Hatfield heard yells off to the south, where the 'jacks and muleskinners lashed the peons on. Haley was heading toward his men, roaring orders at them. It would not be long until a howling army of killers would join the few bandidos.

It took time to ride along the arroyo, to find a slide where he could cross the horses.

The slope beyond eased off but it was still slow going. The bandits kept screeching to mark the Ranger's position for the lumbermen, starting down to cut him off.

He calculated the remaining distance to the flats, where he could make better time. He would not leave Morton. Ahead lay rolling prairie, fairly open, where he could prevent them from ambushing him, at least.

The Ranger, the hope of Maravilla in this crisis, of Texas itself, for he alone guessed the extent of the raiders' plans, now was held back, and death was closing in, for he refused to think of dropping Ban Morton. If he died it would be defending the bronc buster. And, if he died, with him was lost all chance to stop the juggernaut of evil that was fast gaining momentum over Texas.

Not yet had he completely fathomed the plot of the enemy; he knew he must ride hard, ride fast and surely, to gather them all in. There was Avalo, in Old Mexico, near which must be Torquila's lair; there was the great valley of the Maravilla and the northern sections of the state. All of them marked by that wide swathe on the map.

He pushed on, Black Rascal following Goldy. He was but two hundred yards out on the grassy plain when a whole mob of 'jacks and muleskinners, armed with rifles and pistols, dashed from the bush and opened fire. Hatfield swung to send slugs back at the masses of men, to spoil their aim. Goldy was picking up speed on the level and Black Rascal, Morton perilously lurching with his motion, coming on with the sorrel.

The jolting stirred Ban Morton and he opened his eyes in his swollen face, streaked with clotted blood from the whip weals.

"What—?" he muttered dizzily.

"Take it easy," the Ranger told him coolly. "Yuh're on yore way home, Morton."

For a time Morton did not speak; but he was coming fully awake, but on account of the ropes and his weakness he could not right himself on Black Rascal's back.

On the rolling stretches the renegades rode with the wild abandon of their race. They were far ahead of the slower lumbermen, yet Hatfield had thinned them out so only half a dozen stuck on his trail. Enemy bullets whirled in the air, plugged into the earth. A herd of cows snorted off in alarm at the gunfire, throwing up dust that clogged the forward vision, but as he rode through the cloud it helped protect him from his enemies.

"Look," the injured Morton called, "there's s'posed to be a bunch of the boys workin' a few miles east of here today. They'll help us."

Hatfield nodded, grave eyes hunting back over his broad shoulder. They were drawing up and the Mexicans were threatening to cut him off as they opened out in a wide, circling movement.

6

Bowie

HATFIELD'S eyes hunted a spot where he could take cover to fight off the killers in a final stand, for they were coming up and the renegades were now shooting from both flanks. Then he saw dust to the north and turned toward it, guns blasting back the three Mexicans that way.

Twenty Bar W waddies were busy with a bunch of steers, running them out of reach of the lumberjacks. The arrival of the Ranger, the attackers on his heels, threw the herd into a stampede. Hatfield was met by a cursing foreman, a dark saturnine-faced hombre.

"What the hell's the idee, runnin' into my cows thisaway?" Nevada Lewis bawled.

"We brought you some company," Hatfield told him easily, meeting the hot eyes of the lean man.

Nevada saw Morton then. "Afternoon, Nevada," Ban drawled. "I'm back."

At the sight of the enemy the Bar W men grabbed out their guns and started shooting. Howls of fury rose as the 'jacks, balked of their prey, stopped and lined up for battle. Nevada Lewis grunted, brows drawn tight together. He jerked a Colt and began firing at the lumbermen.

"Yuh're aimin' too high," Hatfield told him.

"I can stick in a saddle now, mister," Ban remarked.

Hatfield helped the injured bronc buster to sit up. Ban's face was twisted with pain. Hatfield decided to run him home. "Keep 'em busy," he said to Lewis. "We'll ride ahead."

Guns crackled in the warm air of afternoon, as Hatfield and Ban rode east, Morton pointing the way. The Bar W waddies slowly retreated, and the enemy, after a short scrap, stopped and turned back toward the hills. More armed men were near the ranch and they passed Morton and the Ranger, galloping to reinforce Nevada and his bunch.

"We keep guards out to protect Sam

Ward," Morton explained. He told Hatfield the situation, fully trusting him after the Ranger's terrific feat against the enemy. The story of Black Rascal's strange disappearance interested the keen officer.

"Yuh say this Nevada helped yuh find them tracks?" asked Hatfield.

"Why, yeah. It was decent of him seein' as how I've sorta took his place around the ranch."

It was, thought Hatfield, an interesting point. Remembering Scarface, who had connected with some other spy at the Bar W, he made a mental note to check Foreman Lewis.

Hatfield helped Ban dismount at the rear corral. Morton thought he'd lie in his bunk, but Elsie came running out and she cried when she saw her sweetheart's injured face.

"Ban, what's wrong?"

Ban managed to smile, through gritted teeth. "I'm okay, Elsie. This gent saved my life."

Hatfield regarded the pretty young woman, heiress to the Bar W. Her soft eyes were on the great Ranger's broad-shouldered figure, and she was plainly impressed by the stalwart fighting man, by his manner. The rugged face was calm as a summer sky, and though there was blood on him and he was torn from bullets and thorns, he was entirely unruffled.

Ban Morton, the strain over, suddenly collapsed. His knees buckled and his head went limp as Hatfield caught him.

"Oh bring him inside, quick," Elsie cried, terribly distressed.

The Ranger carried the young fellow easily, following Elsie to a bedroom near the center of the big house, where he deposited Morton on the cot. The Ranger told the worried young woman to bring him a drink and tie up his wounds and he'd be okay.

Morton opened his eyes, and swore after a moment. "Sorry," he muttered. "Didn't figger I'd do that."

Hatfield was rolling a cigarette; seeing Ban's look he gave it to Morton and fixed another, and Morton said awkwardly, "I'm obliged."

"Don't mention it." Hatfield understood that Ban Morton was thanking him, not for the cigarette but for what he had done.

By future actions, Ban Morton showed his gratitude.

Elsie brought in a bottle of whiskey and after awhile Ban felt better and she returned to the kitchen to heat some water and fix bandages for his wounds. By a few casual queries, Hatfield drew out more of the rancher's story.

"Someone's after my hide," Ban Morton ended. "Ross and his pals're all-fired smart; they know ev'ry move we make."

"They were all ready the day Ward was shot, weren't they?" asked Hatfield.

"Yeah."

"Expectin' 'em," mused the Ranger, slouched in a chair, blue tobacco smoke wreathing his black-haired head. He turned the complicated business over in his mind. "Callate I need to get it all straight, 'fore organizin'," he decided inwardly.

Both men were hungry and Elsie fed them. She said, "I'd like you to meet Father, Mr.—?"

"Jim, Jim Harris," Hatfield told her gravely.

He followed the pretty girl across the wide living room to Sam Ward's chamber, where the giant rancher chief lay on his bed of pain. The Ranger's gray-green eyes fixed on the prostrate man, whose ruddy face was peaked by his ordeal. When Elsie told him what Hatfield had done, Ward smiled, straight-looking blue eyes ringed by lines of anguish. In a hoarse voice he thanked the Ranger.

"Ban's come to mean a lot to us, mister."

Riders, then, came sweeping into the yard. Steps on the porch and Elsie turned, with the Ranger, to see who was coming. Nevada Lewis, the foreman, dust-covered, dark face set, stood in the doorway, and behind him was a short hombre the Ranger immediately recognized. The waddy with Lewis was the man from whose hand Hatfield had shot a gun when the Ranger, heading in for Maravilla, had snatched Scarface from the lynch party.

Hatfield was alert, inwardly; but the short cowboy, filmed with sweat-caked dust, looked right at him and gave no sign of recognition; the Ranger had taken care to hide himself when he made that bold play, had even disguised his voice.

"What's wrong, Nevada?" Ward demanded.

A cigarette drooped from the pale lips of

Lewis; for a moment his deep-sunk eyes fixed the Ranger, then swung to Ward. "Boss, somethin's went wrong with the river; it's most dried up, nuthin' but a trickle left. Shorty here jest rode in."

"They got the stream turned into that ditch, boss, and through the old arroyo," Shorty reported. "There's logs floatin' through, but they ain't tried to pick 'em up yet. They can't, not with us gunnin' 'em from the mesquite."

Ward was terribly perturbed. He licked his cracked lips, and Elsie held a glass of water to his mouth.

"That settles it," the old fellow gasped. "We gotta go up after them sidewinders, like Haley said."

"Yore man's right," Hatfield put in. "The Southwest can't float logs to market with vigilantes pickin' 'em off."

"True," Ward agreed. "Only we can't last long 'thout the river. Stock'll die and people get sick. The Maravilla makes this country."

Hatfield knew that. He nodded, rose and went out. From the front veranda he could see the Maravilla; the sides were drying down from the banks, stones showing white and bare, like the bleached bones of a skeleton; in the center of the bed ran a brook, trickles from rills and springs below the spot where the Southwest Company had diverted the main stream. And, from the east, on the road winding along the river, riders were galloping toward the ranch.

The tall Lone Wolf lounged off to one side as this party swirled up, two dozen heavily armed men. They were plainly excited. All wore cowboy clothes save for a very tall, spare man in a black frock coat and straight black hat under which showed iron-gray, crisp hair; his gaunt face was triangular in shape.

"Like a beanpole all dressed up," the Ranger thought.

There was a man of about fifty, in riding pants and black halfboots, Stetson and vest on which was pinned a five-pointed country sheriff's star; sharp-pointed goatee and ragged mustache salted with white. He took off his ten-gallon hat to mop with a red bandanna a head devoid of hair save for some curly fringes around his ears. Also there was a small oldster with a wooden peg-leg, wearing a town marshal's badge.

A bluff, square man with thick brown

hair, sun-seamed eyes, sang out, "Oh, Elsie —where are you?"

Then he caught the Ranger regarding him and he took in the tall jigger, the bullet-ripped clothes, dried blood; suspicion darkened his broad face.

"Who are you?" he demanded.

All eyes swung on Hatfield. They were leary of strangers in Maravilla, and this stranger was obviously just out of a gunfight. Yet the Ranger's appearance awed men and no one made any move against him as he watched them with calm, calculating eyes, and Elsie Ward hurried out.

Only a half dozen, the leaders, of the bunch left their horses; the rest stayed outside, and they looked like armed waddies, followers of the chiefs of Maravilla.

"Hello, Senator and Mayor Yager. Hello, Johnny and all, Dad'll be happy to see you, come on in." Sensing the stiffness in the air she added quickly, "Oh, this is Jim Harris. He saved Ban Morton from death up in the hills; Ban was set on and almost killed by the lumbermen. Jim, meet Sheriff Godey, and this is Mayor Yager;

Senator Ardmore, Marshal Betts. And John Ogalvie of the Circle 5, George Keith who owns the Running R, south of Bowie."

The tall senator cleared his bony throat. "We are obliged to Mr. Harris for saving Ban Morton," he announced sonorously.

Mayor Yager smiled at Elsie, but there was anxiety in his voice when he spoke.

"You know the river's gone. Means the country's ruined. We got to see your father, quick."

Senator Ardmore detached himself from the group, came to Hatfield. "Welcome to our fair land, sir. You've evidently had a long, hard ride and a bloody fight."

The Ranger knew he must quickly gain the confidence of the Maravilla ranchers. His saving of Morton had broken the ice, but he still had not explained his presence in the district.

"I'm a State Forester, Senator," he drawled. "Was up lookin' over them hills when I seen Morton set on."

Ardmore glanced over his shoulder, then said delicately, "Perhaps you have some symbol of your authority, sir?"

"Shore." Without appearing offended, Hatfield drew forth the forester badge he had taken from Ross's suitcase. Mayor Yager's face broke into a smile at sight of that, and he came over, thrusting out a hearty hand.

"Glad to meet you, Harris. We can use you."

Tension eased; stiff suspicion faded, and, with the bluff mayor and others Hatfield went back into the bedroom where lay Sam Ward.

"The river's gone, Sam, you know it," Yager growled.

"Now we got to fight, pronto," John Ogalvie added.

Ward nodded. "Figger yuh're right, boys." Ward looked sharply at Sheriff Godey down whose bearded face the sweat was running. "Godey, if you can't stop them devils, we can!"

"We'll send up every fightin' man in Maravilla," Mayor Yager cried. "Four hundred of 'em."

"Yeah," Ward agreed, "but this time they got to be armed right, and scouts out ahead, gents. It'll take two, three days to collect 'em and see they got plenty guns and bullets."

"Friday," Ogalvie suggested. "That'll

give the outlyin' ranches time to get to Bowie from where we'll start."

"Right," Yager agreed, and Ward nodded.

"Some of Torquila's Mexes gunned us from across the river as we were comin' out," the mayor said. "That's another bunch of snakes we've got to wipe out, soon as we finish up on the Southwest, Sam. The law round here just can't seem to take care of us." He frowned at Godey again.

Godey again took off his hat to mop sweat from his bald dome. "Hell, gents, I'm with yuh. But when I was up there before, this Valentine Ross showed me a lease all legal from the State to cut timber. I got to obey the law."

"Yuh call this law?" Ward demanded angrily, and half rose up; blood suffused his face, as he fell back with a groan.

Yager took up the cudgel for his old pal. "Yeah, Godey. They near murdered Sam and they've killed plenty of our men. Is that law? Is it law to cut off our water supply and steal our stock?"

"You gents went off half-cocked when yuh attacked them lumberjacks," replied the sheriff stoutly. "They had a right to defend themselves. And Ross claims Vasco Torquila's the one who took yore cows."

"You're a fool," cried Yager. "Ross pulled the wool over your eyes, Godey. If you feel so, get out of here, we don't want your help. As for me I stand for Ward and Maravilla." He stuck out his square jaw, glaring at the sheriff.

Fighting talk was hot; the air was tense with the aroused passions of the ranchers. These men were leaders of the Maravilla country through the great area drained by the river; rough, self-made men, used to the saddle and gun, to protecting themselves. There were plenty more of them in Bowie and through the land.

The black shadow of wholesale death hung over the once lovely range.

"Jest a sec, gents," a voice broke in, and surprised eyes turned on the tall Ranger.

As he spoke, easily, with the born power of a great leader, they listened under the spell of that soft but commanding voice:

"Gents, the Southwest Lumber Company ain't so easy to beat. I callate they've switched off yore water to madden yuh. Why else? They know as well as you do they can't run them logs through with yore vigilantes gunnin' 'em with rifles from long range; they can't quit work ev'ry few minutes to chase yore men. Ross is too smart to draw yuh all up there 'less he's ready and wishin' for it. And if he's ready it means yuh run into hell agin."

The sharpness of his logic could not be denied. It gave the hot-headed ranchers pause.

"What would yuh suggest, then, Harris?" Ward asked.

"I've had some experience organizin'," the Ranger told them carefully. "Now, people can get along on what water there is for a few days till we find what Ross is up to."

"And how, mister," asked Mayor Yager, "are we to do that?"

"I'll guarantee to let yuh know. In the meantime arm yore men but do it quiet like."

He nodded shortly, swung and strolled out; he had made his point and to speak further would not help. Hatfield walked back to Morton's room and looked in on the bronc buster.

"Feeling better?" the Ranger asked.

Morton nodded, grinned. "Sorta like a

hunka chewed leather, but I'll be okay after a rest."

The conference in Ward's room broke up, and the men came out, sifting around the big house. Sheriff Godey was first to leave; he went out and through Morton's window Hatfield saw him throwing a stiff leg over his saddle.

"Reck'n I'll be ridin'," the Ranger told Ban, "but I'll be back. Keep yore eye peeled."

As he stepped quickly out into the big living room, Shorty, the squat waddy, eyes gleaming red, ran in from the front and pulled up suddenly. He pointed an accusing finger at Jim Hatfield.

"Gents!" he bellowed. "That there hombre's the one who snatched that scarface lumberman from us! I reckernized his voice"

Shorty was going for his gun; John Ogalvie, and Mayor Yager, too, were swearing as they dropped hands to their holstered Colts. The ranchers froze, however; for with his back to the side wall, Hatfield had his blue-steel six-shooter out and up, hammer spur back under his thumb. The menacing black eye that was the muzzle seemed to cover every heart in the room and they stopped as they were.

Furious eyes, accusing the tall jigger, burned in their heads. The sheriff, called by the cowboys outside, came rushing back, threw himself off his horse and came up on the porch.

"Boys," drawled Hatfield, "yuh've got a name for going' off half-cocked and yuh're doin' it agin. I've told yuh I'm with yuh, and if yuh don't b'lieve me I'll jest hafta prove it. Now I'm leavin' but yuh'll hear from me again."

"He's a spy," cried Senator Ardmore, "a spy for the lumbermen!"

"Put up that gun," Godey called from the front.

Hatfield took a step back, into Ban Morton's room. The bronc buster had heard the talk outside, and he was watching his big friend, the man who had saved him, with troubled eyes. His gunbelt, with six-guns in it, hung from the back of a chair but he had made no move to shoot the Ranger in the back or cover him.

"Jim—Jim! It ain't true, is it?" he gasped.

The gray-green eyes were dark; Jim

Hatfield knew that this event had set him back in his job; he must regain the confidence of Maravilla, even as he worked against the unseen enemies who raged for his life.

"Yuh'll see me agin, Morton," he growled. "Keep yore eye peeled while I'm gone."

Jim Hatfield was at the wide open window, and in a moment he was outside it. A shrill whistle brought Goldy and the Ranger mounted from the window sill, as a rush of men started through Morton's room. A bullet spanged the air, nipping at his Stetson; then he heard Morton's voice. "Cut it out," he bellowed. "Hold it. Yuh've got him all wrong, gents!"

The Ranger did not wish to fire upon the ranchers; though misguided they were decent men whom he meant to aid. He swung at full speed around the line of barns, as armed waddies started for him from the front.

Goldy opened up, legs flashing at full speed that drew swiftly away from the mounted cowboys, whooping it up and shooting after Hatfield. There was plenty of cover to the southeast, and the Ranger headed for it, doubling around to lose them in a burst of clever backtracking.

A mile from the Bar W he rode from the mesquite onto the rutted dirt road leading into Bowie.

"How'd that Shorty waddy reckernize my voice," he mused. "He didn't know me from Buffalo Bill when he fust come in."

He swung, to look back from a little knoll, at the big spread of the ranch, the rolling, beautiful land where the stock grazed so peacefully. The sun was red as a ruby over the hills where lurked the deadly minions of the Southwest Company.

A rider was heading along the road, toward him; he caught the sudden shine on the star pinned to the hombre's vest. That was Sheriff Godey and Hatfield wished to contact him. He drew back, waited until the officer was abreast of him, then shoved Goldy out on the road.

Godey's bearded lips opened in a gasp; his hand twitched toward his gun, as he took in the great fighting man, the thin, quick hands, Colts ready in black oiled holsters. His brows drew into a worried line, for he realized the big man had him.

"I'll ride with yuh, Sheriff," drawled

Hatfield, "and I'll guarantee yuh'll be interested. Yuh got nuthin' to fear from me."

Godey cursed, but he was relieved. The two swung toward Bowie, Godey still wary, wondering what it was all about. Something that sounded like a giant fly buzzed between them, to spang into the bushes fringing the Maravilla's bed.

"That was a bullet," Godey gasped.

"Rifle and a mile off," the Ranger said. "It'd take a lucky shot to hit us."

Godey gave him a sharp look. Then he saw the silver star, set on a silver circle, emblem of the Texas Rangers, cupped in Hatfield's palm. "Jumpin' Jee," the Sheriff cried. "So that's it! What's yore handle, Ranger?"

"Jim Hatfield. McDowell sent me."

"Great. I've heard tell of yuh. But yuh ain't alone?"

Hatfield shrugged. "For a while. But there's four hundred fightin' waddies in Maravilla."

Godey mopped his face. "Yeah, but Ward won't trust yuh now, after what that Shorty claims. It ain't true, is it?"

Hatfield told him about it. "It was a smart play," Godey agreed, "if it hadn't backfired, Ranger. Yuh shore bit off somethin' when yuh come to help these ranchers. I don't know which side of the fence to drop on."

"The Southwest Lumber Company," Hatfield told him, "has busted ev'ry law Texas ever made and is huntin' more."

Godey gave an explosive sigh. "Glad to hear it. I'll fight shoulder to shoulder with Ward. On'y—that timber lease worries me. Them hills're the State's, to use as Austin says. These cowmen run stock on open range."

"McDowell'll look up that lease. I want yuh to send a man yuh kin trust up to the telegraph office with a wire. I'll write what I want done and yuh make sure there's no slip. Yuh any idee who held up the complaints?"

Godey shook his head. "Mebbe it was done at the Austin end," he suggested.

"Mebbe. I'll find out."

Darkness had fallen before they reached Bowie. Lights twinkled in homes, saloons were briskly shining; horses and teams stood at hitch-racks, and around a tree-shaded plaza in the center. Yells of drinking waddies rang on the night air as the Ranger and Godey dismounted in the shadows near the west end of the plaza.

"Ever hear tell of an hombre here called Fat Phil?" Hatfield inquired.

"Why, shore. That must be the gambler who sits in Jack's back rooms. He's fat as a hogshead. Why?"

Hatfield informed him about Scarface's report to Ross. Godey slapped his leg. "That's right. I seen that Scarface one night with Phil!"

The Ranger, by the light of a match Godey held for him, wrote out a note, resting the paper on his saddle. "Askin' McDowell to check the Southwest's sales up to now, and that lease," he explained. "Get if off quick as yuh can and have yore man fetch the reply to Bowie. We'll split; I got an idee, and I don't want to be seen yet with yuh."

"I savvy." Godey took the penciled message and rode off.

The tall man led Goldy to the shadows cast by a great live-oak growing near the edge of the plaza, left his pet, and crossed to the awninged sidewalk. Yager's, the big store, was open, as were the saloons; there were armed cowboys around. Jack's place was next door to the store and the Ranger entered, stood at the end of the bar. A barkeeper came to serve him, and he ordered whiskey.

"Is Fat Phil here?" Hatfield asked in a low voice when it was shoved out.

"In the back room, dealin' faro."

One by one, Jim Hatfield was swiftly marking down the enemies of Maravilla, of Texas. He sensed, from what he had come upon, gigantic menace to the state; there was more to it than Maravilla, and he must check it before it grew too large to stop. That map, now, that cut a swathe through the central and southern parts of Texas—

He was threading a way through the crowd to the rear. A closed door confronted him and he knocked.

"Come in," a thick, heavy voice ordered.

Hatfield opened the door, stepped through. A dozen gamblers sat at a long table. The dealer was an enormously fat man, bulging over his chair; he had flabby jowls, a round body and a round head; he was extremely gross, and the expression on his face was that of a pig. He looked up, all his motions very slow, and frowned at the Ranger.

"Want to sit in?" he growled.

The Ranger shook his head. "Like a word with yuh."

Fat Phil got up; it took him seconds to accomplish it. He had on a gunbelt, shoved out taut by his enormous paunch. His foxy little eyes, set pudgily in the folds of fat, gleamed, and he waddled to a side door after waving a hand to his assistant to take the game over.

Out in the dark side alley, Fat Phil asked softly, "Yes? Who's that?"

The Ranger didn't forget. "S.—W.—L." he replied.

Fat Phil grunted. "Follow me. You're early." He swung around back of Jack's. Close at hand was a small, dark shack which Fat Phil entered. His gruff voice reached Hatfield. "Come in. You can wait here."

Alert, not sure that the password used in the hills was the one for Bowie, not at all certain Fat Phil was not leading him into a trap, the tall jigger stepped inside the inky hut.

7
Raid

A CHAIR scraped. "Sit down and make yourself comfortable," ordered Fat Phil. "The Boss'll be busy for a while but then he'll be along. Have a drink." Fat Phil shut the door, drew the window curtain; he struck a match and touched the guttering yellow flame to a candle standing on the board table. The light shone on his wicked face, glinted from a bottle and glasses.

"So you're a minin' expert," growled Phil. "I guess Ross showed you that coal seam, and told you where to come."

"Shore." Hatfield let Phil call the turns.

"We need a man like you, and you'll come in handy the next few days, a new face, till we're set. D'you know if they finished off that nosey Morton?"

"Purty near; but he was saved."

Fat Phil swore. "He won't be long. The chief hates his guts. We got to be rid of men like Morton and Ward; well, Friday'll do it, we'll settle their hash then. I wouldn't be surprised if the chief had our man at the Bar W kill Morton tonight, though; he's got a real grudge against the bronc buster. I suppose Ross told you what went on here?"

Hatfield had to be careful; he couldn't show too much ignorance nor yet too much knowledge. He hoped to draw further valuable information from Fat Phil, who had evidently been told to watch for a mining expert.

"And how much," the Ranger asked, tentatively, "is there in it for me, Phil?"

"Why, a fortune! There's five in the main Syndicate, but we'll cut you in the way we did Ross if you're valuable enough. Once you get out that coal, there's an iron deposit up in Pecos, and do you know much about oil?"

The Ranger nodded as he drank. "It costs real money to get such stuff out, Phil; we'll need a railroad spur for that coal."

"Don't worry. Once we win here we'll be rich enough to float the whole shebang."

"Labor, that's the most expensive—"

"Not with us, pal. Torquila's the answer. We'll own the entire state of Texas."

Yells, gunshots, sounded outside. Hatfield growled, "What's that?"

Fat Phil chuckled. "All accordin' to plan. Keep sittin'."

There was the pounding of many hoofs and the whoops of cowboys; then the hubbub died off in the east distance and quiet settled over Bowietown.

The Ranger resumed his careful probing. He was, actually, a mining expert; now he was digging for nuggets, digging the gross hombre who squatted across the table like a loathsome crab. He put admiration into his next remark.

"Torquila—there's a great feller."

Fat Phil was laughing, belly silently shaking. "Yeah, Torquila's a great one! That's the best trick of all!"

"Yeah? How so?"

But Fat Phil only replied cryptically, "If everybody knew that, hell would break loose. You'll find out, when you're a member of the Syndicate. No one else knows, up here. The chief's the craftiest devil you ever heard of. Take my advice and make good on the first job he gives you; he may have you kill Morton, since they missed him today."

"I understand this Morton's caused plenty trouble."

"True, but that's not the real reason. We need the Bar W. Maybe you can get Morton the way it was done with Sam Ward."

"How'd they manage it?"

"Oh, Ward was a nuisance; that corridor, you see"—Fat Phil enjoying his superior show of knowledge to this new and supposedly trustworthy thief, broke off, put a fat finger warningly to his lips.

Horses, ridden up, were just outside. A heavy knock on the door, and Fat Phil's pudgy hand went to his gun.

"Yes? Who's that?" growled Fat Phil.

"S.—W.—L.," a harsh voice replied.

As Fat Phil opened and pulled back the slab door, Hatfield rose and stood against the wall. He knew that voice. In the opening stood two men, one a wide, squat figure; it was Bigjaw Haley and the muleskinner's right wrist was bandaged where the Ranger had put that slug.

"We've come in to pick up the stuff," growled Haley. "I rode on ahead with this minin' feller Ross sent—" His eyes suddenly fixed on the figure of the Ranger, off to the right behind Fat Phil.

Fat Phil, with a gasp, suspicion flaming red in his pudgy face, whirled with surprising speed. "Why, he—That—" he yelled.

"Texas Ranger!" Bigjaw Haley howled, and dug for a gun with his left hand.

Fat Phil had his weapon out, rising. The Ranger's Colt blasted straight into the fat hombre and the mountain of flesh quivered, shook violently, as the great arm dropped limp. Fat Phil hit the table, overturned it, the candle going out. The so-called mining expert, behind Haley, let out a yell and turned to bolt into the night. In the sudden dark, the candle smoking on the floor, "Drop yore gun, Haley," Hatfield warned. "This is the next time!"

But Haley was rattled; panic surged through him at sound of that crisp, cold voice, the voice of the hombre who was the only one who had ever made him feel fear. The pistol in Haley's hand blared, as his fingers tightened spasmodically; Hatfield felt the wind of the bullet close to his face.

The Ranger's Colt spat blue-yellow flame; the broad muleskinner's arms flew out, his weapon clanked against the log wall, thudded dully in the dirt. Haley fell in the doorway, a bullet straight through his evil brain.

Acrid powder smoke drifted to the flared nostrils of the Ranger as he rapidly pushed fresh shells into his warm pistol. His ears sang with the boom of the heavy guns in the confined shack.

No one came running at sound of the shots. But a great chorus of yells, and the rapid beat of hundreds of hoofs, took Jim Hatfield outside; he stepped across the dead muleskinner and went through the dark alley toward Main Street. He turned into Jack's, and the saloon was deserted save for the bartenders.

"Where's everybody?" asked the Ranger.

"Vasco Torquila jest raided the Circle Five," a barkeep said. "Killed a couple waddies and run off a bunch of cows. Set fire to some barns, and the boys're on his trail."

"Leavin' the town wide open for Ross," decided Hatfield.

He stepped to the front window, looked out. A large band of mounted men came pushing in from the west. At their head rode Valentine Ross, the pasty-faced devil, top boss of the Southwest Lumber Company. Arrogant, sneering, Ross looked from side to side for enemies as he entered the capital of his foes, the ranchers. With him were two hundred armed muleskinners and lumberjacks, in corduroys, carrying Winchester rifles ready for instant use, pistols strapped to burly waists, a fierce looking, warlike army

They stopped at Yager's, the big general store, still open. Ross got down and a bunch of his men crowded up on the porch behind him; others commanded the plaza and street.

Hatfield went back to the side door, slid out and went to Tincan Alley, behind the buildings. From a rear window he looked into the big store, filled with boxes of supplies of all kinds. A main counter ran from front to rear; there were smaller counters, one for dry goods, another for hardware.

Ross and his 'jacks were already in.

The boss stood up front, and facing him from behind the long counter, an open window at his back, stood Mayor Smiley Yager, glaring in rage as Ross coldly uttered his commands, the rasping voice penetrating to where Hatfield watched, at the back.

"Good evenin', Mayor Yager," Ross said sardonically "We've come to do a little business with you, seein' we're such good neighbors. Want whiskey and your best tobacco; and we could use some of those canned goods boxed over there."

Under menacing guns, Yager and his three clerks had to stand. John Ogalvie was in there, too, and so was Keith of the Running R. Evidently they had just ridden back from the Bar W, and not yet started for the Circle 5, burning after Torquila's attack. They were trapped inside the store by Ross and his killers.

Yager spluttered in fury as he cursed Ross. "Damn your heart and soul! Get out of my store. Get out! I wouldn't sell you 'jacks anything but rat poison."

Ross frowned. "You'll sell us what we want, seein' as how you've cut off our supplies from the railroad, Yager. Tote that stuff out, boys."

Ready hands began carrying out the boxes of canned goods, bottles of liquor and bundles of tobacco.

Ranger Hatfield watched for a clear bead

on Valentine Ross. He had put Fat Phil out of the criminal Syndicate threatening Texas; he hoped to diminish the Syndicate again. But the thin hombre was covered by the counters and by the moving bodies of his men, thick inside the store.

Mayor Yager suddenly gave a howl of fury; he snatched his gun out, fired a hasty shot that whirled close over Ross's narrow head The mayor dived backward out of the window, as Ross fired back.

Ogalvie and George Keith both went for their Colts, but rifles and revolvers poured a death hail into them. Ogalvie went down, mortally wounded, life-blood gushing from a dozen wounds; Keith's right arm was shattered and he stood, proudly waiting for death.

"Let him have it," bawled Ross, gulping with fury.

Hatfield opened fire through his window. His spaced, accurate slugs knocked over one 'jack after another, stung the mob to insane fury. They placed him after the first couple of explosions, and a concerted rush was made toward the window, as they covered it with a thick hail of death.

Ross was down behind the counter. "Get him," he shrieked.

Armed men from outside started around the big store, coming through the alleys. The crashing guns, the yells of hate, made up a horrid bedlam.

There was no cover at hand. The Ranger ducked past the alleyway, heard singing lead as they glimpsed his moving figure. He ran toward the road, past the saloon; they were in full hue and cry on his trail. He paused under the awning a moment; and Sheriff Godey galloped across the Plaza, guns in hand.

"Get back, Godey," bawled Hatfield. But in the din the sheriff failed to hear the warning; he rode his horse straight up to the store, into the massed gunmen, never faltering in his mad courage, the courage of an old-time law officer.

Hatfield tried to distract them by fanning slugs into the 'jacks; but it was impossible to save Godey, and bullets poured into the sheriff. He fell from his horse and was cut up under the dancing hoofs of the many horses and mules, terrified by the shooting.

Ross came out on the store porch, and

saw Hatfield. "That's the man we want," he howled,

A bullet smacked into the wall an inch from the Ranger. Two hundred guns were turning upon him. They were coming at him, roaring on his trail. Goldy stood under a tree, across the road, and Hatfield, Colts barking, melted among the shadows.

From the side of the store, a gun flashed, again and again, and among the wildly fired volley, it seemed to search out the Ranger. He felt the bite of a bullet along his ribs, that stung with horrible agony; he set his teeth, ran to the golden sorrel. There was, in his eyes, the dark coldness of an Arctic storm.

He must, he knew, hurry back to the Bar W; even now it might be too late to save Morton. From the defunct Fat Phil he had obtained information that had made it possible for him to envisage the ruthless, far-reaching plans of the Syndicate. The significance of the map dotted with letters, that he had seen in Ross's shack in the hills smote him, spelling disaster to the vast state of Texas.

As the Ranger rode hell-for-leather westward, a man stamped with an insane fury inside Phil's cabin where Bigjaw Haley and the fat man lay in stiff, ghastly death.

"Damn him!" he raved, "damn him! I'll pay any man five thousand dollars for that Ranger's hide!"

A tall, bony hombre, slouched in the doorway, hissed in sympathetic rage. The glow of his eyes in the dimness was phosphorescent as a cat's.

"You were right, Chief," he snarled. "He's a Texas Ranger. Made us more trouble than the country law and cowmen combined."

"I'll get him," the chief promised, voice thick with his anger. "I'll kill him myself!"

Through the alley between Haley's store and Jack's Saloon could be seen the hundreds of pack animals, forming into a long train under the whips of the cursing, shouting muleskinners. The caravan, dust rising under beating hoofs, was started west for the hills. Square wooden boxes showed, balanced on either flank of the pack animals. An army of guards, with rifles and pistols, rode the flanks and brought up the rear.

"Shall I set everything as you ordered for Friday?" inquired the green-eyed man.

"Certainly. Next Friday."

"How about Ward—and Morton?"

"They'll be dead inside an hour; I saw to that, when I found how things had gone. I'll smash these cowmen into the ground. Can't let a few stubborn old fools ruin my plans."

"See you Friday, then?"

"Okay. And make sure there's no slip."

"There won't be, Chief. Listen, that so-called minin' expert came runnin' out with a face like a ghost, said he quit before he started. He didn't like the way that Ranger acted. I took care of him; so we'll have to find another man."

The Chief's teeth ground together. "The Ranger again," he snarled. "I'll eat his heart when I catch him."

8

The Blow of Torquila

BAN MORTON awoke, a cold sweat on his lank body. He had nerves attuned to his wild, outdoor life, almost animal in sensitivity; besides, his injuries ached, muscles stiff from the terrible beating he had taken from Bigjaw Haley, though with the steel flexibility of youth he was fast regaining his strength.

The silver moon streamed in the open window of his little bedroom. Across the wide living room of the great ranch house, through a door crack, he could see a streak of yellow that came from Sam Ward's chamber.

"Guess Elsie's up tendin' him," he muttered.

He tried to sleep again but a second time started awake, that cold sweat all over him.

Ban lay, intently listening. Horrid terror, a black pall of death, lay heavy upon the Maravilla country. It seethed with danger, men were not safe in their homes. A gigantic, evil brain planned destruction for them. But there should be armed, alert guards around the ranch; those were strict orders.

Morton knew he was in constant jeopardy; a hidden enemy pined for his death; someone had tried to dry-gulch him and that trap had been set especially for him in the hills, when they had drawn him up through his love for Black Rascal.

And, as he stared at the lighter rectangle of the window he saw the tip of a peaked sombrero stealthily rising.

Silently he reached out a hand, gripped the cool butt of his .45 gun, hanging from the chair in its leather holster belt.

A faint scraping from the window, then the sheen of light on a long metal barrel; Ban threw himself out of his cot, streamers of pain shooting through his aching limbs as he hit the boards of the floor. He was blinded by the flash of the rifle in the window; the bed hopped as the long bullet ripped through the blanket, mattress and spring on which he had been lying, and splintered the floor a few inches from his elbow as it buried itself in the pine flooring.

Ban Morton let go rapidly, three shots, through the open window. The rifle clanged on the sill, and as the gun flashes that had blinded his eyes ceased, he saw that the opening was vacant. Ears ringing with the pent-up explosions, he heard running steps, the guttural cursing of a wounded man.

"Reck'n I singed him," he growled, and, coming up on his knee, scurried to the window and cautiously stuck out his head. He saw a dark, stooped figure duck around the rear of the house, out of his sight.

"Hey, boys," he sang out, to call the sentries supposed to be guarding the Bar W and Sam Ward.

No one answered him; even the bunkhouse, where day and relief shifts should be sleeping failed to come to life.

The moon lit the dome of the mighty sky, dotted with star points; the soft west wind rustled the oaks and alders and the mesquite, bringing with it the scent of aromatic blossoms. In the distance a horse whinnied—Black Rascal had heard his master's call.

Ban Morton swore, wondering where everybody was. He strapped on his gunbelt, and, worried about Elsie and her father, went through his door, stepped into the living room. It was late and the fire in the big fireplace had burned down to an ash-encrusted mass of ruby coals.

There was still a light in Ward's room, and he heard old Sam coughing; then a sharp sound which he knew was Ward banging the floor with a stick, calling his daughter.

"Elsie!" Ban said, but the girl didn't answer.

Morton went over and entered the rancher's chamber. Ward lay in bed, dry lips working.

"Ban, what were them shots? I been callin' Elsie a long while, my water tipped over and I'm dry as alkali. Callate the pore kid's wore out, nursin' me; I thought I heard her voice a while back but she didn't come."

A single candle burned golden in its stick, on a small table close to the bed. Morton slid around and picked up Ward's tin mug and pitcher, lying in a wet spot on the floor.

"I'll get yuh a drink, be back in a jiffy," he told the wounded man cheerfully, and, not to alarm him, he added, "Guess the night guard seen some spooks outside and let their Colts go."

Death was closing in upon young Ban, on Old Sam; forces too powerful for them to defeat plotted to destroy them.

Ban could not guess this; he felt only a vague uneasiness, as he took the jug and passed through the living room, headed for the well outside; he thought he'd draw fresh water, cool and invigorating, for Ward. He came to Elsie's room on his way along the hall. Her door was open and a candle guttered on the dressing table. Her bed was empty, though it was turned down, as though she had got up after retiring.

Deep lines corrugated the bronc buster's forehead. "Huh," he grunted. "Mebbe she's in the kitchen." But she wasn't nor was she outside. She did not answer his soft calls.

He stepped into the shadowy yard, unable to shake off that icy dread that gripped him. Then he saw the circle of horsemen, silently sitting their saddles. They sighted him and their guns rose, cries in Spanish challenging him. The voices, the sheen of the moonlight on the crossed bandilleros heavy with cartridges, the peaked hats, warned him who they were.

"Mexes!" he gasped.

He leaped back, as, when he failed to reply to them, they opened fire. He ran through the hall, and as he reached the entry into the living room he saw a big Mexican crossing the front toward Ward's room, behind him half a dozen renegades, cigarettes curling smoke from their brownish lips.

The leader was a giant; he wore velvet trousers trimmed with silver conchas, tucked into spurred boots, scarlet waistband pulling in his paunch, a short, sleeveless brown jacket trimmed with gold braid, and a peaked sombrero ornamented with rows of pearl.

"Torquila!" shouted Morton. He had never seen the Mexican bandit chief but had heard him described.

The huge bandit was framed against the dying fire. Ban Morton saw the dark, cruel face, blotches of mustache and goatee, the white teeth between sneering lips. At sound of Morton's cry Torquila whirled, gun in hand.

"*Cien nil diablos!*" he shouted harshly.

For an instant he failed to place the bronc buster. That instant was fatal, for as his gun blasted the slug missed Morton by a yard and Ban threw up his Colt and let go, the dropped pitcher clanging on the floor.

Torquila bellowed with anguish; he was half whirled around by the impact of the heavy bullet, and he sank, slowly, to the mat, out of Ban's sight behind the sofa and table before the fireplace.

His bandits jumped into action. A volley of bullets whirled at Morton, who threw himself flat, back of a big sideboard. The lead rapped into the walls and tore off great splinters from the sideboard.

More of Torquila's hombres crowded inside, and ran to their chief. Others cursed shrilly as they tried to kill Ban Morton. Behind the cover of blazing guns, the Mexicans quickly carried their leader outside.

The fall of Torquila threw the bandits into confusion, and they did not stand against Morton's gunfire but scuttled out onto the veranda. He could hear their excited chatter, and, seizing his opportunity, he jumped up and ran full-tilt to Ward's room.

The rancher chieftain's eyes were wide with excitement at the mad shooting. "Where's Elsie?" he cried.

Ban Morton shook his head. He swept the candle from the table, plunging them in darkness, as he heard sounds at the windows. There was a mahogany bureau against the wall and the bronc buster dragged it up so it stood between Ward's bed and the windows.

Bullets already were coming in, Spanish curses rising outside. Ban Morton fired back, on his knees back of the bureau, protecting Ward as best he could.

"Gimme a gun!" gasped Sam. "It's hangin' on the head of my bed." In extreme pain, the old rancher showed his cool mettle, the strain of the fighting man's blood.

Ban quickly passed him his loaded Colt Frontier Model .45. Ward couldn't rise but was able to shoot from a reclining position and he helped keep the windows clean of the enemy. The heavy boom of the guns deafened them; they were fighting for their lives against overwhelming odds.

"Where in Gawd's name is Elsie?"

That was what was torturing Morton, the

strange disappearance of the girl he loved. But he had to protect Ward, stay alive himself; she wasn't in the house or in hearing or she'd have come. He heard yelps of pain, knew he had made some hits.

"Burn them out—burn the gringos!" shrieked a bandit lieutenant.

In the feverish nightmare gripping Ban Morton there seemed no help, no relief. The minutes dragged like hours of torture, the insane crashes of deadly guns, the shrill yelps of the killers; and, worst of all, the stifling smell of burning hay and wood, lighted and thrown through the shattered windows. Sam was coughing, now too weak to hold his gun; he lay there with his head on the pillow. The acrid smoke bit at Morton's eyes, and anguish of uncertainty as to Elsie's fate tore his heart as though someone had stuck a knife into him.

It was only a question of minutes till the last charge of hate would bring them in upon the two pressed men, to die under the Mexican's knives. Morton knew that; and as he groped in the smoky dark for cartridges with which to fill his hot gun, he realized it was upon them, for he was out of ammunition. He picked the last five from

Ward's belt and shoved them into the cylinders of his revolver, forced to hold up his fire to conserve them.

His one slim chance to escape was to run, elude Torquila's band by speed of foot, grab a horse, that he could not take for it meant deserting Ward to die at the killers' hands.

They were inside the house, too, at the door, leaping out for a moment to fire in on the two, through the smoke. When he failed to answer a shout of victory went up.

"We have them—now!"

They were rushing Morton, small, savage-faced bandits crowding through the door. He put up his gun, the acrid smoke twitching his eyes, sending smarting tears down his grimed cheeks, and fired twice into the bunch. But it was only a brief respite, their volley tore back at him, and he felt the ripping of a bullet through his left arm.

In such hellish confusion it was almost impossible for Ban Morton to distinguish sounds. Yet, as he rose up, to die in front of Sam Ward in his last stand, the brutal shouting of the Mexicans did change in character. Shots farther off boomed in the sudden strange lull.

His ears shrieked with the deafening explosions but he could hear, and his thumping heart leaped.

"Bar W—this way!" he bawled.

Yet no answering cowboy whoops came to him, and the bandits in the living room started a final charge; he emptied his Colt and cursed at them.

Shrieked orders in Spanish, the thud of many hoofs, the running beat of feet, confused Ban Morton, waiting there with Sam Ward for death.

9

The Death Trail

WITHIN earshot of the Bar W, speeding along with the ribbon of dirt road westward, Ranger Jim Hatfield heard ahead the crashing gunfire.

He had shaken off the pursuit outside of Bowie. The ardor of Ross's killers who managed to trail him for a time, cooled considerably when he shot two of them out of their saddles; the power of the golden sorrel, a fit mount for the mighty Lone Wolf, discouraged them too. After a mile they had swung back to the safety of the mob.

The widespread trouble in Maravilla, he had already diagnosed as the beginning of a greater ruin, the raiding of Texas. He intended to break the criminal Syndicate.

"Fat Phil makes one," he mused. "There bein' four left. Ross is another; Torquila third; there's two more." And one, he knew, was the chief, hidden to him but on whose trail he was riding with the keenness of a bloodhound.

"Hafta head for Torquila's hangout," he decided. Fat Phil had proved valuable, during his brief contact with the Ranger; there was a puzzle about Torquila that amused Fat Phil, and that, Hatfield sensed, might be the answer to the problem he must solve.

The wind blew in his rugged, set face as he whirled off from the river, and saw the dark shapes of the Bar W buildings. The glow of a small fire on the north side of the house framed for him the crowding figures of Mexicans, shaggy mustangs near at hand, who were pouring lead into Ward's room.

Their savage yells, and the drift of smoke to his flared nostrils, told him what was happening. And as he threw up both Colts to attack, he hoped he was not too late. He needed Ward and he wanted to save the stalwart old rancher from death. Such a man as Ward deserved help.

He touched the great sorrel, galloping in with flashing piston legs, with a spur; Goldy whirled and they came in from the northwest, the terrific Colts of the Ranger blasting into the bunched bandidos. The efficiency of his fire as he poured bullets into the nucleus of the attackers, picked with his unerring accuracy and coolness in battle, quickly threw confusion into their ranks.

A shrill screeching rose. "The Ranger! The Ranger!" For some of these men had tried to take him, up there at the lumber camp.

As he hit the end of his run, the sorrel spun on a dime, zigzagging back through the wild slugs the bandits returned. But already they were mounting and riding off hell-for-leather southward into the darkness.

Smashing them, he turned and came back, ever closer to the house, one wall of which was afire. He saw the bunch that had been inside, running and leaping off the porch, hitting their saddles in a panic of retreat.

With the horde on its way, sending bullets back at him, he pushed to the north side where the bandits had dragged an old wagon into which they had thrown several bales of dry hay; this burned fiercely, flames licking at the wooden house, smoke pouring through the windows, sucked by the indraft. The Ranger hit the dirt and grabbed the wagon pole. He dragged the cart off and with his poncho, unfurled from Goldy's saddle, he beat out the burning boards.

From the north, in the distance, he heard shrill cowboy whoops. The Ranger vaulted the side rail of the long porch and hurried into the house.

"Ward! Morton!" he shouted.

There was no reply for a moment, he stood there, faint light rays on his rugged features, powerful figure in a listening attitude, smoke acrid in his flared nostrils. He started toward Ward's room, muscles rippling with the flowing grace of a panther. Cold fury was upon him, for he thought Ward and Morton must have died.

"Now where the hell's that night guard?" he muttered.

His boot skidded under him; he looked down, saw a dark pool of blood. "Ward," he called again, at the splintered door.

"Hey. Who's that?" Morton's voice, husky with fresh hope, answered him.

"It's Jim, Ban. The Mexes've gone. Light up. Where's all yore waddies?"

Cursing in relief, Morton struck a match, found the candle and lit it. His face was grimed with sweat and powder smoke. Anxiously he looked at Ward, and the tall Ranger, spurs jingling, crossed and bent over the old rancher.

"Still kickin'," Hatfield drawled. "He's fainted."

Ban pumped his hand. "Yuh saved us! We were at the last gasp, Jim. I knowed they were crazy when they said yuh was a spy."

"Hafta see 'bout that," Hatfield told him. "What happened to yore guards?"

"Dunno. And—Elsie's gone." Rapidly, the distressed Morton described the events of the night, the attempt to shoot him through his window, the strange disappearance of Elsie, the terrible fight with the bandits.

Hatfield swung on his spurs and Ban limped out after him; paused to light the living-room lamp. Hatfield stopped under Morton's window, stooped to pick up a black circle lying there. Ban held a match for the Ranger, and saw it was a peaked sombrero.

"One of them Mexes tried to drygulch me!" he cried.

Hatfield grunted. He carried the peaked hat, trimmed with silver horseshoes, into the house, looked it over carefully in the lamplight. There was blood on the sweatband, under the bullet hole.

"Yuh clipped him, Ban," Hatfield drawled.

Between his long fingers he picked out several strands of brownish hair stuck to the blood.

From Ban's account, Torquila was wounded; that was a help, thought the officer. The bronc buster controlled himself by a great effort; an overpowering dread clutched at Ban's vitals and Hatfield understood how much he loved Elsie.

"Get some whiskey and we'll see to Ward," ordered Hatfield. They went and poured a drink between Sam's clenched teeth.

"Elsie—Elsie honey," the old rancher moaned as consciousness returned. "They took her out with no trouble," the Ranger mused. "Must've been somebody she knowed or she'd've called out and Morton would've heard, Ward too."

It only clinched what he had already deduced.

The yells of approaching cowboys sounded closer. Ward looked up at them. "It's okay, Boss," Morton told him, taking a cloth to wipe sweat from the big man's tortured face. "Jim's here and he beat 'em off."

Ward stared at the tall fellow. "Say—they claimed yuh was a spy! Shorty and all—"

"That's a lie," cried Ban. "He's shore proved he's with us, Boss."

"Well, reckon yuh're right, Ban," Ward whispered.

Heavy steps banged on the porch, more shouts. "That's the men come back," growled Morton. Teeth gritted, he turned and went out. Hatfield slouched in the doorway, watching.

A bunch of waddies, headed by Foreman Nevada Lewis, crowded inside.

"Yuh was ordered not to leave the yard," Morton snapped. "While yuh was chasin' through the night, Torquila's gang hit us, near kilt the Boss and kidnapped Miss Elsie. What's the idee?" Ban Morton was furious.

"Say, who's askin' all them questions?" Nevada Lewis snarled. "I'm s'posed to be foreman here. I ordered the men out for a damn good reason. A bunch of rustlers started runnin' off that whole herd of cows we was movin' east, and we hadda stop 'em."

Morton's gaze met the saturnine eyes of Lewis, bristling up to him. "Call me a liar," howled Lewis threateningly, "and I'll air yore hide, yuh danged, sneakin' dude." The foreman went for his gun, rage possessing him.

It was Hatfield's cold voice from the doorway that stopped him: "Put up yore hawgleg, Foreman!"

Nevada started, saw him as he turned his eyes; he dared not disobey that icy command. His gun slid back and the bunched punchers stared at the tall Lone Wolf.

"Why, it's that big hombre," Shorty bawled, "the man who snatched Scarface from us. It's the spy!"

"Hold it, yuh fools," bellowed Morton.

They held it; not so much at Ban's warning as at the Ranger's look when he came out to face them. His Colts hung ready; but it was the spell of the man that kept them from trying to draw.

Before him, Hatfield thought, stood a decent bunch—most. Shorty Davis, Long John Betts, "Arizonny," all honest perspiring faces. He came to a halt half a dozen feet from Nevada Lewis, whose Stetson was pulled down to his hard eyes.

"There is a spy in the room," Hatfield said silkily. "Only it ain't me. Nevada, take off yore hat."

"Why?" snarled Lewis. His bony hands hung close to his six-guns.

"Yuh want to know and I'll tell yuh. Yuh're the spy who's been passin' inside information to Ross. But tonight yuh overstepped yoreself." He addressed the bunch, "Any of yuh men see Lewis, after he ordered yuh all out, bunkhouse and night guard?"

Come to think of it, nobody had, not until the foreman rode to meet them as they hurried home at sight of the fire.

"What yuh drivin' at?" demanded Lewis.

"Yuh led the men off, Lewis, started 'em and sneaked back, called out Elsie Ward and handed her over to the kidnapers.

Borrowed a hat from a Mex, tried to kill Morton. Take off yore Stetson."

"Yuh lie! Go to hell!"

Shorty suddenly swept the foreman's hat off. The saturnine hombre's hair was matted with dried blood over a swelling large as a goose egg, which he had tried to hide by keeping his Stetson down.

"That's where Morton creased yuh, Lewis. I'll give you a chance pervidin' yuh tell me who—"

Nevada's eyes flamed hate. He leaped behind Shorty, gun flashing out. The Colt exploded but the boom seemed double and the foreman's slug cracked the floor between the Ranger's wide boots. Nevada, right back of Shorty, threw up his head in a convulsive, snapping movement, then folded up on the mat.

"Right between the eyes," gasped Shorty, staring down at the dead. "Say, yuh cut it mighty close, mister. I got a haircut from yore bullet. Fust time I ever been glad I ain't no taller."

A wisp of smoke rose from the Ranger's Colt barrel as it slid back into its place. Hatfield turned and strode to Ward's room,

Morton after him, the punchers bunching in the doorway.

"I'm ridin'," Hatfield told the rancher. "Whatever yuh do, don't let yore followers attack the lumbermen till yuh hear from me. It's cut-and-dried to wipe yuh out; so do as I order and wait!"

"Where yuh headin', Jim?" Ban Morton asked.

"Hope to fetch back Elsie, for one thing."

"Lemme go too," begged Morton.

"Me, too," Shorty cried, and they all wanted to go.

"Someone's got to stick here and guard Ward," Hatfield told them. "Me'n Ban can do it." To Ward he said softly, "Now take it easy. We'll bring her back."

Outside, he drew Shorty aside. "Who told yuh I was the man snatched Scarface?"

Shorty's honest face was puzzled; he scratched his sandy head. "Why, hell—come to think, Marshal Alf Betts of Bowie slips up to me and says, 'Is it true that big jigger's the man saved Scarface? See if yuh can say.' That made me think I reckernized yore voice."

"So yuh went off half-cocked," growled Morton.

Thud of hoofs from the north sent them outside; dark shapes of burly riders swept down, and, pausing outside the light circle, a rough voice hailed, "Who's that? Vasco—Lewis?"

"The lumbermen!" bawled Shorty, and his six-gun opened fire on the invaders.

A blast of guns flared back in reply. "Take cover," Hatfield yelled. Two Bar W men had been hit; one seriously. Slugs were tearing into the wood, through the night air on the soft wind.

Down behind the rail, the steps, the cowboys poured lead at the enemy. But the 'jacks did not stand; whirling, they rode full-tilt back.

"Come to see how Lewis and Torquila made out," muttered the Ranger. He knew there were a couple of hundred gunmen a few miles above; the half hundred could hold the ranch but could not defeat Ross's ferocious crew in the open. They were worn out from their long ride, the wild goose chase Lewis had sent them on.

"Let's ride, Ban," Hatfield ordered.

They headed south a few minutes later,

Morton on Black Rascal, the Ranger on the golden sorrel. The two horses traveled at a pace-eating clip, under a silver moon. They crossed the Maravilla, its bed nearly dry.

"Don't yuh figger mebbe they'd take her up into the hills?" inquired Ban.

The officer glanced sideward at his young companion; Morton's mouth was a firm line.

"Callate they'll head straight for Torquila's with him wounded—and other reasons. Pick up their trail pretty quick and check it."

The land gently sloped up from the valley. Black shapes of tortured mesquite, shadows of trees, flickering of countless fireflies, were about them; in their ears the steady clip-clop of the hoofs, and the piping of frogs and night creatures. They topped the divide in the darkness, and pushed down through the wild fastnesses of the Big Bend country.

Dawn found them sitting their horses on the north bank of the Rio Grande, wide flowing between shifting, sandy shores.

The Ranger was deep in thought. The stunning blows dealt Maravilla; the expert riposte of the arch-fiend he sought, at each move he made; the savage, efficiency spy system of the enemy, told him he must hurry, and strike unerringly at the heart of the horror if he would win. He must not fail; Texas depended on him, and death snapped at his heels.

"Hafta see Torquila," he mused, "'sides tryin' to rescue Elsie. Marshal Betts looks harmless, but he set Shorty after me. They acted so quick yesterday, must've bin a right smart hombre present; mebbe the one I'm after."

Cactus grew thick here in the flats, of every variety from tiny hairy balls to giants thirty feet high, branching out in eerie pipe-shapes; thick barrel cactus; on the mesquite ridges, green and yellow with star-white blooms, flourished coarse chino and grama grasses. Here were the yucca and prickly pear, catclaw and bayonet, aromatic creosote with oily yellow blossoms; the low, stiff greasewood favored the alkaline soil; feathery huisache trees rustled in the morning breeze. The rippling wash of the river was a grateful sound and men and animals drank.

Red streamers rose in the eastern sky as they crossed the Rio to pick up the south trail. Alert road-runners darted from the path of the big horses, one golden, the other ebony; ladinos, tough, brush-ranging wild cows, galloped off, making a "pop" that could be heard half a mile away when they plunged into the dense tangled undergrowth.

"More blood," said Hatfield, pointing to a dark spot on the spiny, flat green leaf of a prickly pear. "Guess yuh wounded him bad, Ban."

The bronc buster was a good tracker but he was amazed at the skill of the Ranger. It was Hatfield who had certified that the bandido had brought Elsie this far. One tiny bit of white thread on a mesquite thorn had made them certain. Vasco Torquila's wound had been bleeding, kept open by the jogging of the mustang he was carried upon. A broken stick, a fresh hoof mark, drew them unerringly on.

The sun rose higher over the wilderness, and the sky became a fiery, brass oven, beating down on the Mexican land. Before them was Old Mexico.

"And Avalo," thought Hatfield.

The sun broiled them, the two grim-faced riders who pulled up their mounts and stared down at the little Mexican town.

"That's it," said Hatfield.

Adobe huts straggled in two ragged lines, along what was supposedly a road. Clothing hung in the sun; myriad naked brown children played in the shade of walls. An army of mongrel dogs, pigs, chickens and other domestic creatures roamed in and out of dooryards and houses, picking up scraps.

"Wonder what the bunch of hombres're up to?" Morton rasped, throat dry from the rising dust.

He indicated a circle of Mexicans crowded about a shallow bowl under some old trees in the plaza. Cheering came to their ears.

"Cockfightin', I reckon," Hatfield replied. "They do nothin' else down here for amusement."

"Let's go," Morton said impatiently.

"Hold it. We'll see who that is comin' in."

From the southeast a party of armed men rode into Avalo at a fast clip. The sun glinted on rifles and accoutrements. They swept up behind the buildings and, with loud shouts, surrounded the Mexicans absorbed in the spurred fighting cocks. Cries of fright rose.

"Rurales!" The armed riders pointed guns at a dozen young peons, forced them to mount spare animals.

"Torquila's bandits!" muttered Ban, hand dropping to his six-gun.

"Don't shoot."

They watched the armed band, under a lean, mustached lieutenant, turn back southeast with their captives, lost in clouds of dust. The Ranger led the way into Avalo; dogs barked at them, and sad-faced, weeping women peeked from the broken windows. The cock-fight had broken up, those who had escaped arrest hunting cover. Hatfield stopped at a dilapidated shack from which sounded loud wails.

"Senora," he called.

A fat Mexican woman, tears streaming down her cheeks, came to the door, poked fearfully out. Hatfield spoke to her in liquid, idiomatic Spanish.

"What's wrong?"

"Senor, Senor," she sobbed, "they took my son; he's only seventeen. To jail, they say. A new law against cock-fighting. What's wrong with such a sport?"

"You heard of Juan Gonzales?"

"Si, si—he was arrested so, for nothing, by the Virgin! His mother's died of a broken heart, for no word has ever come from him."

"You know Vasco Torquila?"

Her lips shut, fears streaked through her black eyes. These people lived in deadly fear of the bandit chieftain.

"I'll send yore son back to you," Hatfield promised.

She raised a brown hand, waved southeast. "That way. Five miles. A walled hacienda, like a whole town."

Hatfield tossed her a quarter, which she gratefully caught. With Morton, he saw a horse that looked fast, and they bought it, saddle and all, and hurried on.

Dusk had not yet fallen when they sighted a fortified village. Around a collection of huts, in the center of which stood a square white-washed hacienda, was a high paling topped by thorns. The gates were open, guarded by armed bandidos. A corral held hundreds of hairy Mexican ponies; there were shacks and tents. In the center was a bunch of peons, huddled together; women were about and the Ranger estimated that Torquila's army in there must number around six hundred riders.

"Callata that's where they're holdin' Elsie. Meanwhile we'll get some sleep."

Ban Morton's face was grim with despair. How could they hope to strike such a place, swarming with murderous bandits?

10

Jaws of Death

HATFIELD touched Morton's hand to wake him from the troubled doze into which the young man had fallen.

It was entirely dark, save for the streak of moonlight penetrating the dense mesquite on the ridge. The tramp of hundreds of horses, orders in Spanish, sounded from the trail a few hundred yards south. A column of mounted bandidos, Hatfield estimated near five hundred of them, herding a couple of hundred unfortunate captives, passed close by the Ranger's hiding-place in the bush. They turned northwest.

Once they were out of earshot, Hatfield checked his Colts, mounted Goldy; Morton followed on Black Rascal. On the side opposite the gates, now barred for the night, Hatfield stopped. They sat their horses in the shadows of the high palings.

"Stay here and be ready with the spare horse; keep 'em quiet," Hatfield whispered to Ban. "I'm goin' in."

Quickly he noosed his lariat to the saddle horn; let it drop inside the enclosure. The trained sorrel stood like a statue at command, and the Ranger stood up on the saddle, grasped the top of the thorny paling. The clearing was lit by a few lanterns around the hacienda, in which showed lamps. A hundred renegades slept in the shelters or on the ground, while a few stood guard over at the gates.

Thorns tore at him as he vaulted over, knees giving when he landed, light as a leaping panther. He paused in the fence shadow a moment; the sound of a guitar strumming in the house, the high, soft voice of a young woman singing, reached his keen ears.

From patch to patch of scraggly bush he flitted. He noted the man leaning on his rifle at the front of the hacienda.

Near the back was a long window, half open and he slipped into the house.

He went swiftly, silently, toward a light shaft that half lit a long hallway to the front. The lamplight came from a room, furnished in rich Spanish style. On a wide, silken couch lay Vasco Torquila, the giant bandit chief. The dark, Indian face was smudged by black goatee and beard; and the flabbiness of his whole countenance gave the Ranger a start of surprise.

"Mebbe it's the wound," he mused. "Seemed to me he was a lot tougher when I glimpsed him in the hills."

A pretty Mexican senorita softly strummed the guitar, singing to soothe the injured man. Blood-soaked bandages on his right side showed where he had been hit. The music paused, as Torquila swore in fluent Spanish.

"I'll miss it, *si*," he told the woman regretfully. "And what a sight it will be! Four hundred gringos dying in one instant. *Cara mia*, the chief's a devil but a genius too. We have as good as won, and here I die, unable to ride!" He cursed feverishly.

She stroked his brown forehead. "Never mind; you have your Rosa. Perhaps they'll change the day."

"If so, Scarface will tell my lieutenant Arturo. *Si*, nothing can stop us now; the Syndicate has won. We are wealthy beyond all dreams, Rosa. We bleed Texas to death."

"And as for the pretty American Senorita?"

"She's for the chief." Torquila laughed through clenched white teeth. "It will be a good joke, Rosa. He rescues her himself, and so wins the Bar W."

Torquila closed his eyes, waved his hand; the guitar strummed again.

Jim Hatfield, hands swinging easily at his narrow hips, stepped into the room and looked at the giant bandit. The girl gave a gasp of alarm, small hand discording the strings. Torquila's black eyes snapped open, his bearded chin sagged at sight of the tall American.

"*Madre de Dios!*" gasped Torquila.

A huge brown hand started for the belts holding his pearl-handled six-shooters, hanging from the bedpost close to his head; but it paused, suspended in midair, as he stared into the steady muzzle of the Ranger's .45.

"No senor, don't shoot!" begged Rosa.

Hatfield's eyes were on Torquila, back to a blank wall so they could not steal up from behind. He did not miss his chance.

"Senorita," he drawled, "get the young lady brought here today, pronto. If you give the alarm I'll kill Torquila."

She leaped up, the guitar spilling to the floor with a string-humming bang. "No," Torquila growled. "You fool, Rosa, the Chief will kill us!"

But Rosa was hurrying out, past the tall American. "I bring her," she gasped. The ominous figure of the fighting gringo awed her yet her frightened eyes were tinged with admiration, too.

"You die for this," snarled Torquila.

Steps in the hall, and Elsie Ward's voice came to him. "Rosa, where are you taking me? Please let me go home."

"Your sweetheart's here to save you."

Hatfield glided for the door. As he turned Torquila's big hand flashed to his guns, his teeth gritting in rage; he snatched a pearl-handled Colt and fired a shot that passed Hatfield and thudded into the corridor wall a few inches from Elsie. The next one might hit her. Forced to shoot, the Ranger could take no chances; the report of his gun echoed Torquila's, the Mexican bandit was taking careful aim to kill his opponent.

As though painted there by a magic, invisible hand, a round, bluish hole appeared between the murderous raider's black eyes. Torquila flopped back on the pillows, the weight of the gun in his hand pulling his arm down to the floor.

Rosa screamed and ran over to the dead.

"That's two," Hatfield muttered. "Three left: Ross, Number Four, and— the Chief!"

The shooting would bring the guards running, rouse the whole camp. Hatfield grasped Elsie's wrist.

"Ban's outside," he said quickly. Her face was drawn, pale; she recognized him and ran with him, to the back, out the open window. The stamp of feet, yells up front, sounded as rapidly they crossed to the spot where the rope dangled.

"Morton!" Hatfield softly hailed.

Ban peeked over the fence. "Elsie—yuh okay?"

"Yes, Ban, they didn't hurt me much, seemed to be saving me—"

Hatfield swept her up in his powerful arms, soft body a feather in his grip. For a moment he held her and in that moment envied Ban Morton. Women were not for a Ranger, save as passing fancies; he could not ask a woman to share such a dangerous life.

Morton was standing up on Black Rascal. He caught Elsie's shoulders and Hatfield boosted her over the thorny top so Morton could hold her clear.

"Get goin'," ordered Hatfield. "Ride for home and stay there with yore guards, till I come. Don't let the ranchers attack the lumber camp. *Adios*."

"But yuh—what yuh mean to do?" demanded Ban.

The Ranger looked over his shoulder. Dark figures were leaping up from sleep; others running from the house. "Callate I'll stick here a while. Ride, Morton."

He turned, crouched in the fence shadow, as a dozen renegades in the lead, whirled toward him. His Colts flashed death into them, ripping their front, throwing confusion into them by accurate firing. Answering slugs of hate plugged into the palings; one nipped his arm, and blood was warm from his cut thigh and flesh; bullets spurted dust around him.

Giving Morton a minute to get started, and smashing the bandits' first charge,

Hatfield swung, seized the lariat tied to Goldy's saddle horn. He drew himself to the top and, torn at by the thorns, dropped into the saddle.

Yells raged in the stockade. "After them!" a Mexican voice shrieked.

Leaping on their bucking, shaggy mustangs, the bandits swept pell-mell out of the gates, rounded the corner to run into the blasting gunfire of the Ranger. When they jerked their reins, sliding to a stop, dust billowing under the lashing hoofs, to take steady aim at the hombre who had killed their chief, Hatfield pivoted the golden sorrel and headed west, zigzagging in the chaparral.

The raging mob trailed him, whooping with fury. He made another brief stand, and, drawing them off westward by a clever, calculated chase, kept them fully occupied while Ban Morton and Elsie Ward were riding north for the Rio and Maravilla.

The semi-desert, high mesquite patches casting ebony shadows in the mellow moonlight, was covered by a thick, tangled growth that allowed dodging and hiding; innumerable cattle trails crossed and crisscrossed; with the aromatic odor of the plants in his nostrils, the Ranger led the renegades far into the wilds of the chaparral before he gave Goldy his rein along a winding but well-marked trail northwest. The screeches of his baffled pursuers grew dim as he drew away; now and then he heard the distant pop of a gun as a Mexican fired at a shadow.

He dared not pause; Friday was but two days off and it would take him the best part of one to ride back to the Maravilla country. From what he had overheard and observed at Torquila's hacienda, he knew that a diabolical trap was laid, to murder wholesale the ranchers; and, added to Ross's three hundred killers must be the five hundred bandit warriors heading north on the very trail he was following.

"Hafta split 'em," he muttered, looking back over his shoulder at the sweep of the Mexican wilds.

Though obviously much used, beaten by thousands of hoofs in both directions, this track was rougher than the direct corridor from Torquila's to the Bar W. Control of Ward's spread would permit the raiders on Texas a quicker, easier route on which to run up their forced labor. This way sharp, serrated ridges, like the teeth of a giant's comb, smashed the terrain, dead volcanic country traversed by dry arroyos that would present a troublesome problem to a large outfit. There were rocky passes, so narrow at times that only one horseman could proceed.

Day found him still in the fastnesses of Coahuila. The new light spread over the wilderness. Driving on with the unfailing, terrific power of his body and mind, the Ranger looked back from a rocky mesquite ridge, saw in the south distance blue hills a hundred miles off, the bushed badlands between; and beyond, across the dip in which the Rio Grande ran, the rising soil of Texas, the soil he loved, grown over with heavy chaparral.

The wooded mountains forming the Maravilla watershed were sharply outlined against the vast blue-gray dome of the sky, the western slopes still black with shadow. The steady clop of the sorrel's hoofs on the stony trail never faltered. Birds were up with the sun, insects starting to fly. "Figger this here chief won't leave anything to luck!" he mused, obsessed by the vital necessity of reaching Maravilla in time.

Ahead were half a thousand bandits with their prisoners. As the blood-red sun streamed up on his right he took care that all metal was covered so no reflection might telegraph a warning to the Mexicans—such a flash would be visible for miles. Eyes moving first from the immediate trail sign to the distant sky, he saw a springy cactus plant slowly coming back into position, very slowly, and from such traces he could tell how far up the big band, traveling more slowly than he, might be.

On Hatfield alone rested the hopes of Maravilla, of Texas; he must get through, and swiftly.

Reaching the Rio, in a marshy area he found fresh indentations left by horses and mules, imprints gradually filling with water. He started the sorrel into the warm sandy-bedded river, and, on the Texas shore, scanned the sky ahead. He was rewarded by several scintillating flashes, like runaway sunbeams, that he knew were caused by the rays striking on metal accoutrements. Pushing on, he observed a flock of crows winging swiftly to the west.

Their caws were faint on the warming breeze; but the birds did not fly far, but lighted in a clump of huisache trees.

"Camped," he grunted aloud.

He began to circle, with the careful approach of an Indian stalking prey. An hour later, finding a way through threading cattle trails in the chaparral, he paused on a mesquite ridge to scan the Mexican camp, now to the south as he stood.

They were resting for the day, marching at night; armed renegades in high-peaked hats, their sentinels slouched on their shaggy mustangs, chin on breast, Winchester lying across the saddle horn. In the center the main band slept on their guns, ringing the peon captives; the big herd of horses and mules, with a hundred head of rustled beef cattle from the Circle 5 raid, guarded by skilled vaqueros.

The Lone Wolf shoved north on the beaten track left by former parties of Torquila's raiders driving stolen stock and peons to the Southwest Company's mountain camps; the road was ever up, slow going. Foam flecked the giant sorrel's handsome hide, scratched by thorns; the rider was filmed with alkali dust, and dried blood stained his ripped clothing.

Through the fiery day heat they rode; below, through a leafy vista, Hatfield looked over his shoulder at the vast country of the Big Bend, sheening with wild loveliness in the white-hot sun.

It had been dark again for hours when they reached the stands of live-oak and pine forming the watershed of the Maravilla. The man and rider snatched a brief rest, a drink and a quick meal, off the trail; again, resilient as tempered steel, the Ranger rode on.

He knew there were alert sentries around Valentine Ross's quarters. He cut northeast, passing the spot where he had been chased on his first visit into the hills, and struck the Maravilla below the shacks of the Lumber Company.

Timber had been cut off a local area on both sides of the river; he proceeded cautiously, and, seeing through the trees the ruby-red glow of a cigarette, the night wind soughing in his ears, he dismounted and crept from tree stump to tree stump. In the moonlight piercing through the open space he noted the black bulk of the heavy dam that diverted the Maravilla.

The dam was constructed of great tree trunks fastened crosswise by chains in the stream; its upper face filled in by a twelve-foot breast of broken rock and clay. The flowing water hit this obstruction and swirled north into the canal cut by the lumbermen, thence through the dry arroyo. Through this the lumbermen could float timber miles northeast to the plains where teams could pick it up and carry it to the railroad without hauling across the mountains.

He saw, down below, a few hundred yards from the dam, the licking flames of a bonfire. A silent shadow in the forest, the Ranger wished to finish his survey before dawn; he must uncover the enemy's plans.

Part he already knew: the five hundred Mexican renegades would be on hand to mop up the ranchers. But there was more; a stunning blow that would leave nothing to chance in battle. Four hundred determined cowmen, fighting for their homeland, might defeat eight hundred hired assassins.

It was easy for the expert Ranger to cross the dry bed of the Maravilla below the dam.

From a fringe of bushes and trees he looked out upon a large space from which higher growth had been hastily removed. It was as though a great playfield had here been sliced out of the wilderness.

Toward the stream bed, on outcropping bedrock, that bonfire burned, red tongues licking up into the sky, smoke drifting off on the west wind. Crouched on the dried bank, eyes on a level with the fire, the Ranger saw the burly figures of lumberjacks, in corduroy and helmet, as they moved back and forth against the light.

The breeze brought him a whiff of that smoke. The odor was strange, as he sniffed it.

"Glycerine," he mused, "and acid—wood—"

Bit by bit, suspicion turning to certainty in his swift brain, he began to work down, keeping in the river bed, the banks hiding him as he moved. The henchmen of Valentine Ross were alert, and heavily armed; he heard the clang of metal on stones, sounds he recognized as picks and shovels digging deep in the earth. A round stone, disturbed by his weight on the shifty sands, rolled and struck another with a sharp clack.

"What's that?" a snarling voice demanded.

Hatfield froze, a shadow back of the shadow of a great boulder anchored in the river bed. That was Ross's voice, and close at hand. A pistol roared, the flame stabbing straight at his hiding place; the slug spat into the sand, whipped grains into his face, but he did not move the fraction of an inch.

"Jest an animal, Boss," remarked a 'jack.

"Guess so," growled Ross.

The bunch moved off, and Hatfield kept on. Danger was close; he was some distance from Goldy, and, afoot, might be surrounded and taken once they guessed his presence, or glimpsed his stealthy figure.

He left the ditch outside the fire circle and came up toward the clear area from the east. Brilliant moonlight illuminated the wide flat space where the 'jacks were finishing up their task. Men moved rapidly to and fro, shoveling dirt and rocks, leveling off, others walked back and forth from the fire, near which stood Valentine Ross and his bodyguard, throwing empty boxes on the blaze.

That acrid fire smoke drifted full into his nose and eyes.

"Dynamite!" he muttered.

That innocent looking space of cleared land was mined, mined by a huge quantity of dynamite that had come packed in the boxes. Some of the impregnating material had oozed through the wrappings to the wood, giving the smoke its distinctive smell.

The evil plan of the Syndicate was now his!

11

Wholesale Death

COLD fury gripped Jim Hatfield. Ross meant to lead the ranchers onto that prepared field by a clever draw. The great mine would explode, killing and maiming the main bunch of the cowmen, while the Mexican army and 'jacks wiped up the shattered remnants.

Swarming about him were enemies, he heard their calked, heavy boots thudding the dirt, curses as sweating men finished up the death trap that was to destroy all opposition in Maravilla, give control to the Chief and his criminal Syndicate so that they might raid Texas of her natural wealth.

There was no cover so that he could work in closer; the moonlight was bright in the open, and a threat of grayness was coming into the sky behind him. Hatfield crept back to the dip of the river bed, and, crossing it, waited in the thicker bush.

A messenger came whirling up the slopes from the east. "Ross! Ross!" Hatfield could hear him shouting.

The dawn was at hand and details began to stand out in the dew-damp air. The Ranger could see the heaving, lathered horse the messenger had ridden up. Valentine Ross snatched a paper from the rider, put his pasty, evil face close to it so he might read it in the dimness.

"Scarface!" bawled Ross, his voice echoing though the forest aisles to the officer's hearing. "Quick! Take the fastest horse we have and ride south!"

South. The Mexicans lay that way, five hundred guerrilla fighters; they might prove an overwhelming force if brought up at the right moment, and he knew he must hold them up if that were possible.

The Ranger faded away, and picked up Goldy, waiting in the bush clump as his master had left him. With that dynamite trap set, Hatfield would not pause in his vital, dangerous work until its awful menace was removed. A ghost rider, he watched and glimpsed Scarface, on a swift gray mustang, crossing the dry Maravilla bed, heading on the trail to Mexico.

Half an hour later, as Scarface rounded the turn on the downgrade south, Jim Hatfield pushed Goldy out onto the trail, the sorrel sliding down the rocky side.

"Scarface!" the Ranger said sharply.

The lean hombre jerked on his rein, the gray dancing sideward to a stop. The messenger's twisted face drew up in terror, and a great gasp heaved his lungs.

"Jim!" he quavered. His eyes were like saucers and he sagged in his saddle. Sheer fright actuated him, he thought he was to die and he dug a spur into the gray's ribs, and whirled the horse against Goldy, who snorted and lashed out with an angry hoof. Scarface had grabbed for his gun, and a shrill squeak issued from his constricted throat.

Hatfield grabbed the gray's bit as the mustang jumped from Goldy's kick; a touch of his knees and the sorrel crushed in. The Ranger yanked back the gray's head, slewing Scarface around so he couldn't shoot. As Scarface fought to come back into firing position, Hatfield hit him across the forearm with his gun barrel.

A sharp crack sounded. With a yelp of anguish, Scarface dropped his pistol from his helpless, numbing hand, and the tall jigger with a cold surety of movement that appalled Scarface, grabbed his prisoner's shoulder, leaped down to the trail, yanking the messenger to earth.

He shook Scarface violently.

"Pass over that note," he snarled viciously.

Utterly cowed, whimpering with the pain of his cracked arm, Scarface's left hand shook as he extracted a paper from inside his shirt and passed it over. "Stand quiet or I'll drill yuh," Hatfield snapped.

Scarface was half sobbing; he held his injured wrist tightly with his left hand. The Ranger glanced at the paper; there was writing on both sides, one in a bold hand that said:

Ross. Make it Thursday morn instead of Friday.

And a hasty scrawl on the other where Ross had dashed it off in pencil, using the same sheet:

Torquila: rush up your men at once.

"Thursday—that's today," growled the Ranger. He stared into the cringing, twisting face of the lanky hombre. "Yuh ain't deliverin' this," he told Scarface. "I know plenty, and there's some things yuh're goin' to tell me; don't try to lie." His voice was an icy stab that seemed to penetrate the miserable captive's heart, for he shivered.

"Who's chief of this dirty bus'ness?"

"Vasco Torquila," Scarface replied instantly.

Hatfield's hand shot out, grasped him by the scrawny throat; the long, viselike fingers tightened and blood purpled Scarface's cheeks, his eyes bulged from his head.

"Yuh lie," snarled the Ranger.

Scarface was trying to shake his head; Hatfield relaxed his grip a bit, so he could talk: "So help me, that's the truth!" choked Scarface. "Don't kill me, Jim! Torquila gives Ross orders sometimes."

"Not this time. Ross is givin' the orders to Torquila, ain't he? And who sent this note up to Ross, givin' *him* orders?"

"I dunno. There's a guy named Fat Phil in Bowie but yuh kilt him yoreself, Ranger."

"This note come from Bowie?"

"I figger so. The only bosses I know are Phil, Ross and Torquila; they got a political connection but I couldn't say who he is." Scarface's earnestness convinced the Ranger; like most of the rank and file, Scarface was unaware of the identity of the savage chief the Ranger sought.

He pumped Scarface dry, but obtained little more information than he already had ferreted out for himself. The sun was rosy in the blue sky dome as he finished his catechism of the prisoner.

A few miles south the Mexicans were camped, awaiting their orders from Ross. And, very dim, from the northeast sounded a number of faint yet distinctly staccato cracks.

"Gunfire, and heavy," growled the Ranger.

His clawed hand started again for Scarface's throat, his eyes searched the lanky hombre's soul. "That's—that's the ranchers attackin'," gasped Scarface, shrinking from that clutch of steel that shut off his wind and took all the strength out of his muscles.

Hatfield's eyes darkened. They had disobeyed his orders, and were rushing up to stunning, wholesale slaughter. They were rushing into the dynamite trap laid by Valentine Ross.

He snatched the lariat from the gray's saddle, and swiftly bound Scarface, left him gagged and tied to a tree back out of sight of the trail. Forking Goldy, Hatfield rode full-speed back toward the dynamite mine.

Minute after minute passed, minutes of time precious, that meant the life or death of Maravilla, of Texas. The golden sorrel's legs flew at full speed, as the Lone Wolf urged him on, crooning to him a wild song of battle. The great horse dug in his hoofs as he fought on uphill, swinging into the forest south of the Maravilla.

"Got to make it," Hatfield growled, eyes fixed ahead through the leafy vistas. Vines and bushes forced them to swing, zigzag this way and that to get through. The seconds seemed to speed, as the vital time passed.

When he came up on the south side of the Maravilla, below the dam, he could see through the trees a hundred and fifty of the lumbermen, in their brown corduroy and flannel shirts, and helmet caps, down behind the clay banks of the canal. They were heavily armed, with Winchester rifles and spare pistols, boxes of ammunition open and waiting. Eagerly they scanned the eastern bush for the approach of their enemies, the ranchers running full-speed into certain death.

Four hundred yards below, close to the dry river, were Valentine Ross and half a dozen burly 'jacks, his personal bodyguard. The pasty-faced, green-eyed killer, gulping in fury, watched the east, too, as he squatted among a nest of rocks.

To the north, fifty yards off, the bonfire was dying away, most of the wooden boxes consumed, smoke drifting off on the gentle, sweet west wind, And below, not far from Ross, began the open area purposely cleared, where the great dynamite mine was planted.

The gunfire to the east was terrific, mingling with it in the short lulls the yells of furious cowmen. The defiant shout of Ross's second gang arose, leading on the ranchers, as Hatfield had guessed they would.

Jim Hatfield quickly took in the situation. There was no time to warn the ranchers, stop them; so he headed Goldy down the south bank into the river bed.

Digging in his spurs, rising up from the saddle, Hatfield was abreast of Valentine Ross as the great sorrel headed up the north bank.

Down through the bush, Hatfield glimpsed the attacking citizens of Maravilla. Riding in full battle array, the ranchers were well-armed; in the van he recognized young Ban Morton's slim figure on Black Rascal. There were other leaders, the Bar W waddies, among them Shorty and Arizonny, and men from the Circle 5, fighting hombres drawn from every outfit within two hundred miles of Bowie. Four hundred splendid young men, the heart of Maravilla, were riding up to drive out the murderers who sought to ruin their home range.

One hundred and fifty mounted lumbermen were slowly retreating before the spirited onslaught of the cowmen. The 'jacks fought a smart, drawing action, feigning to stand, then running on back up the slopes toward the dynamite mine. Men and animals were being hit on both sides, though the rough ground, the motion of jolting beasts made close aim difficult.

Valentine Ross squatted in his pile of

rocks, and in his left hand he held a matchbox. In his right Hatfield could see, in the bright yellow sunlight, the white match stick with red-and-blue tip, that the boss had ready to strike. Hatfield's eyes were on a level with the ground, as he came up from the river bed; through the heavy fringe along the Maravilla he glimpsed Ross's pasty face, green eyes shining with a tigerish glow, as Ross looked around.

"Huntin' for them Mexes," Hatfield muttered. "He's at the fuse end."

The bunch of 'jacks leading the ranchers to death was at the east edge of the mined area. Hot curses and hotter gunfire ripped the cowmen, blinded by the fury of the fight and their long pent-up hatred for the destroyers.

No shouted warning could reach to the ranchers in such a din, and no time remained to tell them what they were riding into. Above, back of the clay banks beyond the canal, lurked the second half of the lumbermen, waiting in ambush to wipe up any possible survivors of that terrible explosion.

"It's the only thing to do," Hatfield mused.

He had sized up the danger-fraught, fatal situation at a glance, knew he had but a half minute in which to strike. Then Ross would be surrounded by the 'jacks coming in from the east. Hatfield knew that what he attempted was practically suicide but he had no choice. Unless he could seize that scant time-fraction it was all over for Maravilla, even for Texas!

Squatted low with his match ready to strike and light the fuse at the proper instant, Ross looked like the devil himself. His white, slim hand—a dude's hand— would touch off the wholesale murder.

The golden sorrel's hoofs dug into the sandy north bank of the river bed, kicking back loose rocks, the noises drowned in the battle din. Jim Hatfield urged Goldy through the bushes.

Ross could not fail; squatted at the gray connection to the tremendous mine, he would time the death stroke perfectly. He was ringed by half a dozen 'jacks, his guard and the rocks helped protect him from any long shot the Ranger might try.

As Hatfield, low over the golden sorrel, touched Goldy with a spur, the horse lunged out from the screen of bush. At that moment, Valentine Ross looked impatiently back over his shoulder again, for Torquila's men.

Ross saw the tall jigger as Hatfield whirled straight at him. At sight of his arch-enemy, Ross gulped and uttered a shriek of astounded rage, pointing at the tall rider galloping in. The 'jacks with him had their eyes glued on the fight below, and they swung at his warning, threw up their rifles as Hatfield opened fire with both Colts.

His bullets thudded into the flesh and bone of the men grouped around Ross.

"Kill him! Kill him!" screamed Ross, vitriol of fury burning his slender throat.

The seconds fleeted. Each one brought the bunching ranchers nearer the trap, upon that ripping, tearing death.

Two of the men shielding Ross fell at the first blasting volley of the Ranger's guns. He let go again, and the bullets tore an arc of death along the small group of 'jacks. The terrible accuracy of his fire, the grim, rugged face of the great fighting man, appalled them; he was almost upon them, and still he rode hell-for-leather straight into what seemed certain death.

Slugs from their rattled guns whirled about the Ranger's head and body, one missed him by inches, another tore the saddle and cut Goldy's hide. The sorrel gave a tremendous bound forward, shoulder knocking down a lumberman, his rider's guns flaming the end for a fourth and fifth. The sixth man with Ross turned with a scream of terror and ran off in mad retreat, arms over his face.

Hatfield left his saddle in a flying leap as Valentine Ross, dropping the box and match, snatched out his small-caliber pistol and aimed at the Ranger. Ross fired pointblank at the moving officer. The lead hit Hatfield as he traveled through the air, pierced between the tendons of his neck and shoulder, stinging with horrid anguish. Then his spurred boots struck Ross in the stomach, knocked him flat as the Ranger's weight came through.

Hatfield's hand found the green-eyed hombre's scrawny throat. He held the furious chief, writhing like a six-foot rattler, in a grip of steel, and banged Ross's head against the jagged rocks until the blood flowed scarlet from the smashed scalp.

A fraction of a minute remained; he knew that, even as he fought Ross for control of that great mine. To kill Ross would not stop the slaughter; the incoming lumberjacks would light the fuse as they came from the open space. And the bunch above, across the canal, had seen the Ranger as he attacked Ross in a mad swirl of power.

The golden sorrel gave a sharp warning whinny, seized his master's shirt in his teeth and shook. From above, the lumbermen in ambush were starting across the canal, and their bullets were rapping into the rocks, close to the Ranger, though they dared not shoot too close for fear of killing the prostrate Ross.

Ross relaxed under him; Hatfield snatched up the match box, struck a match and touched the flickering flame to the gray fuse. It sputtered bluish sparks, took hold with a low, swishing sound. The gray line grew rapidly black as the fire ran swiftly along it.

Like the jaws of a giant pincers the two bodies of lumbermen were closing upon Hatfield. The gang leading the ranchers on was now over the mined space.

"Look out, he's lit the fuse!" That shriek, shrill with terror, came from the mob bearing downhill on the officer.

Hatfield whirled, guns spitting death into their bunched ranks. Suddenly they all saw that faintly smoking, blue-sparked train to hell, and with precipitate haste they turned and fled for cover. The 'jacks on the mined area, deafened by gunfire, backs to the rocks, did not realize the fuse was lighted. Only a few happened to turn, and realize the import, but it was too late.

Eyes staring in horror, they tried to point to the running flame. With horror-gripped eyes they followed the spark that would touch off the percussion caps attached to the dynamite.

The Ranger leaped to Goldy; the explosion might kill, so close were they to the mighty mine. He was stopped as a claw-like hand clutched his booted ankle, tripped him; Ross made his final play, trying to take his arch-foe along.

Even as he fell, weight taken on his outstretched left hand, the Ranger twisted his body around, lashed at Ross's face with his Colt. The sharp sight cut down across the green eyes that flamed with hatred. He raised his thumb from the hammer and Valentine Ross let go, fell back on the jagged rocks, head a bloody horror.

Hatfield scrambled to his feet. Only instants remained; he hit the saddle in a single bound, and Goldy, seeming to guess the danger, leaped with tremendous strides for the depression of the river bed. The sorrel flew over the brink, sliding and half turning on the steep downslope. At that moment the whole universe exploded, and horse and rider were knocked flat, rolling over and over across the rocky dry course of the Maravilla.

12

A Ghost Rides

HATFIELD'S next impression was that he was caught in a terrific cloudburst, a heavy downpour that spat upon the leaves and sand.

Yet the drops were stinging, hurt as they struck his head and body; he put his arms over his head as he lay flat in the stream bed. He realized that it was not water that was falling but a violent hail of stones, dirt and rubble. There were worse things than inanimate matter in that rain: arms and legs, parts of the bodies of men and animals.

After seconds that dragged interminably the worst of the downpour ceased, spattering off as smaller fragments landed. He sat up, shook himself, fighting off the stunned blackness that the shattering dynamite had brought over the world,

His vision was obscured by a giant smoke pall drifting into the brilliant heavens. The biting odor of the discharged explosive was in his flared nostrils as he came up on his knees, rocking from side to side as his equilibrium returned. His face was bloody from abrasions caused by jagged flints, and his skin blackened by powder and dirt.

Goldy was scrambling to his feet; the golden sorrel's eyes were as wide as saucers, flaming red. He pawed furiously at the sand and rocks, kicked out wildly at the leg of a man that had fallen on his back, the dismembered limb strangely clothed in corduroy with hobnail boot intact.

"That did it," muttered Hatfield aloud, but his voice was lost in the banging of his shattered eardrums. No living creature could stand near such an explosion, nor bear it without terrific shock.

Then, over the mighty wilderness, a brooding quiet reigned. Life seemed to suspend animation for minutes, eerie time interval that was unbearably long.

Pulling himself together, shaking his head in an effort to clear his hearing, Hatfield slowly stepped over to Goldy and touched the quivering gelding's velvet arched neck. The horse quieted under his hand, and the Ranger led him up the north bank and mounted.

Now he could look, through the clearing drifts of smoke and dirt, upon what had been the cleared area wherein Valentine Ross had planted his gigantic dynamite mine. A raw, bleeding crater, many yards in depth, showed there, the entire earth blasted away to bedrock and clay. Nothing remained of the lumberjacks who had been standing on top of the mine, only fragments with here and there an entire corpse, killed with the brutal vagaries of the explosive.

He wiped his stinging eyes with the back of his long hand, and his gaze sought the spot below where the ranchers had been coming. The explosion had stunned them all, and several had been injured by flying rocks, but the main army had been spared, saved by the Ranger's play. Horses were rising up, and riders, thrown from the saddle, were on their feet, rocking dizzily from shock.

Jim Hatfield picked out young Ban Morton's slim figure and he started down toward them, skirting the crater of death. Sounds of life once more rose over the Maravilla wilderness: birds were flying off in the brilliant sky, and the excited voices of the cowmen were audible to his quieting eardrums.

Then someone opened fire on him, the bullet spanging into the clay side of the crater. Looking back, he saw that the 'jacks beyond the canal had come to life and were shooting again. He drew a Colt and rattled them down behind their breastwork as his slugs spat up flies of clay where they peeked over the embankment.

Morton recognized Jim Hatfield as the tall jigger pushed Goldy among the massed ranchers. Some were more dazed than others, running their hands over their faces as though the skin were brittle and might break, eyes round as circles, breath fast. Coughs and sneezes from dust-clogged throats, and the monotonous cursing of a nerve-shattered waddy broke the quiet.

"Jim! Jim!" Morton croaked hoarsely, spitting out dust.

"Howdy, Ban," the Ranger told him. He was rolling a cigarette, and lit it as he coolly scanned the faces of the cowmen, turning toward him. Silently, they began to gather about Hatfield and Morton, and their eyes, meeting his, fell before his stern gaze.

"How is it," Hatfield drawled, "yuh come up here, gents? I left orders yuh was to stay put till yuh heard from me."

The sunlight gleamed on the rugged fighting jaw of Jim Hatfield; and it glinted back from the silver star, set on a silver circle, emblem of the Texas Rangers, pinned to his vest.

"Ranger! That big jigger's a Texas Ranger!" The whispered exclamation traveled like wildfire through the great crowd.

"I knowed it, we oughta guessed," a cowman growled. "Nobody could ride and fight like that 'cept a Ranger!"

Suddenly a hoarse cheer welled from them as they shouted for the hombre who had saved them. Hatfield, modest as he was courageous, raised a hand to quell the ovation.

"Nobody could stop 'em comin' up, Jim" cried Morton. "I was close to home, bringin' Elsie up from Torquila's, when I met the whole parcel, four hundred men, ravin' for the hills. Word had gone out Ward was murdered and Elsie kidnaped; yuh know Ogalvie was killed and Keith bad wounded by Ross when he raided Bowie.

So's Mayor Yager hurt, so bad he can't ride.

"Every man who could be spared from the ranches took up his guns and started; Senator Ardmore was so riled he advised 'em to attack the lumbermen and drive 'em out, though he's always been for lawful means afore. Yager ordered 'em to go ahaid and so'd Keith. I done told 'em all yuh said, that yuh was okay and had saved Elsie and Ward, but they jest kept a-comin' all the same."

Marshal Alf Betts, the little old town officer of Bowie, wooden leg sunk in the soft earth, frowned up at the tall Ranger.

"I'm for cleanin' out that nest of snakes," he growled.

Shorty, from the Bar W, drawled, "Lucky for us that dynamite went off when it did."

Ban Morton was staring at Hatfield. "You—you set it off, Jim, and saved us," he shouted. "So that's what they had planned; it was a trap, to lead us up here and blow us all to hell!"

Hatfield shrugged. The ranchers, watching the mighty Ranger, suddenly realized that he alone had preserved them. Another cheer split the warm air.

Hatfield was regarding Marshal Betts, with a deliberation that made the small hombre shift uncomfortably. Betts cried, "That's so, Mister; I got a telegram for yuh."

He reached inside his shirt, pulled out a yellow envelope. The Ranger took it, and scanned the message, written in a careful hand.

It was a reply to his wire, dispatched by the deceased Sheriff Godey's messenger:

"Southwest Lumber Co. lease okay and legal. Prevent citizens from attacking. Take no drastic steps till you hear from me. McDowell."

The gray-green eyes darkened; then a puzzled light fleeted in them. "Huh," he mused. "Sounds like the captain's gettin' soft. Hell, no, he couldn't be, not that old tiger!" He swung again on Betts.

"Look, Marshal. One or two things I wanta know: who told yuh to jog Shorty's mem'ry that day at the Bar W? And who gave yuh this message to hand me?"

Betts scratched his sunburned, bald head. The Ranger, carefully observing the watered blue eyes, decided that while they did not show much intelligence they were honest. "Why" the marshal replied, "come to think, it was Senator Ardmore who told me he'd heard yuh was the man snatched Scarface from the boys. And the senator's a mighty good man and a powerful help to the community. It was him figgered this telegram must be fer you; I asked around, seein' as how Godey's man, the sheriff bein' daid, left the message at Jack's saloon."

Winchester bullets, at long range were plopping into the dirt and bush from above the canal; the remaining lumbermen had taken cover behind the clay banks.

"Hafta clean them out fust of all," remarked the Ranger, tossing away the stub of his cigarette. "Load up, gents."

As the unwounded members of the vigilantes swiftly checked pistols and rifles, shoved fresh shells into empty chambers, and pacified the alarmed, wide-eyed mustangs, Hatfield drew Ban Morton to one side.

"Take that black horse of yores and ride fast as yuh kin to Lenox. Ask the telegraph operator to give yuh copies of all telegrams sent by Captain McDowell from Austin."

Morton hated to quit the battle but he could not disobey the Ranger. He swung Black Rascal and with a wave of his hand the bronc buster lined out northeast down the slopes.

"C'mon," ordered Hatfield, as the ranchers gathered before him, ready to dig in. "We'll wipe up that gang."

He led the way, skirting the crater of destruction. The lumbermen's bullets were rapping closer as Goldy snorted and stepped over the corpse of Valentine Ross, ripped by rocks, doubled into a constricted shape, lying sixty feet from the rock nest where the fuse end had been hidden.

"That'll be Number Three in that Syndicate," the Ranger thought.

He swung toward the dry Maravilla, the cowmen bunching at his heels, shooting back at the 'jacks. His keen eyes, traveling from right to left, looking over the debris, suddenly stopped. The explosion had blown the bonfire to pieces; the blackened circle of earth showed where it had been. And there were several pieces of the wooden boxes of which it had been composed; one was nearly intact and a corrugation came across the bronzed forehead of the Ranger.

"Huh," he muttered aloud.

A bullet bit a chunk from his Stetson crown; he knew there was work to be done, and quickly. It was possible that the explosion and heavy firing would bring up the Mexican army, and he wanted to deal with the lumbermen separately; his strategy had split the two armies.

Hatfield went across the Maravilla and worked up through the forest. They did not stop till they were above the position of the entrenched 'jacks.

"Flanked 'em," bawled Marshal Betts, throwing up his old horse pistol which boomed like a small cannon in the shadowed sweet air of the wood.

From partial cover they raked the line of lumbermen. The heavy gunfire from the cowmen tore into the now unprotected 'jacks, rolling them up; they fought to get behind one another, and they were disheartened and shocked at the terrible loss of their leaders and mates. Scattered shots came back, as the remnant of Ross's once powerful band stood hesitantly before the charge of their enemies.

"Bust that dam right now," bawled Hatfield, and he sent two cowmen to clean up the 'jacks, who had broken and started running.

A loud cheer rose, as the remaining ranchers set about pulling down the dam that diverted the precious water of the Maravilla. Once the break was made the water assisted, swirling through the holes and carrying rocks and clay, turning aside the big logs.

Up on the north bank of the river, the ranchers watched the stream going back into its proper channel. And then, from the south side, among the thick bush and trees, a tremendous fusillade of bullets whirled at them. A half dozen ranchers were hit, before the Ranger's mighty voice penetrated to them, ordering them to hunt cover.

Turning on this new threat, they saw among the trees over the Maravilla, riding with the mad abandon of their race, half a thousand Mexican bandidos, charging with hot cries of hate upon them.

"Torquila! Torquila" a cowman shrilled.

Jim Hatfield, pushing up erect in his stirrups, stared at the charging Mexes. In the van rode a giant figure, dark face smudged by mustache and goatee, a black cape wrapped about his body, peaked hat strapped low over his flashing eyes.

Vasco Torquila led the bandit charge.

13

Number Four

TAKING advantage of tree trunks, of huge boulders and piles of cut logs left by the lumbermen, the dismounted ranchers opened up on the bandits. The Mexican charge came to the brink of the muddy river, still carrying debris and clay as it rode eastward.

Hatfield was trying to pick off the chieftain, but the swift movements, the rising dust and smoke, intervening bodies of Mexicans, spoiled his chances. The other bunch of cowmen, hearing the new shooting from the river bank, left the scattered fugitives running for the tall bush and returned, whooping it up, to the fight. At sight of them the renegades faltered; the odds were nearly even, and the ranchers had a protected position.

For minutes the Mexicans fought bravely, but their ranks were bitten into by the accurate hard-shooting cowmen. A hundred were hit to twenty ranchers; the Texans roared in triumph, fever heat of battle flushing sweated, stained faces. Mad with victory, at the fierce joy that is the thrill of revenge, they jumped up at Hatfield's order and charged through the running water of the river.

The charge sent the wavering bandits back. As Hatfield, shoving the dripping Goldy up the south bank, swung to hunt the giant leader of the foe, he glimpsed Torquila as the chief galloped hell-for-leather south among the trees.

Between his position and the fleeing Torquila interposed the main body of the bandits. The cowmen charged, and Torquila's hombres, having failed to find a bloody, shattered remnant of Texans to clean up, knew they had run into a hornet's nest of hell. The flight of their leader broke them altogether; every Mexican swung to escape, horses bumping, piling up. Utter rout followed, and the ranchers attacked them viciously, taking prisoners, shooting those who resisted.

For mile after mile, picking off the bunches of bandits, leaving dead, wounded or prisoners, the victorious vigilantes raged south. They reached the camp of the Mexicans, where the new bunch of peons was held under skeleton guard that fled in alarm at sight of the disastrous rout.

Hatfield freed the captives. To several of the more intelligent he gave advice: to get in touch with the Mexican rurales and inform the police of Torquila's perfidy. With the main band smashed, the rurales could clean up the hacienda, and break the power of the bandits.

His gray-green eyes hunted from corpse to corpse, from batch of prisoners to batch of prisoners, for that big rider. But the chief, mounted on a fast, fresh horse, had faded away, disappeared.

Worn out, torn and blood-stained, but filled with jubilant emotion, the ranchers straggled back at dusk to the mountain camp of the Southwest Lumber Company. Wounded men had staggered up here, and prisoners were being collected. They were turned into the stockade from which the miserable Mexican slaves were released. Hatfield saw to it that the peons were provided with mounts and food for their journey home.

In Ross's shack he found that map that

had told him much of the Syndicate's plans. He smoothed it out and looked at the vast territory that had been in their plans. He put it in his pocket, its significance entirely clear to him.

"Hafta take him," he mused, as he watched the ranchers setting fire to the shacks, destroying the enemy camp. "An hombre who could get up such a scheme can figure out others!"

His power and skill had saved Maravilla; but he knew he was far from through. Texas must take the perpetrator of the wholesale horrors that threatened to engulf her.

Dawn found him down below, near the spot where the dead bonfire had burned. Young Ban Morton, riding a lathered and heaving Black Rascal, pushed up to Hatfield as the Ranger curiously looked over the half of the wooden box he had noted the previous day.

"Here's yore message," Morton reported; he was covered with dust and his face was drawn, from his hard ride. Curiously, he stared at the wooden container, its edges scarred with black. "What yuh got, Jim?"

In the clear light, Ban could see that the box end contained bits of sawdust; and when Hatfield ran his fingers along the inner wood they came away shining with an oily substance.

"Dynamite was packed in this," the Ranger drawled. "And—I've seen these boxes before, Ban."

He accepted the telegram copy Morton held out. Quickly he scanned it, and his eyes lightened.

"I'll be ridin'," Hatfield told Ban.

"Can I go with yuh?"

"Yeah, if yuh can keep up."

Leaving the main body of ranchers, Hatfield and Morton headed eastward down the slopes.

Another night was on Bowietown, which looked like a deserted village with most of its citizens out, up in the hills to fight the lumbermen, as Jim Hatfield and Ban Morton, ahead of the main army, dismounted in the tree-shaded plaza, with its little speakers' stand empty in the darkness.

They had stopped at the Bar W on their way, for Ban to change horses, for Black Rascal was done in from the hard run to the railroad and back, and also to make certain that Elsie Ward and Sam were in no danger.

The settlement was quiet; the saloons and Yager's store were open but only a few oldsters, too crippled to ride far, were around. Every able-bodied man, save for skeleton guards to hold the ranches, had headed for the west mountains to drive out the invaders. Punchers wounded in the early stages of the fight had straggled back home, and brought news of the cowmen's victory.

Hatfield, Ban Morton limping at his side, made a swift survey of the store and saloons.

"That big place is Senator Ardmore's, Jim," Morton remarked. "Yuh said yuh wanted to talk to him."

The Ranger stared at the square mansion, pretentious for a Western town, standing back in a cut lawn planted with trees and flowers, enclosed by a picket fence.

Dark shadows rested around the gloomy building; at the rear a light gleamed yellow in the kitchen windows. The rest of the house was dark, shades drawn.

"Don't look like the senator's home,"

exclaimed Ban. "Reck'n Mayor Yager would help us; he was wounded bad when Ross raided his store, though he can walk and talk some."

"We'll try the senator first," Hatfield drawled.

He pulled back the gate and strolled along a gravel walk, rimmed by flowering shrubs and ornamental cactus plants. Wounds stiff and aching from the terrific pace at which he had been going, Hatfield could not yet ease up.

There was work to do, for though the armies of the bandits and lumberjacks had been smashed, the evil brain which animated them still rode free, and Texas would never be safe until the chief of that criminal Syndicate was dead or arrested. Such an hombre, Hatfield was aware, could easily start again; tools were plentiful.

Eyes watching the shadows from side to side, Hatfield went quietly around the square house to the kitchen. He rapped on the door with the butt of his Colt.

"Who's there?" a gruff voice demanded, after a moment.

The Ranger nudged Morton and Ban replied, "It's me, Ban Morton."

"What yuh want?"

"Tell the senator I wanta see him."

"He ain't here. Started for Austin this afternoon."

The Ranger tried the knob but it was locked.

"Open up," he ordered.

"Go 'way. Yuh can't come in."

Shoulder to the panel, the Ranger shoved. A bolt pulled out of its socket and the wood groaned and squeaked, then the whole side gave way and Hatfield stepped into the kitchen.

A man in a rusty black suit, evidently a cast-off of his master's, scowled and swore at them angrily.

"What's the idee," he growled, "bustin' in here?"

But his eyes fell under Hatfield's cool look. The Ranger brushed him aside, strolled through the hall and glanced into the big living room. It was dark, empty, but a closed door to one side attracted him and he tried it, found it locked, no one answered his call, so he shouldered it in.

A wide bedroom opened before him. He saw the white of the counterpane on a tester bed in the middle of the chamber. The curtains were down save for one that looked out on the front walk; that was up a few inches, a lighter space under the shade, as though it had been used to peek through.

Hatfield struck a match; on the bed lay a lank figure. The tall jigger touched his flame to the black wick of a candle standing on a bureau and the little light came up.

The long man on the bed was covered to his triangular chin by a sheet. His mop of iron-gray crisp hair was wildly awry on the pillow, and his body was rigid, sunken eyes wide.

"What's the meaning of this intrusion, sir?" Senator Rathburn Ardmore angrily demanded. "How dare you force your way into my private chamber?"

"Senator," broke in the officer, "I don't like botherin' yuh since yuh've rode to Austin, but there's one or two things I wanta know. Yuh told Marshal Betts to prod Shorty at the Bar W on me bein' the man who snatched Scarface from the rope."

"You did," Ardmore snapped.

"How yuh knowed it is what interests me. But this telegram haunts me more. Listen: here's the one yuh give Betts to hand me, 'case that dynamite blast yuh so handily didn't go near failed to kill us."

Hatfield nodded at Ban Morton, who took up a position at the hall door, on guard. The Ranger read the fake wire, ordering him to give the Southwest Lumber Company a free hand.

"Now," he went on, "this is the real wire that come to Lenox for me: 'Southwest Lumber lease forged. Only granted limited cutting permit in small area north of Maravilla. On your advice traced money paid for incoming timber to Austin office of Senator Rathburn Ardmore of Bowie. Rumors in capitol Ardmore has offered bribes to members of legislature for support in obtaining leases on other public resources of Texas. Clean up Maravilla. I stand behind you all the way to hell and back. McDowell,' "

The thin man in the bed trembled violently; his strange, bony face contorted, flushed a deep purple.

"Get out," he shouted. "Get out! You can talk to my attorney, sir. Leave my home at once."

Hatfield shifted closer, steel fingers seizing the bony arm hidden under the covers. The circling grip held Ardmore helpless; Hatfield took a small pistol from his hand, as he pulled the senator's arm into view.

"Yuh ain't got the nerve to use thet," the Ranger drawled.

"Don't—don't!" whispered Ardmore, suddenly cracking as the gray-green eyes drilled deep into his soul. He was a physical coward and the pain of the hold shook him; plainly he was under a great mental strain.

"Callate yuh're Number Four," Hatfield told him. "Number Four in the Syndicate to raid Texas. Yuh ain't got the murderer's nerve yore chief has." His voice turned suddenly harsh, terrifying; Ardmore jumped nervously: "Talk, and talk fast, Ardmore. Yuh want to hang by the neck?"

The senator moaned, writhed, "I—I only handled the legal end, Ranger. I swear it. I never shot anybody."

"Not even Ward?" asked Hatfield grimly, "I seen the rock pile where he was wounded."

"Why, I wasn't even up there that day! *He* shot him during the battle!" He broke off with a gasp. "He'll kill me," he yelled, reddened eyes bulging with terror.

Papers rustled in the Ranger's hand. "See this map? These letters mark the natural resources of southwest and central Texas, timber, coal and iron. The man who made it wrote this fake message to me."

Again his steel fingers closed on the wincing senator's bony wrist; it was a battle between two fears for Ardmore, fear of the cold, tall officer who had caught up with them, and dread of the hidden chief. The former won.

"I'll talk," Ardmore cried, "I'll tell you everything, Ranger! He forced me to give Betts that message for you, to slow you up; all we needed was a little time to get that timber out of the hills, win a fortune with which to finance our Syndicate."

"And who," Hatfield drawled, "is yore chief? Callate I can say now myself, but I want yore evidence."

Ardmore gulped, as Hatfield leaned ominously toward him again. "He's—" he said quickly.

"Watch it," shouted Ban Morton from the door.

Hatfield was already in action. The slight sound at the window where the curtain was up a few inches, warned him.

His Colt was out and rising as he whirled in a crouch, on the balls of his feet. The boom of guns roared in the confined space of the room, window glass shattering as the muzzle of a double-barreled shotgun was thrust through. Hatfield had let go at the window as a bunch of unscattered slugs tore into Ardmore's chest, ripping him wide open, the blood spattering the tall jigger.

14

Chief of the Syndicate

THE second load from the shotgun fanned within an inch of Hatfield's moving head as he went down on one knee for better aim. The vicious whir of the bunched shot passed him, slugged into the wall, bringing down a rain of plaster.

An instant later Ban Morton swept the candle from the bureau, plunging the room in darkness. Glass smashed in other windows; there were gunmen outside, and they began shooting into the room from three angles. Bullets hit the floor, the walls, and the furniture.

"Lie down flat, Ban," called Hatfield.

He drew his second Colt, covering one window after another with lead. The heavy flashes of the gun blinded them; Morton was shooting from the floor.

Hatfield came up on his toes and started

like a panther for the door, to get outside and take the hombres attacking. But loud yells, the drumming of hundreds of hoofs, sounded over the din around Ardmore's home. The gunmen outside quit, and as Hatfield crossed to a window and looked out, he glimpsed several dark figures scurrying away, leaping on waiting horses.

When Morton and the Ranger emerged, the assailants had escaped, mingling with the great army of ranchers returning in triumph from the hills The shouting, victorious cowmen fired their guns into the air, roared with victory.

Bonfires of empty boxes and brush were lighted in the plaza; the platform, weathered by sun and rain, was framed in the red glow. Gleaming faces showed as the cowmen began to whoop it up. Saloons overflowed, hungry and thirsty citizens tanking up.

Senator Ardmore was dead the shotgun blast having torn his heart. John Ogalvie was dead, and Sam Ward lay wounded at home, as did George Keith; Mayor Smiley Yager, pale and shaky from a head wound, around which a bandage was tightly bound, appeared, supported by two friends.

The citizens gathered about the platform. Yager was the only one of their old leaders present, though there were many lieutenants. Alf Betts took the floor, thumping the creaking boards with his wooden stump.

"Gents," shouted the marshal, "we've beat the lumbermen and Torquila too. Maravilla's safe."

A mighty cheer echoed across the plaza. Alf Betts stumped over, assisted Mayor Yager to rise; the mayor leaned on Bett's arm, smiling cheerily at his people.

Yager's voice was weak but silence fell on them as he began to talk. Jim Hatfield, at the front, stared up into the bluff face.

"Boys," Yager began, "you did it and I'm proud of you. They near finished us, but we've won. I was always in favor of hittin' 'em and hittin' hard, and that proved to be the right way."

They cheered him. Yager grinned out at his friends. "I heard some of how it was done," he went on. "Texas Ranger Hatfield here, from Austin, saved you from being blown to hell. We're mighty grateful to him and he deserves a yell."

A shout went up for the Ranger. The tall jigger put a spurred boot on the platform and stood beside Yager. The people quieted as they stared at the majestic officer; his eyes were dark as he faced them, easily. Hatfield was not a man to talk much but what he said counted.

"Gents," he began, voice hardly raised yet penetrating to every ear, "there's still some things left undone. Five men formed a Syndicate to take over our natural resources and ruin Texas. They started with Maravilla. That timber up there was the quickest way to pick up a million dollars to finance 'em. Their plans was big, to raid coal, iron, oil and other natural wealth through the state.

"Torquila was one, and he supplied cheap labor, runnin' up peons wholesale; they wanted a corridor to fetch 'em along, and Maravilla, 'specially the Bar W, was it. Fat Phil, the gambler, Torquila, Senator Ardmore, Valentine Ross—they're all gone, 'cept the chief of this vile Syndicate.

"You ranchers was in the way and they

tried to wipe yuh out; enough dynamite to blow up a mountain was sent for, but they couldn't bring it through yore waddies. It might have been exploded by bullets. So it was switched here to Bowie, and that was why Ross made that raid: to pick up that dynamite."

Spellbound they listened to his crystal-clear exposé. "Why how could Ross do that?" Yager asked.

"That dynamite was boxed and ready only it wasn't marked as such," Hatfield replied smoothly. "I found one of the boxes it come in, one that didn't altogether burn up. Morton's holdin' it. Bring it here, Ban, and let 'em see for themselves."

Hatfield's weight rested on his left leg; he half turned from the people, as Morton shouldered through the crowd, that opened a way for him. Ban handed up the half-burned box the Ranger had brought down from the hills.

"I seen the boxes the night of Ross's raid, gents," explained Hatfield, "so I got suspicious when I came on this one. Though it's marked 'Canned Tomatoes' its been packed with sawdust, to cushion the dynamite; some of the oil oozed out, too." Beside the box, Ban Morton handed the Ranger a pair of stuffed saddlebags.

"These here bags belong to the chief who run this shebang," continued the Ranger. He opened the bags, drew forth a folded silk Mexican cape. "Torquila's," he growled. There was a vial with dark liquid in it: "Berry juice to stain his face. And some glue and a mustache and goatee of horsehair, to stick on. This here sombrero is so fine made it kin be folded into a small ball, to stuff in the bag, too.

"Gents, Torquila could hit two places at once because there was *two* of him. The real one, the Mexican bandit leader, and a second, who rode in the dark fixed up like Torquila. Nobody knowed, 'cept the Syndicate; even the Mexes didn't savvy who this second Torquila was—the two-faced snake who shot Sam Ward in the side, up there that day, for Ward wasn't hit by a bullet from in front."

From the back of the spellbound crowd, a gun suddenly flashed its roar. The Ranger staggered as a bullet ripped through his black hair, creased his scalp; a trickle of blood showed on his bronzed forehead, running into his eye.

Pandemonium broke. The dry-gulcher, a dark-browned hombre in cowboy garb, was seized as he tried to reach a horse; in an instant he was knocked down and the furious mob tore at him.

Hatfield whirled, as Mayor Yager flipped his big body backward off the platform, landing in the mêlée. The Ranger's Colt was out but Marshal Betts was on his feet, and stood between. A slug from Yager's pistol, fired from behind the platform, tore a chunk from the officer's left arm as he jumped after the mayor, who had so suddenly thrown off his weakness.

Through the stamping mob, ducked low, Smiley Yager tore a way. Hatfield was after him, watching for a chance to shoot without hurting any excited citizens. Yager reached a clump of oaks, leaped on a great black stallion, dug in his spurs.

The Ranger, coming to the outer circle of the mob, as yet unaware of their mayor's perfidy, whistled three shrill blasts. A few moments later Goldy came galloping up, and Hatfield hit the saddle, whirling south in pursuit of his quarry, the chief of the Syndicate.

Yager was two hundred yards ahead; he swung to shoot back at his lone pursuer, the flashes of his gun spitting his hate for the man who had caught up with him. The Maravilla intervened; Yager's horse, cruelly goaded, bounded down the bank into the current.

Yager turned in midstream to shoot again at the big jigger inexorably shoving after him. Hatfield, the stream licking his thighs, held himself in steel control, fighting off the weakness of wounds and the pace he had undergone for days.

"That's him, shore as hell's hot!" he muttered.

Before him rode the man who had raided the Maravilla range in the guise of Vasco Torquila, at the same time posing as a loyal leader of the ranchers, mayor of their capitol. Driven by the mad lust for wealth and power, Yager had broken every law of decency and of Texas.

A bullet hit the water close to the swimming sorrel; another bit Hatfield's shoulder. Yager's horse was at the south bank, scrambling up. The black slipped as

Hatfield's answering slugs rapped rocks and dirt into his glaring eyes.

Close upon his foe, Hatfield threw himself bodily from the saddle, clutched at Yager's leg, yanking the burly mayor from his leather seat. The two big men locked, slipped on the slimy bank, rolled into the water. Hatfield's fingers sought the beating throat of his thrashing, powerful adversary.

The Ranger twisted his lithe body on top; the mayor went down under the surface, but the slippery mud coating Hatfield's hands helped break his grip as Yager fought with the mad desperation of the drowning.

Yager broke free, lashing up, boots digging into the bed of the river. Then he fell back, hand still gripping his Colt, stood there thigh-deep in the running water, and as the mayor's gun covered him, Hatfield raised his thumb off his own hammer.

Yager's slug hit the water a foot in front of Hatfield; the mayor staggered, a black blotch on his furious, twisted brow, from which the bandage had come, showing no injury. Then Yager lost all volition, splashed down, under the surface of the Maravilla.

The Ranger waded slowly toward him, got hold of the limp body, and towed it to the bank.

Captain Bill McDowell stared at the tall Ranger, reporting at Austin Headquarters.

"So yuh got all five," he growled. "And that skunk Mayor Yager was chief of this Syndicate?"

"Yes, sir. It was Yager's plan." Hatfield laid the stained map he had taken from Ross's suitcase on the captain's desk. "He had the natural wealth of Texas marked out, Cap'n. Meant to get a fortune quick by sellin' that timber to put the scheme through. Plenty of cheap labor was to be had in Mexico.

"This Yager posed as a hearty, good feller, but all the time he was workin' underground, and ridin' as Torquila. Yager and Ardmore held back them complaints to us; Yager's spies was all around, and he knowed ev'ry move the ranchers made. It was Yager egged 'em on, to rush up and get slaughtered; he put a bullet into Sam

Ward's back ribs that day, for he wanted the Bar W himself, and he figgered he'd marry Elsie Ward.

"Fact, he had Torquila kidnap her and meant to pretend to save her so she'd be grateful to him. Only she was in love with a bronc buster named Morton. Figger Ban Morton and his wife Elsie'll keep a sharp eye on the watershed from now on. Ward never savvied what hit him that day, thought it was a ricochet from Ross's 'jacks."

McDowell listened to the tall jigger's account of the dynamite mine, of the peonage, of Yager's attempts to cover himself.

When Jim Hatfield had finished, Cap'n McDowell put a hand on his powerful shoulder. "Callate yuh've earned a long rest," he told the Ranger. "Yuh got sorta battered up down there in Maravilla."

Then he chuckled, at the troubled darkening of Jim Hatfield's gray-green eyes. "I was goin' to pass this complaint to another Ranger," cried McDowell, "but since yuh feel that way, Jim, yuh've shore earnt the right to it.

Read it." He thrust a telegram before the tall jigger.

> Four men murdered here in two days. For God's sake send us the Rangers.

Later Jim Hatfield, on Goldy, headed north out of Austin. There was work to do, work for a Ranger, and Hatfield was happy as he rode to lock horns with other enemies of the Lone Star State, kept livable by the Texas Rangers.

THE END

This book is published under the auspices of the
ULVERSCROFT FOUNDATION,
a registered charity, whose primary object is to assist those who experience difficulty in reading print of normal size.

In response to approaches from the medical world, the Foundation is also helping to purchase the latest, most sophisticated medical equipment desperately needed by major eye hospitals for the diagnosis and treatment of eye diseases.

If you would like to know more about the
ULVERSCROFT FOUNDATION,
and how you can help to further its work, please write for details to:

THE ULVERSCROFT FOUNDATION
The Green, Bradgate Road
Anstey
Leicestershire
England

GUIDE
TO THE COLOUR CODING
OF
ULVERSCROFT BOOKS

Many of our readers have written to us expressing their appreciation for the way in which our colour coding has assisted them in selecting the Ulverscroft books of their choice. To remind everyone of our colour coding—this is as follows:

BLACK COVERS
Mysteries

★

BLUE COVERS
Romances

★

RED COVERS
Adventure Suspense and General Fiction

★

ORANGE COVERS
Westerns

★

GREEN COVERS
Non-Fiction

WESTERN TITLES
in the
Ulverscroft Large Print Series

Gone To Texas	*Forrest Carter*
Dakota Boomtown	*Frank Castle*
Hard Texas Trail	*Matt Chisholm*
Bigger Than Texas	*William R. Cox*
From Hide and Horn	*J. T. Edson*
Gunsmoke Thunder	*J. T. Edson*
The Peacemakers	*J. T. Edson*
Wagons to Backsight	*J. T. Edson*
Arizona Ames	*Zane Grey*
The Lost Wagon Train	*Zane Grey*
Nevada	*Zane Grey*
Rim of the Desert	*Ernest Haycox*
Borden Chantry	*Louis L'Amour*
Conagher	*Louis L'Amour*
The First Fast Draw *and* The Key-Lock Man	*Louis L'Amour*
Kiowa Trail *and* Killoe	*Louis L'Amour*
The Mountain Valley War	*Louis L'Amour*
The Sackett Brand *and* The Lonely Men	*Louis L'Amour*
Taggart	*Louis L'Amour*
Tucker	*Louis L'Amour*
Destination Danger	*Wm. Colt MacDonald*

Powder Smoke Feud William MacLeod Raine
Shane Jack Schaefer
A Handful of Men Robert Wilder

MYSTERY TITLES
in the
Ulverscroft Large Print Series

Henrietta Who?	*Catherine Aird*
Slight Mourning	*Catherine Aird*
The China Governess	*Margery Allingham*
Coroner's Pidgin	*Margery Allingham*
Crime at Black Dudley	*Margery Allingham*
Look to the Lady	*Margery Allingham*
More Work for the Undertaker	
	Margery Allingham
Death in the Channel	*J. R. L. Anderson*
Death in the City	*J. R. L. Anderson*
Death on the Rocks	*J. R. L. Anderson*
A Sprig of Sea Lavender	*J. R. L. Anderson*
Death of a Poison-Tongue	*Josephine Bell*
Murder Adrift	*George Bellairs*
Strangers Among the Dead	*George Bellairs*
The Case of the Abominable Snowman	
	Nicholas Blake
The Widow's Cruise	*Nicholas Blake*
The Brides of Friedberg	*Gwendoline Butler*
Murder By Proxy	*Harry Carmichael*
Post Mortem	*Harry Carmichael*
Suicide Clause	*Harry Carmichael*
After the Funeral	*Agatha Christie*
The Body in the Library	*Agatha Christie*

A Caribbean Mystery	*Agatha Christie*
Curtain	*Agatha Christie*
The Hound of Death	*Agatha Christie*
The Labours of Hercules	*Agatha Christie*
Murder on the Orient Express	*Agatha Christie*
The Mystery of the Blue Train	*Agatha Christie*
Parker Pyne Investigates	*Agatha Christie*
Peril at End House	*Agatha Christie*
Sleeping Murder	*Agatha Christie*
Sparkling Cyanide	*Agatha Christie*
They Came to Baghdad	*Agatha Christie*
Third Girl	*Agatha Christie*
The Thirteen Problems	*Agatha Christie*
The Black Spiders	*John Creasey*
Death in the Trees	*John Creasey*
The Mark of the Crescent	*John Creasey*
Quarrel with Murder	*John Creasey*
Two for Inspector West	*John Creasey*
His Last Bow	*Sir Arthur Conan Doyle*
The Valley of Fear	*Sir Arthur Conan Doyle*
Dead to the World	*Francis Durbridge*
My Wife Melissa	*Francis Durbridge*
Alive and Dead	*Elizabeth Ferrars*
Breath of Suspicion	*Elizabeth Ferrars*
Drowned Rat	*Elizabeth Ferrars*
Foot in the Grave	*Elizabeth Ferrars*

Murders Anonymous	*Elizabeth Ferrars*
Don't Whistle 'Macbeth'	*David Fletcher*
A Calculated Risk	*Rae Foley*
The Slippery Step	*Rae Foley*
This Woman Wanted	*Rae Foley*
Home to Roost	*Andrew Garve*
The Forgotten Story	*Winston Graham*
Take My Life	*Winston Graham*
At High Risk	*Palma Harcourt*
Dance for Diplomats	*Palma Harcourt*
Count-Down	*Hartley Howard*
The Appleby File	*Michael Innes*
A Connoisseur's Case	*Michael Innes*
Deadline for a Dream	*Bill Knox*
Death Department	*Bill Knox*
Hellspout	*Bill Knox*
The Taste of Proof	*Bill Knox*
The Affacombe Affair	*Elizabeth Lemarchand*
Let or Hindrance	*Elizabeth Lemarchand*
Unhappy Returns	*Elizabeth Lemarchand*
Waxwork	*Peter Lovesey*
Gideon's Drive	*J. J. Marric*
Gideon's Force	*J. J. Marric*
Gideon's Press	*J. J. Marric*
City of Gold and Shadows	*Ellis Peters*
Death to the Landlords!	*Ellis Peters*
Find a Crooked Sixpence	*Estelle Thompson*
A Mischief Past	*Estelle Thompson*

Three Women in the House	*Estelle Thompson*
Bushranger of the Skies	*Arthur Upfield*
Cake in the Hat Box	*Arthur Upfield*
Madman's Bend	*Arthur Upfield*
Tallant for Disaster	*Andrew York*
Tallant for Trouble	*Andrew York*
Cast for Death	*Margaret Yorke*

FICTION TITLES
in the
Ulverscroft Large Print Series

The Onedin Line: The High Seas	*Cyril Abraham*
The Onedin Line: The Iron Ships	*Cyril Abraham*
The Onedin Line: The Shipmaster	*Cyril Abraham*
The Onedin Line: The Trade Winds	*Cyril Abraham*
The Enemy	*Desmond Bagley*
Flyaway	*Desmond Bagley*
The Master Idol	*Anthony Burton*
The Navigators	*Anthony Burton*
A Place to Stand	*Anthony Burton*
The Doomsday Carrier	*Victor Canning*
The Cinder Path	*Catherine Cookson*
The Girl	*Catherine Cookson*
The Invisible Cord	*Catherine Cookson*
Life and Mary Ann	*Catherine Cookson*
Maggie Rowan	*Catherine Cookson*
Marriage and Mary Ann	*Catherine Cookson*
Mary Ann's Angels	*Catherine Cookson*
All Over the Town	*R. F. Delderfield*
Jamaica Inn	*Daphne du Maurier*
My Cousin Rachel	*Daphne du Maurier*

Enquiry	*Dick Francis*
Flying Finish	*Dick Francis*
Forfeit	*Dick Francis*
High Stakes	*Dick Francis*
In The Frame	*Dick Francis*
Knock Down	*Dick Francis*
Risk	*Dick Francis*
Band of Brothers	*Ernest K. Gann*
Twilight For The Gods	*Ernest K. Gann*
Army of Shadows	*John Harris*
The Claws of Mercy	*John Harris*
Getaway	*John Harris*
Winter Quarry	*Paul Henissart*
East of Desolation	*Jack Higgins*
In the Hour Before Midnight	*Jack Higgins*
Night Judgement at Sinos	*Jack Higgins*
Wrath of the Lion	*Jack Higgins*
Air Bridge	*Hammond Innes*
A Cleft of Stars	*Geoffrey Jenkins*
A Grue of Ice	*Geoffrey Jenkins*
Beloved Exiles	*Agnes Newton Keith*
Passport to Peril	*James Leasor*
Goodbye California	*Alistair MacLean*
South By Java Head	*Alistair MacLean*
All Other Perils	*Robert MacLeod*
Dragonship	*Robert MacLeod*
A Killing in Malta	*Robert MacLeod*
A Property in Cyprus	*Robert MacLeod*

By Command of the Viceroy	Duncan MacNeil
The Deceivers	John Masters
Nightrunners of Bengal	John Masters
Emily of New Moon	L. M. Montgomery
The '44 Vintage	Anthony Price
High Water	Douglas Reeman
Rendezvous-South Atlantic	Douglas Reeman
Summer Lightning	Judith Richards
Louise	Sarah Shears
Louise's Daughters	Sarah Shears
Louise's Inheritance	Sarah Shears
Beyond the Black Stump	Nevil Shute
The Healer	Frank G. Slaughter
Sword and Scalpel	Frank G. Slaughter
Tomorrow's Miracle	Frank G. Slaughter
The Burden	Mary Westmacott
A Daughter's a Daughter	Mary Westmacott
Giant's Bread	Mary Westmacott
The Rose and the Yew Tree	Mary Westmacott
Every Man a King	Anne Worboys
The Serpent and the Staff	Frank Yerby

We hope this Large Print edition gives you the pleasure and enjoyment we ourselves experienced in its publication.

There are now more than 1,600 titles available in this ULVERSCROFT Large Print Series. Ask to see a Selection at your nearest library.

The Publisher will be delighted to send you, free of charge, upon request a complete and up-to-date list of all titles available.

Ulverscroft Large Print Books Ltd.
The Green, Bradgate Road
Anstey
Leicestershire
England

(B, 3/19)

DNS/NFFS   ① AUTHOR